Christian Stannow

The Bed in the Tree

A baroque tale

Tr. John Weinstock

Christian Stannow

Sängen i trädet

En barock historia

The Bed in the Tree
Translation © 2013 John Weinstock
ISBN-13: 978-0615850900 (JMW Books)

Cover art by Beth Brotherton and John Weinstock

An earlier version of this book was published in
Swedish by Atlantis Förlag, Stockholm, 1989

to consider:

Was not the first Man, by the Desire of Knowledge,
corrupted even in the whitest integrity of Nature?
John Donne

Why does man feel so sad in the twentieth century?
Walker Percy

Everything is bound in rings.
Gutasaga

He always had the little dark round magic piece of glass with him, on a thin platinum chain around his neck. He liked to keep it open to reality, even when he was without his movie-camera. The contrasts became clearer, the contours sharp; shut one eye, squint with the other, like now: toward the coast. The Olympic powers were pouring silver into the Corinthian gulf on this divine day. Reflections from the sun flickered everywhere, bounced off the waves onto the railings' shiny varnish, splashed from the chrome and glass of the portholes into the corners of the eyes. The islands toward the west couldn't be seen yet. Haze obscured the area outside of Cape Papas. But diagonally to starboard Oxia was already sticking up its wild peak, or more correctly, its twin peaks into the sky that was as blue as blueweed. Every time he passed by here he imagined that it was right up this mountain that Sisyphus rolled the rock. It still felt nice to know that he wasn't entirely alone in this: pushing reality in front of himself without getting rid of it.

One of his all-time heroes lay there once and died, emptied of his feverish blood by a bungler of a doctor; in love with a boy from Cephalonia for the very last time. It was spring then too and the lord wrote about the birds, "on the way north – spring is here – I saw a swallow today – and it's about time!" How often hadn't he read those letters of Byron without understanding what it was that actually got him to sacrifice everything for something so uncertain and unusual as truth and freedom. So absurd, this rebelliousness that no one can escape.

But the swallows were still there, then as now still on their way north; some of them were certainly going to spend the summer months soaring under high, stacked clouds over Austers or Skär.

He really ought to have felt fine, although it was painfully cold in the apparent wind. He remained for a while with his stomach leaning on the railing, felt deep within his body the vibrations from the motors far down in the vessel's interior; as if it were a pleasure to finally get some sun on his winter-white upper body and rolls of fat on the sides that serious training no longer seemed to be able to overcome. He drew his belt in one notch. A few days with crude, rustic mutton salads, dry bread and a couple glasses of retsina, just a couple, would certainly help!

A little farther forward on the deck a couple of American girls were hanging onto each other. Indeterminate age, wind-ruffled hair, tight jeans, giggles. There was still time for everything, plenty of time; also for American tourists. He sank down in the shade between two benches full of old ladies dressed in black and the hot metal wall in toward the restaurant. The smell of fried lamb and strong coffee percolated in steaming blasts out of the half-open door. Alongside of him lay the camera, tripod, tape recorder, the battery belt, the little silver box filled with lenses and filters. For the third time he was on his way to Ithaca. Certainly not without a little anxiety. How many times did Odysseus return? Had any of the thousands of Homer researchers bothered to figure that out?

He thought: does it really matter when so much is still going on constantly in the intervals which are worthy of investigation; the barely visible ones, at the outer edge of the field of vision where the spaces are broken up and merge with each other as if time didn't exist. It had also been his generation's great mission to fight for freedom and truth, rebel against the absurd, controlled and controlling society. That was presumably every generation's most important task. His was, to be sure, beginning to get middle-aged. Byron's never did.

He continued to think: where space ends time begins. That thought actually caused him a bit of anxiety. As if space could shrink, time grow.

For several years he had preferred to work alone. A much more restless traveling, preferably to places he had visited before, somehow to confirm his own presence in something old and familiar instead of challenging new spaces, new people; that which was his real task to depict. He had become a maverick of civilization, among mountains that had undoubtedly shrunk since the last time, plains that had become smaller, dirtier cities filled with foreigners. Every year that passed he was looked at with increasing suspicion at the frontier stations when he came along hauling his unwieldy equipment and presented his note-book to customs to get it rubber-stamped and signed as required; journalist, okay, film-maker, okay, permission to work, okay.

He was out of phase with himself, that was, of course, the simple truth. Blockages, obstacles, laziness. The critical eye had become cloudy. More and more often there was a blurriness on the strip of pictures that only he could see, interruptions on the sound tape only he could perceive. Everything was actually quite unpleasant. As if he was on the verge of being invaded by something. But, by what? Not by insidious diseases at any rate or treacherous ideologies. He knew how to take care of himself during the breaks, kept in shape with selenium and vitamin C, the Nouvelle Observateur and the New Statesman. Just the right amount of jogging. Could still keep the Finn fairly straight on a ten meter per second tack.

From behind, something was on the verge of catching up with him. When he sat down somewhere, he now more often made sure there was something solid behind his back, a tree trunk, a rock-face or like now the thick hot metal plate of the ship with its rugged sun-warmed security. There is no good way to explain this, it is difficult to get people to understand what was happening. If it is possible to explain at all. Was he actually on the verge of remaining in the interval, becoming an intermediate person, like all the rest?

It should always be the first time. Everything. Repetition is punished with the death penalty. He sometimes noticed a pressure in his diaphragm, a tension in the back of his neck, aches in his knee. That at least was new. Somewhere inside of him a stranger was moving about freely, making himself broader and broader at his expense. If this creature had come with peaceful intentions or on an entirely different errand he couldn't make out. Whether it was a supervisor or an anarchist.

Once upon a time he was the first man. Then only life was necessary in order to live.

The vessel changed course several degrees or, too, the sun had changed its attitude. Like a savage blowtorch it hovered above the sea. It hurt to look into the light. His chest began to get blotchy red. But the rolls of fat above the belt didn't want to melt away. And the girl opposite him was still stubbornly squatting!

"Hi! Are you an American?" she wondered.

"I am Odysseus. From Sweden with love."

She stretched out her hand. Narrow, high, almost black veins was the pattern on the back of her hand. There was an insidious, subtle smile on her very exaggerated fresh sunburned face.

"Wow, what a coincidence. I am Pen. Penelope from Santa Monica."

"Hi sweet Pen from Santa Monica."

She kept her hand in his. It was strong, almost sinewy.

"Hope you actually have a very nice, convincing scar to show."

He played along.

"In time you'll get to see it. But actually isn't there something that doesn't fit. We weren't supposed to meet again here? You were supposed to stay at home on Ithaca and wait. Feed suitors. Dream about me. The mighty eagle."

"I know. But there is so much else that isn't included in that old story. Mary Lou for example, she isn't included at all!"

She nodded over toward her friend who raised a half-empty wine bottle as a greeting.

"Are you absolutely certain about that?"

"Swede Odysseus, I think you're pretty funny! We have a little cheese and some olives left if you want to taste them."

She got up and pulled him up onto his feet. Never before had he felt so very old. He pulled on his sweater and smoothed his thin hair, smiled back at her. She couldn't readily know that he actually did have a scar!

The darkness was rocking, certainly because of all the strong Raki that had just crystallized large parts of his liver. It was cool in the room. He tried to close things up down around his feet so that the entire night wouldn't run in under the blanket and the far too short sheet. But it didn't help. He crept together into a fetal position with his arms between his legs, stared out into the darkness. After a while a weak hole appeared in the black. The open balcony door was squeaking against the rail. Otherwise it was ghastly silent.

The next time the blow was clearly felt, the surging from the earth propagated through him all the way into his heart. His pulse doubled. He reached for his chest. But there was no pain. Just a sudden dark silence, a hole so intensively full of anxiety that he had never felt anything like it. He turned his body around out of the bed, put his feet down against the cool marble floor. It wasn't him at all that was shaking.

He knew that he ought to hurry out onto the balcony, preferably jump down onto the dock below, immediately sit down in a secure place. The silence was quickly filled by roosters crowing and dogs howling, donkeys braying, an infernal uproar from everywhere; agitated human voices, grumbling, tears. He pressed the soles of his feet harder against the floor. It was the earth's heart that was beating. He wanted to feel the shakings as his own. The blind fury that gradually merged imperceptibly with his body's own breathing. All his pores were wide open.

Afterward, when things quieted down, he moved out onto the balcony with the blanket as a tent around his body, his legs drawn up against his chest. The dawn was the usual one, as it should be, as he remembered it; rosy-fingered. Although actually the index finger of gold is the very first thing to come, all the way to the right on the mountain top on the other side of Vathi bay, if you want to be pedantically precise about the details. And you should be. If for nothing other than the sake of credibility.

The deposits in his body after the previous evening produced the expected result. Rotten, to put it mildly, he wriggled out of the hectic final repetition of his dream, awakened by normal sounds, the high RPM rattle from the mopeds, the motor cars' more damped throbbing. Already quarter to eight. In a half hour he was supposed to meet the girls at the harbor café. In the high mirrored door of the wardrobe could be seen the wash basin, his shaving kit on the narrow shelf above, his clothes in the usual pile on the floor, the battery charger's lamp which was blinking green along side the wall socket. He rolled around in the bed but without climbing out, crumpled the sheet and blanket together around his body, huddled up, shut his eyes hard before he slowly, slowly opened them again. The change wasn't especially great. Into his field of vision came the open suitcase too with dirty underwear and socks, the tripod, the camera equipment. The thin white curtain got caught on the door handle, fluttered like a poorly set foresail in the morning breeze. Outside, everything was blue, stratified; lighter water between the balcony railing's wrought iron, the shadows on the mountains in nuances of violet, the sky like a well above. Workday.

He was the only guest at the Hotel Mentor. Down in the dismal bare reception room sagging chairs were probably awaiting the first eccentric spring tourists. It was completely empty. He put his backpack and camera down behind the counter, laid the battery belt alongside. If you didn't know what it was, it could be easily mistaken for a cartridge belt. It had happened. He straightened out the backpack. This particular morning he felt least of all like some bold warrior in the service of the public, the knight without fear, with spotless objective and the whole world as battlefield. The last champion of truth, freedom and human dignity. There weren't many left now. One by one they had fallen. Sometimes he felt very alone. Middle-aged. He hated the mere thought.

In the key slot lay a folded-up message. Call Sweden. Home? Work? That could wait. He crumpled up the telephone note and stuffed it down among the crumpled drachmas in his back pocket.

He ordered the same frugal breakfast as the girls, dry white bread, sweet marmalade, a piece of cheese, coal black, bitter steaming coffee. Their faces were morning shiny, untroubled, thoroughly rested. He didn't even dare to think of his. The baggy eyes, pecked open; the sparse reddish gray stubble that was supposed to transform him beyond virile recognition but that on this trip, too, didn't show any sign whatsoever of developing beyond a pubescent downy stage. He felt cold and shivery in his thin red and white checked summer shirt. It could be clearly seen how his new found friends were also freezing around their bare arms. All the surrounding Greek natives were naturally clad in warm sweaters, which were appropriate for this time of year, under jackets and substantial long pants. The girls at least had jeans on. He glanced furtively down at his winter-white thighs, which came forth where the shorts ended. Nice, well-trained muscles, he tried to console himself. It looked quite ridiculous.

While Pen and Mary Lou got warmer clothing, he negotiated a decent taxi price out on the dock. They stopped at the Mentor where he got the equipment, minus the tripod. It would have to be a freehand day. There was plenty of support against old olive tree trunks and Cyclops-like boulders to lean against if necessary.

"My name is Nikos," said the driver.

He drove with his side window rolled down. The inrushing morning cold was followed by the smell of the chain of cigarettes that never left his fingers. In a completely incomprehensible way they wandered from hand to mouth, between lips and hands and lighter at the same time as he shifted up and down with ever greater speed, steered past the citadel, the cave of the nymphs and over toward the steep serpentine climb at the very back of

Molo Gulf. Morning breezes were drifting in narrow streaks over the water surface, ribbed strips of dark blue that abruptly collided with the shadows of laid-up rusty boats at anchor vainly waiting for better shipping conditions. The narrow strip of beach was crowded with shiny strips of plastic with all kinds of richly colored wrappings that had floated ashore from the sea. The sand was gray, dirty, and had somehow infected the low vegetation. Higher up all that disappeared. When he turned around and looked down, time sank away. Everything was washed clean. The horizon lifted the islands and the distant mainland. Only depth and distance in the all the more over-whelming blue, all contours suddenly absurdly sharp. You could make out trees miles away. The road turned one last time and straightened out toward the north, high above the sound toward Kefallinia. A herd of goats moved quickly to the side, the herd dog barked. Nikos tooted like a madman at every new curve. The girls were holding on to each other and just laughing. But for him it was the wrong day. The transformation failed. He was and remained Hans Jörgen Kineman.

They unloaded outside of the Homerikon at Stavros. He tried to make it clear that they wanted to be picked up at four o'clock at the latest, pointed distinctly at his watch. Nikos shook his head resolutely.

"The car and I will wait here until you need us. Not much to do this time of year. Good driver, many trips, lots of money!"

The loads were divided fairly equitably. Mary Lou took the shoulder bag with microphones and mini tape recorder, Pen the blue plastic bag with the victuals. He himself pulled on the backpack which was full of new film, sound tape, charge bag and all kinds of odds and ends, a few lenses and the little black repair kit with tools. The camera he carried alternately in his right and left hand. Now he was changing sides often. Before, he used to train his strength and steadiness with long hours of holding it out from his body, dead still. Always extremely careful to stand erect and relaxed, breathe calmly from the diaphragm, like the saxophone players. First the one arm, then the other, until the weight became too much for him. At that time he never needed to use the tripod. But they were distant now, the barricades in Paris, the shiny flower-adorned bayonets in Berkeley, the student union in Stockholm, the ore fields in Lappland. Then these two weren't very old. One of them could even be his daughter. The new naive egocentric success-oriented generation.

And he himself? The comfortable withdrawal? You could get cold and sweaty for less.

The little expedition marched down toward the sea along the red, eroded sandy road that meanders forth to the edge between the fields and the precipitously steep cliffs up toward Pelikata. If they had time, he was thinking about showing them the paltry ruins of the city and still farther away the boulders that are called Homer's school and beyond, the little white church Ayios Athanasios. They rested a while and loosened their clothes. It suddenly became warm in the shelter of the hillside. Everywhere you could feel the suddenly fine and strong smell of the spring's first spices. There was a weak ringing in the air. But nowhere could they catch sight of the goats or the man tending them, just hear; hollering, barking, bleating.

He picked up the Minox from the backpack and took some pictures. They were spoiled of course by a stupid cheeeese in unison.

Everything was absolutely wrong. He got up.

"Shall we go on!"

The last bit up to the cave is difficult. Rocks have been tumbling down for millennia. Where there once must have been a fine strip of beach with good round pebbles to pull the ships up on, today it is practically speaking impassable. The smell from rancid dung was mixed with the sweet scent of humble flowers on scrubby bushes. Higher up on the hillside the stiff breeze was poking about in the sparse tops of the pines. The murmur of the waves took over the sound from the invisible goats. The light reflections from the water competed in strength with the blue light of the southern sky. Kefallinia's silhouette was just as coal black as the ravens above the steep slope; the gulls drowned in the thick white light above the sand.

As a matter of fact there isn't much left to the cave, rather a chasm, a cut in the porous rock; far too much shade left to permit work. He drove his hand down into the cool gravel inside, strained it between his fingers. Here is where the tripods were found, gift of the Phaiakes. A long, long time ago the English were there and dug them up, certainly scrupulously British. He took a couple more fists full, deeper down. The sand felt damp, raw. Finally he found something after all. A thin porous grayish brown potshard, not larger than a thumb nail. He blew it clean. It heated up in the palm of his hand.

While waiting for better light he took a roll of breaking waves and shore rocks, blue violet tree trunks, cloud formations, squeezed in a few gulls against the light, hung onto a beautiful high-stemmed fishing boat that was leaving the pier way back in the bay. The girls were on their way back from the sandy beach. He put in some new film. Then he used the charge bag as a black cloth over a table-like projecting rock and picked up some small, shriveled salty olives, bread, slices of ham, tomatoes, cheese. Opened the retsina bottle and poured into the abominable plastic glasses.

It could never hurt to ask!

He took off his shirt and kicked away his sandals, went out into the water and poured water onto himself. Their exhilarated voices were very close.

Worse than a no it could hardly be.

"Now, right away, or will it be all right after the food?"

Mary Lou stuffed an olive in and touched her waistband. Pen giggled so much that she could have peed in her pants.

"I'm a very moralistic girl," she said and turned off her smile. It was difficult to tell whether she really meant that seriously. Actually he saw only himself in her ugly black sunglasses, double, distorted, white, quite fat. He already felt sorry.

"On one condition," continued Mary Lou.

"Certainly."

"That you also take off your pants!"

He got his pictures. Without clothing, the age differences were clearer; more mother daughter than siblings. Pen's smooth powerful flesh, muscular rear, small firm breasts. Her juicy patch of hair run wild. Their faces still remarkably of the same age under equally fuzzy short clipped nut-brown hair. He zoomed in and focused on Pen's oddly slanted eyebrows, panned over to Mary Lou. There the differences were visible. Small broken blood vessels in the whites of the eyes, heavier eyelids, fine wrinkles like a thin blue shadow all the way down into the corners of her eyes. Her entire body spoke so strongly of experience that he had difficult problems with little Rousseau that grew with alarming speed. She was shaved, completely clean, not a suggestion of excess fat. Like a danseuse for whom no movement is any longer impossible. Her dark violet nipples glistened with the same color as her pussy.

After lunch they bathed together, dried in the sun.

"Tell more about your Danish grandfather, the silent film director. And my dear, please say Mary Lou in Danish. I want to hear how it sounds."

"In Swedish it sounds like this: Marie Louise."

"Say it again, say it many times."

"Marie Louise. Marie Louise, Marie Louise. Is that enough?"

"Like when grandmother says it! Exactly like it. Louiiiiise."

"The two of you are certainly related, or you will be soon the way you're carrying on."

Pen sounded a little sweet and sour.

"Just as certainly as you are my own beloved, eternally young waiting wife," Hans Jörgen said and tried a careful smile. The shade from the overhanging cliff slowly crept out over the flat rock where they were sitting. Somewhere up there the sound of thin bells became denser. Small stones fell down the precipice. Goats can find their way everywhere.

"I love sweet old dumb men," snorted Pen.

Hans Jörgen Odysseus pretended to look around.

"Can you see anyone like that here?"

"Tell me more about Denmark," interrupted Mary Lou, serious, determined.

Pen threw her hands together over her face, took them away just as quickly again, guffawing.

"This is just crazy. I love it. I love you, Mary Lou. I love you, Odysseus. Right now I love the whole world. It's so terribly stupid, everything. Can anyone help me?"

"I love you both!"

It became dead silent. They looked at him, both at the same time, and then at each other. He felt over his whole face how extraordinarily comical he had to look. Thank god everyone burst into laughter. Pen almost choked.

"Sweet Swede Odysseus. I think I'm dying!"

The sun worked on toward the zenith. The light finally began to be right for the cave. When he was done with the shooting and returned to the base camp on the shore rocks, the girls had disappeared. But they couldn't be far off. Their clothes were still there. Unfortunately, they had drunk up all the wine. He stretched out on the hot rock and let his body lose its grip, sank into the sunny blue, all the way down to the eagles. The images didn't let go. Calypso and Circe in the same sequence. Navel shadows. Sunny down on an upper lip. Grating teeth.

The pain stretched far into the dream. The attempt to draw away failed. It didn't help to wake up either. He tried to turn on his side so as in that way to be able to get at a stubborn wasp. But he was stuck, got nowhere!

She pressed him against the flat rock with her belly, sat up high on his chest, pressed hard with her legs against his sides, pressed down. Her narrow back stood up in the air, the skin on her spinal column shone. The other one was standing alongside, the younger one. She was holding a sharp thin pine branch in her hand. Sun streaks in her hair, the color like a ripe field of rye. There were cones in it. Around her chest she had daubed red earth.

"We didn't find any scar on you. For safety's sake we've made one now, under one of your shoulders."

She let her index finger move along the tip of the pine branch, brought it to her lips, licked it off. Around her waist she was wearing the battery belt, drawn tight.

"The pine resin is just great for infections. You won't have any problem at all from this. Just a little souvenir. There was one other thing too. We thought we would collect the honorarium in kind. If you don't have anything against that, of course."

She let go of the branch.

The first one, the older one, bent down over him. He felt something sticky from her chest against his belly, damp earth between their bodies. She touched him with her mouth. Then the other one came on. He turned his head to the side. The sea seemed completely unperturbed. He turned in the other direction. Deep inside in the blue shadow on the hillside above stood someone with a coarse black jacket hanging over the shoulders. Movements between bushes and rocks, white, brown animal bodies. The sound is difficult to describe, it ricocheted like playful metal between the rock faces, got a reply from the heights on the other side of the cove, scattered but still close; variations, modulations, ringing layers through sour air. The guy up there calmly laid aside his staff, opened his coat. He too was moving.

00

He had expected higher mountains and the smell of hot spices far out at sea. The coast was so low that the surf time after time obscured the dark blue contour of the forest and the thin white strip of beach or breakers. To starboard a gray treeless cape stretched out. Far out in the surge of the sea could be seen the silhouette of a sea-mark, surrounded by hazy back light. Farther in, three compact clusters, sooty black, pyramid-shaped.

He too had once been in Laestrygonia. Dogs followed him along the beach. He looked for his friends, the fools who would never listen to him, among the cadavers of washed-ashore seamen. Swimming, he came out of his dream.

The rigging creaked, the hull drifted without steerageway. The shabby black-backed gull who had joined him rode in toward land. There were strong updrafts under the clouds, bands of breezes ahead.

Intervals, he thought. Intermediate man.

He leaned over the railing. With his fingers he poked into the water, let his hand drag in the reflection. Everything was moving around him, the first man.

Where space ends time begins, the thought continued.

The moment he takes up his hand he will meet a face.

For the moment we can provisionally call him 0.

The curtain hem needed repairing. As usual it had gotten caught in the hasp. The whole curtain was wildly hitting against the window frame. The wind took hold of several manuscript papers and really made a mess on the desk. She caught them and stuffed them into place in the salt and pepper colored folder. For safety's sake she laid a fossil clump on top. Slowly she pushed the stone over the handwritten text of the jam jar label: Olympia in Asgard.

The floor cooled the soles of her feet.

It had been a remarkably breezy and cool summer. Maybe it was going to change now. The weather systems succeeded one another. In steadily new patterns, the cloud columns drifted over all of the island's skies. She walked over to the window and released the curtain, put her finger on the cut seam and tried to remember who had used the sewing machine last. Presumably one of the girls from the excavation. Perhaps Hans-Jörgen had repaired one of his many sails?

Far out on the narrow inlet, near the horizon, a boat had apparently gotten stuck in an icy blue shiny sea. One never knew where he was, her baby seal. He lived in the sea. She seldom worried, not about him at any rate. The Other One though ...

She leaned out. The sun at once grabbed her hair. In the strong light the corners of her eyes narrowed. A fine net of wrinkles fell down over her high cheekbones. Her bangs hung far down over her forehead, a little bit uneven, amateurishly cut for the summer, they reached all the way down to her sharply slanted eyebrows. She breathed in deeply, opened her mouth wide, closed her eyes. Sun spots danced under her eyelids. Her pulse increased slowly inside her ears. She held her breath, a long time.

What the landscape saw was an open window, a dark hole with a woman's figure in the row of all the closed windows that reflected the pine grove below the building wing, the barn and the big tumble-down storehouse, the road that slanted across the rubblestone earthworks and the damp shore meadow above the sheds at Fitegarda. From the farms could be heard the drone of tractors. Late larks exchanged codes. Red shanks were still making notes wildly from the stone fence.

The slam from a car door opened her eyes. She shaded them against the light with her hand, winked at the project leader's dusty jeep. It was completely impossible to see who was driving, he or one of the girls.

We live on the edge of time, she thought.

At the same time there was a ring inside the house.

The woman in the window was completely naked.

"Yeah, hello!"

The sound of the carrier wave thinned out in the receiver, thickened again around the distant voice.

"This is a person-to-person call for Mrs. Kineman."

"Okay, I'm ready."

"Hold on, please."

She leaned her long narrow back against the cool limestone wall. Her skin shriveled when she touched it, became wrinkled; all of her thin body shook. The tone in the ear changed pitch again. The new voice sounded clear and strong, her brother-in-law's.

"Is it you?"

"If it's me?"

"To hell with the existential questions, that would be much too long and too expensive for the authorities. I'll take the practical first and the interesting last. I'm flying home tomorrow. Mimmi and the kids are already in Skåne. You can count on us, you know that. We do not intend to miss the party, that's for sure."

Through the open door she saw the old man coming. He cut across the courtyard toward the shed, pattered into its shadow.

"There won't be any party this year. Didn't that get across the Atlantic? There's just no reason any more."

"Stupidity. It is clear that there will be a party. A huge celebration even. Are you sitting down? Hold onto yourself or else."

"If you're interested, I'm standing just fine."

"Blame yourself, for now comes the interesting part. He is back, the very object of the party. The dear runaway!"

Now he came out again, straightened his peaked cap, promenaded slowly over the gravel with his shuffling gait. She looked but didn't see, heard but didn't hear. What was there to say?

"It's two thirty here, what time is it over there?"

There was silence. Her heart was certainly still beating, but just as much outside the cage as inside.

"Hello! Astrid! What's with you? It's eight thirty here, why?"

Everything was blocked for the present. She looked down at the floor. The joints between a couple of the Höganäs tiles were cracked. The dark red toenails alongside actually needed mending. She should really also get that expanding birthmark under her navel removed. But that sort of thing you don't need to tell an embassy counselor on the other side of the globe; that would be too expensive for the authorities.

"I'll take it up promptly with the consul general in LA. For this sort of thing should not be permitted to happen. He was already there a week ago. Anyhow we have looked very seriously at his absence this time. Everyone. You too. Or what? Hello!"

"It's already afternoon here. And so nice that you called."

"Now everything's under control, here at any rate. We can't do any more from our end at any rate. Do you know how dad is? And the boy?

Everything okay there at home as it ought to be?"

"Otherwise, everything is fine. Naturally everything is fine. Why shouldn't it be fine. It's always fine in this house?"

She hung up in the middle of the distant guffaw. The Old One was already clinging to the outer door, but, of course, he pretended not to have heard a thing, even less to have seen her.

"Is anyone home," he shouted, just to confirm what he already knew.

"Aren't you ever going to grow up," he continued and emptied his abominable pipe against the doorpost.

A badly mishandled gull landed on the roof of the barn, stretched out its wings testingly as if putting its pinions in order after a long cruise, balanced on the ridge a few seconds, then lifted against the wind and flew away out of sight. The Old One sat down on the sandstone steps, turned away, unpleasantly present, already with a new match against the striking surface. She looked at the back of his blue overalls with all the pockets, inundated with tools.

Obscenely slowly she crossed over the hall.

"Greetings from your sons, both of them by the way," she said.

"Time to open up the Danish horse," he mumbled.

It is not certain whether she heard. The roar just increased.

"Dear Mother, best greetings from your brother and aunt Muck. They're nice and worry a lot about when I'm going to drown. The wreak of a car held up and the boat wasn't crushed by the roof rack. I hope you are getting along without it, because I'm thinking about popping over to Denmark for a couple of days after the sailboat races. Met a big red-haired Dane who has the same name as me, and we figured out that we had to be third cousins or something like that. Thought I'd look into it. The preliminary races went rottenly, shitty, damn difficult to find the way. But the third cousin seems to know the Öresund waters damn well, is going to the European Championships after this, the lucky guy. Take care. Yeah, by the way, saw a guy in a boat here in the harbor who was almost uncannily like father, strange, huh. Take care. Read the sports pages, there may be results there. Enclosing a postcard I meant to write on but there wouldn't have been any room for this novel. DS."

Bad reference, undated, not signed, DS without PS. She looked at the postcard. The flag poles with all the Nordic banners hoisted on the pier. The harbor basin full of sailboats. On the dock in the foreground a bunch of upside-down orange optimist dinghys. Greetings from Viken in a lopsided border right across the sky. Her childhood. She laid it down quickly together with the letter on top of the pile of mail and old newspapers that were crowded around the telephone. Then she looked right at the envelope. The postmark three days earlier. It probably would take ages to sail here from down there; through the door she saw the sea and caught sight of the poor creature who was stuck in the calm outside the holm.

29

She had jeans on now and the faded blue shirt with rolled up sleeves. There was a band around her grayish blond hair so that it stood out from her narrow neck. She stepped out onto the steps and shouted straight out into the quiet afternoon heat between the houses:

"I'm taking the car to the Konsum."

The answer came from inside the shed.

"It's at Blue Thorp. Is it your damned archaeologists who messed up the tools again!"

"Hans-Jörgen took along a few to Skåne. Did he really forget to tell you. He surely knows how angry you get. Do you want to eat with us this evening?"

No answer, of course. But an extra large au gratin potato dish should be enough for everyone.

She bent down and tied bows on her cranberry and milk-colored run-down jogging shoes, squatted a while with her elbows against her knees and rested her chin in her intertwined hands. There was a bit of a tightening back there. She would probably never get fat?

It smelled warm from the ground, of summer well under way; all the scents flowed together in the hardly noticeable breeze. The swallow-wort that she'd never really been able to put up with. The thyme. The sweetness of the lady's bedstraw. Ground lilacs they were called on the island; virgin Mary's bedstraw.

She straightened up and jogged the sparse alder avenue down to the fishing booths, whirled around as in a dance, swung her arms exaggeratedly, jumped over the ditch and crept under the barbed wire; continued over the lamb pasture between junipers and whitebeams and alder buckthorns and heavily bitten-down rowan bushes, the whole time in the same way, very lightly.

He looked after her.

Incomprehensible. She'd probably have to get old sometime too. Clearly some never grow up. Some are never anything but.

It was getting dark much earlier now, the end of July. The girls were trying to find the glass covers in the big room, put in candles and set them out on the table. The flies got tired after a while. The old man finally went home after a few hours of brilliant acting, since he usually knew most and best, criticized and corrected; in his time they still felt respect for knowledge and experience, understood the art of listening and learning, independent of the topic of conversation, to be sure. Nagging, more repetitive. Jabber.

Everyone was quite exhausted. Still they remained.

"One more glass, madame!"

"You know that I won't decline. How about you?"

"Is that perhaps supposed to represent a reproach?"

"I reproach you all."

The two female aides exchanged glances, invisibly they thought for sure.

"You want some too?"

They got up instead. Their names were Ler and Långhalm. Always at each other's sides, at least when she was present. The giggly understanding, the crazy conversation, their own codes that no one on the outside could understand. Now they stand there and know precisely what is going to happen between the big buck and his magnificent ewe. Oh, how she occasionally missed that community between girls of the same age. She read their quick facial expressions, the signals from the corners of the mouths, the hardly perceptible contraction at the corners of the eyes. Strange, really, that they didn't understand that she understood!

Ler was really named Lisa and was actually a very prominent expert on ceramics, an amanuensis at the archaeological institute in Stockholm and assiduous summer digger on Gotland. A little stuck up perhaps, with an ironic, almost snotty manner with her boss. But she could afford that. She was irreplaceable.

Långhalm was more difficult to figure out. She was a product of the island: scrupulous, strong as a Gotland pony from Lojsta, broad-shoulderd and radiating such a strong femininity that all men within ten miles used to shrink at her mere presence. But she almost never said a word. Just wrote her reports, did her digging, vacuumed the fields with the metal detector, disappeared for a few days here and there to the mainland and won orienteering competitions. Brittgun. You can be called anything.

"Is there something we can do in the kitchen," wondered Ler.

"Certainly," she answered, but changed her mind at once.

"There's so little, I can take care of it. But you could clear the table if you want."

She lifted up the black Cretan wool shawl from the back of the chair and swept it around herself. Low evening moisture drifted up from the shore meadows. Her fingertips got very wet when she moved them over the shiny white lacquered ribbed table. He laid his hand over hers. She drew away, lightning fast, stuck both of her hands down between her thighs, as if she were freezing.

To tell the truth she was still shaking.

"Hans-Jörgen is on his way home."

She said it so quietly that he hardly grasped it himself.

"Did the sailboat races go well?"

"The other one."

The interval between the breaths, where most of life is played out, can be just as silent as the silence between stones.

"And I who have it so damned good with all my women!"

"You're a big bastard."

"I know," he said.

"Some time I'm going to …"

But she interrupted herself and instead got up from the chair with her eyes firmly, almost convulsively drawn together.

"I know," he said one more time, very calmly.

Let me begin with a statement: everything, or call it rather by a more solemn word for life, is in the end a question of secrets and control. It can just as well be expressed in terms of memory and consciousness, history: stories in short. In this competent forum it is enough to mention names like Bergson, Freud, Baudelaire, Proust, Benjamin so that you'll understand at once what I mean. But I don't want you to be frightened by all of your predetermined and precisely limited prior knowledge.

I want you to make a clean slate!

For you, control is a plus word, control of facts, of life itself; secret is something negatively loaded. If you are to have any benefit at all from the following reasoning I ask you to allow these words to change overtones.

Now you no longer have a clean slate. Then we can begin!

I amused myself by calling this prologue Odysseus in the Baltic, although it is of course just a way of cajoling you with my old well-known and thrashed-over ideas about Gotland's narrator stones. The treatise I always rehearse. But now Olympia's visit to Asgard will soon be arranged. However, I have to warn sensitive persons from the very beginning. Where gods live there is nothing holy. Least of all any self-evident scientific truths.

Notice how I talk about stories, not about circles of motifs, symbols, the idiomatic language of images. It is clear that I have a purpose with this. I of course want you to totally forget that you ever saw these so-called picture stones.

If you will be so kind as to wipe the slate completely clean again! Otherwise, this will not work!

At the end of the presentation you will naturally get to defend the preconceived notions you then can still be thought to hold; it is after all still science we are dealing with, reality itself, isn't that so?

The discerning listener – others are not of concern here – will say to themselves now as a matter of course that if it is impossible to give answers to fundamental questions, then it is highly unlikely that we will ever arrive at a well-grounded understanding of how the Homeric poets got up here. And note well that I am not talking about the legends which we know were performed here on the island.

I of course agree with the discerning sceptic.

Once and for all we have to forgo the tempting thought that these songs were performed in holy places, at big meetings, ritual festival-like entertainments around the island. That would lead to immediately unlikely consequences for the interpretation of the Homeric material that synchronically circulated around the Mediterranean, with the same content as recorded by Säve here on Gotland, by others around the entire Finnish gulf, in Lithuania, at Rügen.

Every work of art ever created is intended to be used in one or another way. No painting is painted for the blind; no ship is built where there is no sea. The classical question remains: who really has a use for Odysseus?

She paused as if to check the effect of her words. They had all obviously grown closer; scarecrows with footnotes rattling around their necks, hirsute folklorist organs on the way out of the sheaths, art veterinarians, cocksure diapered structuralists. No one was missing. All one hundred and eight, or was it 129, archeologists were also present around the shrinking table. She put herself at ease, prepared for the chaste agonizing; the same old apathetic enjoyment as always at these solemn meetings.

The sun shone in under the curtains. She rolled around, returned to the secure morning slumber. The bed rocked. Like a tree full of buzzing insects and sweet scents from fruits still hidden under the petals. Her nightgown had twisted together around her chest, caught in her armpits. She always slept dressed, like a very young girl.

The invasion was well prepared. It wasn't possible to squeeze a single hamburger into the ice chest. The responsibility for all practical arrangements was, of course, hers; there wasn't anyone who even questioned that. Ler and Långhalm had to work at Gamlehamn, there just wasn't talk about anything else. Besides it didn't have to be done so specially, bake your bread, whip up a few salads, fix the lamb; you were so good at that! Wine, people bring along nowadays. Prehistoric drink they would get from Austers. As if the idea for this whole party was in some way hers. It would've been much simpler to fix everything over at the excavation, when everyone was still there. Fit perfectly such hearty types like Björn and the colleagues he was going to show off for, the professors in the shiny, worn leather shorts with long sheath knives at the belt or in well polished black party shoes, right suit and high shiny, sweaty foreheads after the strenuous promenade from the bus to the actual scene of the crime, through a frightening reality full of mosquitos and prickly juniper shrubs full of ticks and staring sheep; the doctoral candidates with their lap-top computers in their backpacks and virile beards over their entire bodies; all the cocksure female amanuenses with smoothly lustrous flesh and obvious menstrual difficulties; cleansed, sinewy and weather-beaten relic inventoriers of both sexes and all ages; relaxed museum people who long ago understood the seamy side of research and instead wisely concentrated on automatic promotion with corresponding moves up the salary scale and summer symposia, preferably on Gotland with expense allowances and the appurtenant free entertainment.

She was morose. Completely morose. Outside and inside. It smelled warm around her. She hated it. Just as much as she hated this sudden anxiety. Absence. Homecoming. She had nothing to be ashamed of. They had promised each other fidelity and freedom, once and for all; there was nothing remarkable about that. There was no reason whatsoever for her to feel this way. Yet she did. He had been away before, come home before, tarried too long. They had lived their parallel lives in peace, allowed their own strengths to grow.

She couldn't stand to think about it.

And then the scene with Hans Jörgen when he came back from the sailboat races in Fiken and the strange excursion to the Danish relatives whom they never had any contact with any more, apart from a few occasional, usually unanswered Christmas greetings, letters with the mourning border and a few newspaper clippings, the old photo albums deep down in the secretary. He comes home dark brown on his neck and face from the sun and real Kattegatt salinity, handsome as a young curly god and she runs out toward him as she always does to hug him, her own little boy: wonders how it went. But he just pushes her away, really maliciously, hard, so that it hurt against the car door. Bad, he answered, can you help out a bit so we can get this shit-boat down from the roof rack. You expected something else perhaps? Not the slightest glance by way of thanks, although her back almost broke in two.

"To hell with this shit, going home to Lidingö for a while so you can do whatever you want here."

Angry, furious, infuriated, rigid in his body, absolutely stiff; so that it hurt you yourself. No sweet baby seal anymore. A very strange youth.

"Why didn't you all ever tell me the real story about Denmark."

Yes, why haven't you done it. The truth was quite simply that she didn't have anything to tell about Denmark.

"It's your blood, your relatives. You can talk with grandfather about that. Or your dad."

"You know very well that you don't talk with grandfather. And there's barely been any dad."

That certainly made sense. Then he tossed her the car keys, hard again. They fell down in the gravel in front of her bare feet. Still, she couldn't get angry, bop him on the nose, just stood there and looked into her son's expressionless face. It was wet! From tears, I suppose?

He dashed into the house. Amazed and surprised she turned after him. Do you really have to tolerate anything whatsoever, cope with exactly everything just because you are a mother, happen to have been born a woman.

The sun-warmed sheet metal burned against the back of her thighs, but she needed that support.

"I've got time to make the 12 o'clock bus. You can always say hello to Dad when he comes back. The Danish relatives said that he passed by, was on his way home. Let the boat lie there. I'll fix it some other time. Bye!"

"Say hello to Björn, by the way. I actually finished twelfth. Out of sixty Lasers. Not too damn piddly considering it was Öresund."

They found her where she usually hung out, way out on Auren. Her bike with the bast fiber basket clearly signaled refuge. The beach was still quite full of people although it was late in the afternoon. There had been some prudes out there again, not at all the same wonderful unconcerned naked community as a couple of years ago. But it still happened that there were enough swinging old men's cocks and plodding old women's butts, bare feet splashing around in the seaweed at the edge of the water, hands filled with smooth, sun-warmed stones that wanted to melt into the skin. Youth were dressed now, in flapping jogging shorts or shiny clinging stingily cut tank suits. Of course it was still the same old normal summertime of anarchy, dancing of happy bodies on satin sand, in the velvet water, under high summer's blond crown.

She would have preferred to be alone, to herself, by herself. They were swimming together in all the luster. Ler and Långhalm with their bikini shorts on, Bamse with his hat and modestly controlled erectile tissues. She was swimming along the shore, in the deep beyond the sand banks, where the cool of the water was both pain and pleasure. Nothing is more beautiful than this condition of movement and rest, the calm strokes, her legs high in the waves. The sea full of hands, her body open to everything, no demands.

With her arms stretched straight up and wide-open eyes she sank down to the bottom. The patterns of the waves over the sand's grooves came closer. She huddled up down there but the air in her lungs wanted to get out and go up or burst her. She emptied herself completely, exhaled and pushed away with strong legs, lay on her back, drifted with the weak current below the swells. Terns swaggered and shrieked. Under the high, piled-up clouds over Näset late summer buzzards were already whirling.

When she waded ashore the girls had long since jogged off toward the lighthouse. It was meaningless to try to get in a race. But she too ran a few steps, let the motion merge into dance; the wind got to lift her, lacking Baryshnikov. She got goose pimples in spite of the afternoon heat. The water shone on her breasts, dew glittered in the twisted knot of her sex. She caught sight of him up there, whoever he was. The eternal man? She was at any rate the first woman.

It tickled in the side; hurt in the armpits. She must have dozed off.

"Ah! Lay off. It pinches. And think about the girls."

"It'll be a while before they come. They're real joggers."

He got up and looked over the edge of the dune, nodded sort of affirmatively, threw together some more strong lyme-grass straws.

"A little beating might be nice, huh."

But he just crumbled the spikes over her, in small yellow down that fell over her body. She liked it. She liked him too. There wasn't anything more to it. It felt nice. He stretched out alongside of her, on the side, close by, lay his wet hat where the stomach's huge muscle mass merges with various limbs. His free arm he placed over her, with his hand on one breast.

"You better lay off."

No one moved. They lay there, completely silent, a short while.

Then he got up one more time, walked up to the edge of the dune, squatted like an Indian.

She turned around, her tail in the air.

"That surely wasn't the idea!"

"I don't want to get a bunch of sand on me."

She sat up and rooted around in her backpack among note pads and cans of Nivea and chapstick and nail clippers which she cut herself on. First, she carefully licked her fingertip clean from the little drop of blood.

"Well. Can you put it on yourself or should mama perhaps help?"

Of all the wives of all the heroes who persisted in fighting year out and year in she is said to have been the only one who withstood the sweet temptation of meanwhile amusing herself with various lovers. Now it is not at all certain that anything is true just because it's in a book; some thoughts on a papyrus fragment from the area of Alexandria; scribblings on a wall in Athens itself; genuine type in Chalkokondyla's Florentine edition; a recent cheap edition pocketsize.

It is actually also asserted, and from what I understand, with at least as good a right, that she threw herself into the sea from pure and simple desperation since the rumors had reached her that her husband had also descended below the walls. That time she was saved by gulls. Long-tongued cormorants brought her ashore to a continued extended waiting for the homecomer. Meanwhile, she amused herself by shacking up with all one hundred and twenty-nine or one hundred and eight suitors, the information is uncertain, to see which one had the softest skin. At any rate the great Pan maintains that he was conceived during this mass copulation.

Besides, it is claimed that at the homecoming, instead of bringing about an unnecessary mass slaughter of completely able-bodied and fit-to-fight men, he satisfied himself by killing her, because of the supposed infidelity with Amphinomus. Then he took off out into the world.

However, no one has denied that she once was a young girl standing at the gate and waiting.

Hawthorns and rowans, badly treated by the winds from the sea, were crowded into a brushy cluster by the gate. They're still there today, just as alive, just as knocked about. Besides, the rowans should sometime be feted in the same way as the hawthorn at Combray. The fingers of the leaves grown together in constantly new forms should signal the memories, in the same way as the epoch evoked Balbeck or the uneven paving stones Piazza San Marco in Venice.

Of course, it's not that simple. Yet, I can picture him quite well. Everything is contained among the words which were then still entirely usable, not worn-down like counterfeiters' glass coins with thin films of gold, soiled by all sorts of reality, worn by time and printer's ink.

The war was forgotten in an afternoon. And then summer vacation came. So, a brushy low-grown cluster of trees crowded around the gate. The terns' irritating hoots could be heard clearly. They were diving unnecessarily at some invisible person down on the beach. From what he heard and saw he was finally possessed with a great calm. Gone were all the sarcastic commentaries about how big and clever he had become; the usual scornful grin that was several sizes too big for Tomas' pimply face; the smell from Annastina who on the other hand had really grown a bit. The last bit from the ferry berth they traveled under normal, sullen cousin silence. Everything would certainly be normal, the eternal summer vacation match on neutral ground between Skåne and Stockholm, or Lidingö and Helsingborg to be precise.

There was an unknown girl standing at the gate. She unlatched it, opened it, curtsied and held out her hand. She could hardly have been from the island, for she had on only a canary yellow bathing suit, tied on with a big bow around the neck.

"Do you have any pennies on you," Tomas said appealing.

At the same time the girls exploded into guffaws. He got his hand up out of his pocket as quick as lightning where he of course had immediately begun to search. She, the new one, shut up and climbed up onto the wagon bed.

"Does anyone want some," she wondered and dangled a strawberry filled blade of grass. She actually smelled of strawberries too, she's always smelled that way, sun sweet, freshly warm; also when she spread her legs the first time for him.

"You're first, because you're new," she said and reached out, but Tomas got there first, grabbed onto the straw and crushed the berries in his clumsy fist.

"Damn kid," shouted Annastina angrily and tried to punch him. But her brother just grinned and dried himself off on the edge of the driver's seat. He cracked the whip and the ancient horse toiled on ahead on the dry loosely packed road. Raspy larks climbed from the shore meadow through the early summer air, disbanded high up in hovering drills.

"Annastina has a companion with her this year," Tomas nodded. "For safety's sake, sort of. As if we aren't good enough any more."

With the suitcase which was supporting his back he settled down with the soft knapsack between his knees. His sandals were much too new and pinched near the big toes. But his nails had survived, were still completely whole and uncracked. The previous summer had been a barefoot summer. Now he was grown up. Alone and strong. The whole holiday without unnecessary parents and brother. The island completely to himself. His own sea.

There have always been foundlings and changelings, he thought, little people who thrive best in corners and intervals that no others know about; presumably they never need to become properly grown up, yet do just fine.

In any case no pimply cousins and totally unnecessary girls were going to disturb this summer. Besides you could never know whether it was the last one; not even he, the first man.

All four sat stone silent. But it was hardly noticeable, the rest of reality unperturbed was still making as much noise as possible, mostly the birds of course and the waves which were fighting with the rubble-stones for room on the shore.

He looked without looking. One thing was absolutely clear. There wasn't going to be much pleasure from those two girls. He remembered Annastina as something completely different than the woman who was now sitting alongside of him; then a daring tree climber and swimmer in forbidden storm waves. That one could change so quickly! Now she just looked big; not to talk about that other one who seemed if possible even more useless with all of her bulges.

Someone nudged him in the side, and he glared angrily at Tomas. But it wasn't he who had pushed.

"Do you want some? You should always have reserves in the wilds. My name is Astrid."

You Tarzan, me Jane – who in the hell did she think he was? Somewhere at this second, Cheetah had to be crouching behind the stone fence and roaring his chimpanzee laughter and hitting himself on his hunched hairy thigh. What should he do?

He stuffed the little chapped, hairy, yellowish-red berry into his mouth. But her smile he couldn't cope with. And then it was so little and short that only he in the entire world could have perceived it. It was just that precisely in that insignificant tenth of a second Tomas of course turned around to check on what was being furtively offered behind his back.

"Are you sick or something else serious?"

The damn redness, that was his illness. If it at least had been normal, innocent heat from the sun that had spread out, if you could blame it on sunburn. But his face was still schoolroom white, homework white, exam white, cribbing white.

"You weren't thinking of burning up or what?"

Sometimes stoic silence is the only way to survive, not to reveal with a single word your own enormous strength, how you could knock all quick-witted super scoundrels to the ground with a single lightning rejoinder.

He jumped off and let the horse and wagon go on.

"Oh, don't sulk so damned much. Climb up now."

"You can certainly understand that he doesn't want to the way you're carrying on. Make up, huh!"

The girls' faces. They looked at him seriously, brightly, as if nothing had happened. He slowly followed along, stuffed his hands down deep in his pants pockets, really bored down so that he felt the seams. The unevenness in the road penetrated through the thin soles of his sandals. He kept a distance from the wagon.

I'll come entirely alone, he thought. There isn't anyone else. The first man. I'm the only one in the entire world. The world exists only for me, through me. It is best for them to be careful up ahead. If I don't want them, then they don't exist. I still remember clearly the girls' faces, that one of their mouths finally broke into a pearly laugh which easily could have competed with the call of the wading birds.

That it didn't have a thing to do with me, I can almost swear to that.

Everything is there, simpler of course, not worn, mistreated by either memory or time. Alongside, immediately below, next to, very close to the words. Figures.

But the feeling of uneasiness he couldn't get rid of. He often used to get directions when he was running and it was no longer fun or he wasn't among the very first ones. It was the same thing now. It took so damn little for everything to capsize, a whole summer to start out completely wrong.

He jumped up on the bed again, with his back against the others. The girls were chattering. Tomas bellowed right out into the air:

"Biggest, prettiest, best; kicks like a horse; just say when if you want, said the horse!"

And then a raw laugh and a scornful grin that burned in his back.

The road went on under the wagon, not much more than wheel tracks with thin tufts of coarse grass that disappeared to the rear. The stiff wheel axles responded immediately to all the large rocks and kicked straight into the butt. The legs dangled, sickly white. The sandals were dusty from swirled-up limestone dust. He dried them off against his calves, the one after the other, spit on the broad leather straps to get more shine and missed of course; the gob ended up under one knee. He let it be. It was now above all a matter of emptying himself, not getting irritated by anything, so as in the simplest way to again become the first man, perhaps even the only one. Everything was really quite simple. What he didn't see didn't exist. But his cousins and that other one could still be heard. What could you do about that?

"Hopp-la my swift steed!"

You could go crazy at that cheerful type. Everything would certainly have been much better if instead he had taken the bus all the way to Lassorkröken and walked the last bit, then this entire painful arrival could have been avoided. Of course, it was part of all the stupid customs of the summer that you were supposed to be picked up in this ancient way down at the beach restaurant on the other side of the island. You were supposed to notice that you were in the right country, in some sort of middle ages. As if there weren't any V2 bombers now and jet planes without propellers. Soon half the century would actually have passed.

But the first and presumably also last man didn't succeed in extinguishing the voices. After a while the reality got the better of him. He turned around and checked. It was only to bitterly ascertain that two girls were sitting there looking remarkable and then the coachman who also turned around but who all of a sudden was transformed and looked very nice and friendly and pimply and even smiled when he pointed with his funny homemade whip:

"Damn, it's pretty nice in any case."

Sometime he would express all that much better, so that the world around would be dumbfounded; with at least as much life and reality as in the deerfoot books and in the forests of words around the log house at Licking river. Although the landscape of course was very different, deep forests with mystical quiet streams instead of flat open wind-tormented heaths and thin gray rubble-stone fields where it was incomprehensible that anything could grow at all; the prairie's buffalo herds exchanged for lambs and staring cows with wet muzzles, Sioux and Apaches for rather peaceful old men and old women who talked their incomprehensible language and offered rolls and sour bread and laced coffee on saucers when no useful civilized people were around and you helped with the hay and raked and drove it in. Happiness, when at last the fishing village's low gray houses popped up with the boats in front and the nets' silvery wooden racks and the whole sea. It should at least be possible to express this much better than with a meager: how nice it is at any rate. With the recorder perhaps or on a rolled up, chalky canvas which he had gotten together with many fine oil paints with the money he got for good grades. Or why not with the little snipe that some friendly soul had already driven down to the shore from the winter lodging up in the shed – it only needed to be varnished and rigged then he would be able to say what he wanted to through perfect tacks and bold jibes way beyond the breakers, under clouds of gulls and seagulls and the giant sea-eagle that swept happy days over the bay.

The sun cut obliquely through the very clear water as it does in the early summer, toward the sandy bottom. The light painted the whole wide bay in ultramarine and green or dark, dark blue-violet where the seaweeds swept forth in the shadow of the seal rocks where the waves finally broke and burst in a breeze and gleaming sun sparks.

The house too lay as it should, firmly anchored between high pines that no northwest storms were able to dislodge, even if some of the trunks were leaning precariously after extra hard shoves from the eternal wind. The sloping roof and the few windows gossiped about prehistoric times when the building was still new, it showed clearly, for it was still newly whitewashed, should have been grayer; like the farms on the other side of the shore meadows or like the hotchpotch of fences all over the place, that divided field and pasture, carrots and oats, hop-poles, asparagus plants; cows and lambs from all the good green summer goodies.

"Let's go down and take a swim together, huh. You'll go along! Then we can play something."

"How cold is it?"

"We'll get strawberries for dessert. Edla has been picking them."

"Can you stay in for a long time?"

"As long as you want."

"I'm not swimming. Don't have any extra fat layer like the girls here."

"You're so damn disgusting. Just cowardly and filthy and pimply."

He got rid of them. Instead he waved to uncle Selfrid who was sitting astride the ridge of the roof straightening dormers with a rake. He raised it straight up in answer, saluted militarily before he handed it down to the ground in a wide arc. Tomas swung the whip and finally succeeded in getting a crack. The horse flinched surprised, stopped, twitched with his ears and peacefully began to munch along the ditch-bank.

"Damn horse!"

He pulled in the reins and tried to get in a few smacks.

The girls jumped off, but then whatever her name was crawled back up again and tried to grab the handle of his suitcase. When she saw how heavy it was, she just laughed and rushed off again and raced Annastina. The draft from the wind smelled sweet. Her bathing suit cut into her in back. Her buttocks showed clearly.

"Damn. Typical. They're going to laugh like hell at Austers."

The coachman jumped off, took hold of the halter and pulled and dragged the poor surprised horse head, which very easily shook loose and snorted and showed its foul yellow teeth. He left Tomas to his well-deserved fate, put on his backpack and lugged the lead suitcase the last hundred yards up to the farm. The alders had hardly blossomed, there were still bunches of spring blossoms in the ditch among all the compact, lavender orchids.

There was someone sunk down in one of the summer's lethal easy chairs, alongside the high steps, in the shade under the lilacs; someone whom he didn't immediately recognize. Aunt Molle of course appeared in the wide-open door, in the usual same old blue and white checked dress as in all the other normal old summer vacation summers, wavy, wavy, wavy.

Actually, you could see only a pair of black pants and a wrinkled white linen jacket with gray vest underneath. But the voice still talked of life in the little remnant of a body.

"Hello, my hale fellow."

Surely he understood that it was Danish he was hearing. Yet, it was a thousand years before it occurred to him that he actually knew that miniature man, that that was all that was left of the round, strict good old grandfather from Denmark. A big stone grew in his mouth. But, even if it got so heavy that he could hardly move, he succeeded in putting down his suitcase, stepped forward, held out his hand and bowed.

"Hello, grandfather," he said.

"I really wanted to come here once, again. I have been here before, you see. And I brought along the horse. I think you should have it back. We did win the war finally, I believe?"

At last he dared to look at the face under the old tropical hat. It was very yellow, the corners of the eyes too. But it smiled.

The summers at that time were divided into a number of phases, I would almost venture to say fixed situations, rules of the game that were followed by most of the people involved so that as peaceful conditions as possible should prevail. Among these unwritten instructions were to be noted the following: You should help out as little as possible. You should for safety's sake pay attention to the dinner hour. You should stay as far away from the kitchen as possible. Look out for all civilized adults, especially those from the Stockholm environs. Willingly help the original inhabitants with hay-making early in the summer and with the threshing work in the late summer. Pretend that you are very interested in nature and learn by heart the names of a number of birds and flowers. Generally have a book close by, as if you were studying ahead for the fall term.

The one who didn't follow these and similar directions to a T risked being hit at any time and for no reason whatsoever with the most repulsive punishments. Any sort of higher court to appeal to didn't on the whole exist. In short, the summer was a society of lawlessness and anarchy for the one who knew how to exploit the intervals, the controllers' nightmares. Yet, terrible, fateful accidents often occurred, when you least of all anticipated it.

The first days it was easy to keep out of the way. Especially for Hans Jörgen who obstinately and carefully was scraping his boat clean, trying to get rid of the woodrot between the ribs and planking; he blamed it on the moisture which hindered the varnishing in spite of the fact that the sun was shining brightly and offering remarkably dry weather days at a stretch. As a matter of fact he was afraid. Deathly afraid. Already from the first moment it was clear to him that he was exposed to the very last summer on earth; many signs pointed to that. It wasn't just that grandfather was sitting up there in a chair and dying. After a few days everything began to go seriously wrong..

He worked on the mast. It lay between two sawhorses with himself under it on his back in the prickly grass. His back was still tender and pink and he had had the first round of peeling around the shoulders. Yet he had no shirt on. By getting brown as quick as possible you were through with that bother from then on for the rest of the summer. That extra effort that had to be made before the fall's first gymnasium lessons, when you were supposed to be the brownest in the class, could be taken care of by the usual strict sun treatment among the dunes the last days before the trip home.

"Hi!"

"Hi."

It was Astrid, the new girl; Annastina's summer pal.

He rubbed the sun out of his eyes and of course hit his head on the mast when he sat up.

"Shit!"

"Whoops."

Larks. Lapwings complained. Hysterically jabbering redshanks. An awful bird din filled the ensuing distress pause. She sat down just opposite, with her legs crossed, rubbed the thyme and grass with her hands.

"How soft it is. Have you felt it?"

He pressed his palm down on the ground and felt inexpressibly foolish.

"And you just paint and paint."

"Varnishing actually."

"Varnishing then. Apropos that, would you have anything especially against my borrowing your paint-box. I mean of course just while you're working on your boat. And if you don't want to, just say no. I know that oil paints are expensive."

Now she was undoubtedly looking at him. He suspected it by all at once looking in all directions except into her eyes. There stood the racks for drying the nets, the old, upside down rowboat like a shiny insect black as tar, weathered gray fishing booths, rippled water between shore and horizon; all of reality in its right place. He already knew that her eyes were brown, annoying and forward, always inquisitively staring into others. He had also noticed that. There was something special with her presence. As if it told about coming catastrophes.

You could feel all the more clearly that the last summer was there.

"Everything is under the bed in my room. The roll of canvas too. You can take a bit if you want."

"Are you sure, are you absolutely sure that I can?"

"Sure you can. Otherwise, I probably wouldn't say it."

"You never know. I mean ..."

She was silent. Now she could just as well go. But she stayed on anyway.

"It's nice here," she said.

"You could stay here a lifetime. Almost, at any rate."

She stretched out one hand and grazed as if by accident his bare upper arm. It burned.

"See you. I should also say thanks. Thanks! Did you know by the way that I have my name day on your birthday. We could have a party together! My name is Karin too, you see."

Astrid Karin. Aha. He shivered at the mere thought. But the summer was still eternally long, August just an ugly word; a party with cherry juice and blond pigtails a remote and loathsome threat which certainly could be gotten out of.

"Bye," he said and remained sitting a good while too after she had gone off, for he could neither lie down and resume a supine position under the mast nor politely get up as you're supposed to do when women get up; every movement was of course totally impossible because of the state of things in his tight bathing suit.

And this was only the beginning of an unusually nightmarish day!

He was at home for a while and cleaned his fingers with turpentine, had a quick snack and guzzled down a half jug of luke-warm milk that was still standing in the pantry and not doing so well. The house was empty. No trace whatsoever of life. Just death. He quickly slipped past the easy chair. It was unbelievable how thin a human body could become. Yet it was there somewhere under the blanket. There were presumably things to explain between him and grandfather or vice versa. About the man in the interval for example. Some time he too would become one of those, fill the space between father and son with presence and absence; take the place as the obvious first man, who nevertheless is always between others.

He had fortunately grown out of the Indian age. But for safety's sake he transformed himself as quickly as possible into Sitting Bull when he passed the shore booths and invisibly succeeded in getting by all the pale faces in the form of various relatives with accompanying coffee thermoses and rolls. He moved a pine branch aside. Tomas lay roasting his fowl pimples. Annastina glistened from the disgusting, greasy Nivea cream. It smelled faintly of resin from pine needles, sour from the black stagnant pool in the middle of the grove. The gravel path swept past close behind shabby wind beaten pines that separated the shore from the actual main forest where the real trees were, the lamb pastures and the huge dunes which wandered far in over the island.

Cling clang, cling clang!

Two of the old women from the boarding house cycled past and waved cheerfully at him. The first summer the family had also lived up there, before the house was ready enough so that you could live in it, if it should ever be that. It was always the same types that returned, one or another score of guests spread out over the summer. Those two belonged to the early summer round and were distinguished primarily by dreadful hats that they always had on during the dinners where they roared out drinking songs with the old boys or were just silly in general terms.

He popped quickly in among the orchids and the gray grass from last year under the pines and rushed so far out onto the beach that he became quite alone. He managed the world's quickest dip and then made himself comfortable in the soft hot sand. After a while he jumped up, carefully observed the closest surroundings, pulled off the wet bathing trunks and again stretched out. He shook the sand out of the whodunnit magazine and definitively left this world for a while.

Song! There was someone singing. There was another one singing. Shrill. At the top of their lungs. He must have dozed off in the middle of the murder. His head was heavy and his eyelids sticky. Reality must have literally ground on. The voices came from down in the water. He crawled up onto the edge of the dune and pushed the lyme grass aside. They were apparently engaged in shocking behavior, totally naked at the water's edge. He got up carefully, squatting, so that they couldn't see him. The beach was completely empty, apart from the tiny family dots far away at the booths. The witches just continued, laughing, singing. Now the hags danced around with each other, the water splashed; laughing, singing. Ancient; certainly forty, fifty years.

He tried to squash himself flat the best he could, but in the end he still had to loosen his stomach and try to get rid of all the sand that had penetrated far in under the foreskin. Suddenly the voices drew near. Impossible to get on his bathing trunks! Appallingly sparse between the pines where he was lying and pressing down! The only possibility for salvation would be the world's fastest sixty meter dash to date to the protective forest curtain on the other side of the road. Yet he remained there, petrified by the song that now went over into an ever crazier two-part humming. A quick transformation into lead would possibly suffice for allowing him to sink down into the lower regions. Another possibility would be to turn into a gull as quickly as possible. Only a miracle could save him from eternal ignominy, shame and degradation. From the dining-room of the bread and breakfast via the store the jungle telegraph would reach their kitchen as quick as lightning, his parents would be called home from a business trip to Germany, his brother, disgraced, would have to leave cadet school in Karlberg, he himself at the beginning of the term be openly branded in front of all the classes of the same grade in the gymnasium. The captain would call him forth with his dry voice from the peaceful existence in the third squad, with the C people, and order his pants down; the stain of all time would be revealed in front of all the people. A sunburned butt!

The unexpected and sudden silence had its very natural explanation. They passed by in the dune alongside and never noticed the flattened creature. He carefully raised his head. Still entirely naked and with swinging rumps they disappeared along the road during an ever weaker song, looked carefully around before they hurried over and continued up toward the shack they were renting from the Ljungholms. For some inexplicable reason he followed along; bewitched, quick, low so that no one could see from over at Fitegarda, crossed on his bare feet over the hard, hot limestone-covered surface, to safety among the low small pines that were crowding around the red limbed trunks of the real hefty chaps. The song could be heard clearly again, through open windows. He sneaked ahead, unresisting, it was impossible to stop. He didn't know at all what he was going to do with them, just that he had to see, see more, much more of the wretchedness.

The singing was still going on inside when he felt the quick grasp around his body. Something warm fluffy soft that was pressing against him, clung fast and wouldn't let go.

"Vera, Vera, you have to come out quickly, hurry up, and see what I've found!"

He made himself as narrow as an eel, broad as a ram, sharp as a pike tooth, hard as rock crystal.

"But it's just sweet Hans Jörgen, as you can see!"

The other one came forward into the door opening that was filled with huge dangling breasts and masses of coal black curly hair below the stomach.

"Do you think he is big enough yet?"

"I think we'll let him go. Hardly legal. He'll have to improve in looks. By the way, do you know when mama and papa are coming down, then we can begin to play bridge with them?"

The slap behind released him from the spell.

"Besides, you will certainly want to have a glass of milk before you go down and swim again."

He didn't walk, he flew.

He was simply in such a hurry that he saw absolutely nothing. The cyclist succeeded though at the last second in making way. It was Astrid. She had the paint box in the basket. In one hand she was balancing a piece of canvas stretched on masonite.

She turned toward him, astraddle over the frame.

"Has anything serious happened?"

"No, why."

Before the heat in his face totally wiped him out he could still perceive the weak song from the forest with the high voices; as well as her close, increasing voice:

"In any case, you don't have anything on."

He didn't get any closer. Without wind the hull was rocked by the swells. The water surface shiny between bands of seaweed, broad yellow bands from the pollen of the pines. There on the island, inside the white strip of beach, there was possibly a father, a son, a wife. Sometime the truth about the horse would probably come out too, who built it, who carried it. The little horse in the boy's knapsack.

Three times he had visited reality's Ithaca. Three times he had left the island, at dawn on the ferry to Patras, under the sunrise described definitively once and for all. The gulls flocked over the wake. The sinking mountains. The low invisible mainland where Byron died.

Heroes, he thought. It's been a long time since they disappeared. Yet the war goes on.

The first time he took the pictures home with him, to honor a poet who got a big prize, but had to die bitter.

The second time an involuntary slave in an ever larger organization.

The third time the trip away began.

Now he was again almost home. The evening breeze carried him down toward Svavar Huk. The night was still rather light. Below land he found some wind which was enough all the way into the sound.

There is no reason to mention him by name yet. The face is invisible in the dark.

On the other hand the dark is filled by the face.

Danish National Filmography is teeming with interesting information about the many different film companies that turned the film during the tens and twenties into great folk art and grand fiasco. Many projects fortunately never came off. Others probably should have met with another fate. It is actually entirely possible that Nordic film is lacking one or more unrecorded masterpieces among all the competent productions that are now nostalgically played in the film clubs and raised to masterpieces by over-read film semanticians who never understood what history actually is, neither in the meaning good cock-and-bull story nor *wie es eigentlich gewesen.*

The little Danish Film Company had a studio and office in the idyll Birkeröd, quite near the sea, and within walking distance of the station. Hans Jörgen Kineman had just taken over the shares in the concern with the help of insurance money he had gotten after an awkward shipping bankruptcy. Practically speaking, the entire tonnage had perished during the war. For the right man the film business seemed to be an absolute industry of the future.

One problem was possibly that there were too many honest men with shady business plans in relation to the number of really great stars. Director Kineman wasn't especially bothered by this. He knew who he was and what he wanted. Originally, his name was Sörensen and he came from a family of capable farmers and station-masters on Jutland. Through the right contacts at the Inner Mission he had met Frida who was the daughter of the court chaplain at the garrison church in Copenhagen. This meant a family situation with many small children at home and demands for success in society.

The relationship to the father-in-law and the contacts connected with him together with the support from the banks had gotten somewhat worse though after the conversion to the sinful entertainment activity, with the concomitant change of name.

Director Kineman straightened out various desk accessories, the almanac of leather with gold letters HJK, the ink-well in its solid silver holder, the beautifully carved crest that was a memento from the trips with "Denmark's Honor" to the old West Indian colonies, St. Croix and St. Thomas. The old shipping company's flagship and pride had gone on the colonial trade and brought home coffee and sugar from the compatriots' plantations. He got up from the squeaking chair, arranged the watch-chain over his vest and got ready to solemnly walk over to the door to call in little miss Tone for the day's first dictation. Before he reached it, it was pulled up, just as he was going to grasp the handle. She stood in front of him, frightfully pale, if it were possible to become more pale under all the make-up.

"The director has a visit," she got out with a forced voice, which toward the end thinned out into a whisper. "I think it is Asta!"

"I see," he smiled encouragingly at the girl, "I see, that's not so dangerous."

There was already a catastrophic wind in the door opening.

And when Asta Nielsen had an idea, then anything whatsoever could happen, even if the result in this special case only qualifies as a footnote in Danish film history.

The star was going down to Berlin over the summer. There was accordingly no time to lose and the expedition had to be fitted out immediately. Already after a couple of weeks, the last day of May to be precise, "Pernille" thus headed past the Karl islands with a company aboard that was still elated and hopeful. Outstanding filming locations had been secured on Bornholm for the scenes from Calypso's island. Gotland was next in line for the quickly written manuscript and the reconnoitering trip. If there was time left over or if the Swedish authorities made trouble, there was always Åland as a conceivable Ithaca for the future great film, Odysseus in the Baltic.

So as to avoid unnecessary and trying conflicts during filming if it possibly came to that, and besides to somewhat more easily guarantee the honorarium which nevertheless sooner or later had to be signed by director Kineman on the contract with her, Mrs. Nielsen had insisted that she herself should take care of all the larger female roles, Circe, Calypso, Nausicaa as well as Penelope, of course.

Director Kineman had really just one great weakness in life. Otherwise, he stood out almost as the perfect citizen; devout and hard-working wife who at regular intervals made sure that new little Kinemen saw the light of day, even if the proportions between the sexes should have been evened out, because for the time being there were besides Hans-Jörgen – the eldest son in the family always got the father's name – already six girls; a beautiful house in Hellerup; a fast return to business after the most recent bankruptcy; a masculine and pleasant exterior already characterized by the powerful paunch of the successful forty-year-old together with a certain weakness for light gray suits with the associated multicolored silk vests.

The weakness was little miss Tone. She followed along on the trip as stenographer and secretary. She herself had no plans for the future whatsoever other than to become a good mother to an unknown number of children with an equally good father as her beloved employer, and it should be pointed out at once: she was by no means lacking offers. Miss Tone was, you see, very sweet. And young.

Director Kineman had plans for Tone. She was, as a matter of fact, his great investment in the future. For a very low stake in the form of friendly treatment and, at most, a normal salary he intended to transform her into the Danish Film Company's most important capital. She was also going to be a star or why not the Star. Therefore, sooner or later he had to take up the delicate question of the casting of the Nausicaa role. It was going to be difficult, he knew that. The eternal question of the passage of time and man's age is always just as sensitive. No one had any objections to casting Asta as Circe on great Karl's island, that was an excellent suggestion. But as said … "Pernille" swept close below the high dramatic bird cliffs and anchored, by way of precaution a good bit outside the shallow and difficult-to-navigate harbor. They opened anew a bottle of champagne and stared together down into the deep under the sun's reflections on the waves and saw all of them very clearly the glimmering treasures Valdemar Atterdag left behind deep down.

Mr. Kineman didn't have the heart to disturb the fine mood at anchor outside of Norderhamn. When they arrived at Visby in the evening, though, it had to take place. Because Visby was going to be the capital of the Phaeacians, that much everyone was agreed on.

"Pernille" caused a great sensation when she later in the evening lay to at the dock in Visby. She was so pretty in her slender form with the characteristic bowsprit which at the front expanded into a little round platform. This could be used both as a place to sit for intimate conversations and for partaking of mahogany colored grog high above the prow's wet wave splash and foaming white glitter. Actually, that protuberance was intended for bold photographers to work from during filming at sea. "Pernille" was, you see, a valuable common asset of the Danish Film Society, just as usable for pleasure trips away from gossips and families as for the sort of more serious sailing she was now chartered for.

The good residents of Visby did not fail to walk down to view the magnificent motor yacht and furtively glance up on deck so as if possible to catch sight of passengers if any. The following day's Gotland newspapers contained a notice with reference to the list of arriving and departing tonnage. There you could read – and moreover can read even today if you take the pains of opening up the old file:

"The steam yacht Pernille from Copenhagen, with a cargo from the Danish cinematographic society, is well worth a visit to the harbor. In various shapes sometimes disguised as a viking ship, sometimes as a many masted freebooter on the Baltic she has amused both old and young in our cinemas. Departs tomorrow for Fårösund and then is going to sail to her home harbor via Åland. I wonder whether the conjecture is not too bold, that some spectacle is going to take place on our island?"

For Asta Nielsen this entire trip was exclusively a question of pleasure and rest. It had really taxed her strength, breaking with the company, and the negotiations with Berlin were still far from completed. Thus, it fit her perfectly to launch Ludvig's completely impossible idea of making an adventure tragicomedy about all of Odysseus' affairs with women while waiting for the reunion with his old wife which was constantly postponed by friendly gods. Hans Jörgen was also a sweet and innocent gentleman, and it would certainly only be good for him to get a little help over the threshold through her name and person, especially now when he had been so kind and stood surety for her when she had to buy herself free from her contract. Favors and favors in return. To a certain limit. Perhaps she could get him some contacts in Berlin some time. For that was where the money was and all the other resources too; there they were big enough to be able to make use of a star of her immense luminosity. She didn't at all understand hare-brained dreams of America and that little comical hole Hollywood that believed it should become some sort of film capital far away, on the other side of the globe. So silly.

"Skoal, Hans-Jörgen!" she said. "You are so sweet and good."

He had a tough time with his face. She sent him an even darker red smile over the dram glass. Now you're certainly going to want to know what is going on behind my pretty forehead, she thought. And you too, little goose. She even included little miss Tone in her circle of rays. Ludvig, the dummy, was inaccessible at this time under his phoney captain's cap.

She walked up to the brass-framed round window and peered out. The little city, to say the least, looked romantic in the early summer twilight. The battlemented façades and ragged church ruins stuck up above the roofs.

I definitely must do something for those two virgins, she thought while the smile died a natural death. She absent-mindedly watched the thin line of evening strollers who were casting long purple shadows over the cobblestones. Where were the jubilant masses? She suddenly felt very tired.

"Good night everyone," she said rapidly and hurried off to her cabin without even condescending to take a single look at the magnificent sunset.

There are stars and Stars!

Tone slipped out of her mustard yellow silk pajamas and voluptuously stretched out, as much as possible in the little nook. One, two, three, four. One, two, three, four. She rocked on her little bottom and rubbed her thighs with the terry cloth towel. Eventually it got warm and very amusing. From the water jug she poured water into the diminutive marble washbasin that was squeezed in under the oval window between the narrow bunk and the brown-painted wall on which was hanging a sensationally large photograph of Mrs. Nielsen. She stuck out her tongue at it and splashed even more water on her face and tousled her short cut, unfortunately much too naturally curly, frizzy hair. Loud voices could be heard outside.

The dock was full of wood and large piles of stone. There was Ludvig in all his splendor gesticulating with his priceless facial expressions, pointing first at the shiny dark automobile and then at the gangplank of the remarkable boat it had just been rolled onto. He was so funny.

There was a hard knock on the door.

"We're going now if you are coming along!"

"Coming, coming."

She had overslept, but what difference did it make? It had been so pleasant yesterday evening, on the foredeck in the sparkling Baltic night.

Then she stuck her tongue out one more time. This time at her blond self in the mirror. Humming she jumped into the dress and pulled up the zipper at the side.

Little butt, little butt, little butt!

Hans Jörgen Kineman inspected the equipment. The expedition was solidly prepared, for all conceivable hardships. In the food basket were stuffed delightful red sausages with just as delightful shiny round cheeses, crisp French breads wrapped in stiff napkins, the obligatory bottles of champagne and as the crown of the creation a crate of the very most essential, the royal Danish beer. Just as he was going to close the trunk lid he was stopped by a shout. Asta came tripping toward him in her impossible shoes with her arms full of towels and sheets, clean and wrinkled, ironed and used, side by side. She stuffed everything in, around and on top of the food.

"Be careful, be careful!" Hans Jörgen shouted. "What are you going to do with that?"

"Surprise, my own little darling!"

She wriggled past the car and over to the other two in the company. They stood way out on the prow, quite close to two horses and their wagons and gaping farmers who were also crowding aboard the little steam-driven ferry. A blue pulse was beating in her neck which was almost marbled with whiteness. The hats with the long soft brims effectively prevented the sun from reaching her transparent alabaster complexion. That Ludvig was not ashamed of standing there and disguising his intentions for the little goose. Men are characterized first of all by a unique lack of taste. He was reading aloud from a book and the girl was nodding and pretending to be interested. How innocent can you really make yourself?

Ludvig glanced over the edge of the book at her and raised his drawlingly deep baritone:

"I am reading to little Tone from Linné's trip to Gotland. You can borrow it later. By the way, it is a very good Danish translation, extremely interesting."

"You are always so intellectual, Ludvig. That suits you."

So, on the other side of the sound lay their Ithaca. Islands upon islands. Some are hilly, others flat. It didn't make any difference what it was called or how it looked. The only important thing just now was that some sort of suitors and swineherds lived there, just like in that funny manuscript Ludvig was lugging with himself everywhere.

"No, he's going ta Ajkes an' Austers."

They had at long last ended up at an intersection, far, far away from the church with its funny black-tarred bulbous dome. The hefty blond chap kept a respectable distance from the growling car and pointed to the north, judging from the clock and the position of the sun. Hans Jörgen rotated the map and pushed up the motor goggles on his forehead to see better.

"It sounds like pure Greek to me in any case," said Ludvig and continued the efforts to get into a new gear without having to break off the shift. There was a brutal howl of metal under the hood.

"Well, we've come to the right place in any case. It was about time."

Asta Nielsen began to get heartily sick of everything. They hadn't done anything else the entire day than stare at odd stones that were standing on the edge of the water or at houses with shaggy roofs and a bunch of bad-smelling sheep around them. The island at least did justice to its name, Fårö, sheep island!

"Now I want lunch," she said determined. "Somewhere by the sea. And it should be just warm enough and not be windy and there should be shade so that I can take my hat off."

"We want to go down to the beach," explained Hans Jörgen Kineman, slowly and with clear lip movements. The native apparently understood. In any case he pointed both to the right and to the left.

"If we had just been smart enough to keep Gotland after the war at the time of that peace then you would all have spoken good Danish with each other," Ludvig commented on the language confusion and chose to turn to the left.

"The Peace of Brömsebro 1645," instructed little miss Tone with a frank and saucy smile. She remembered, she was the last to have left the Danish education system.

68

Just think, to have only a belly and sit there and think you are some-one! And Hans Jörgen should be careful. She certainly saw how impressed he was as he watched that anemic young secretary. You just wait, she thought and took hold of the wide hat that was on the verge of flying off and flapping apart in the increasing apparent wind. At the same time she gave them all her very most timeless smile, melancholy, fierce, cat-like. A very careful observer would possibly claim that the severe contours of her lips and the ample curve of rouge spoke about bad weather.

"And now we're going to play in earnest. Or more correctly, my dear friends, now we are going to work, rehearse. There has to be an end some time to this idle pleasure trip. Come on, up and at it everyone! Ludvig and you too, Hans Jörgen, will you be so sweet as to fetch the laundry from the car!"

It had been a divine early summer afternoon. All the others seemed just sufficiently tired and turbid in the eyes. Hopefully, though, not worse than that the gentlemen would still be able to rein in the vehicle as well on the return trip over the island. It was still mild and beautiful in the air that was full of the racket from a bunch of birds with ugly long red legs and bills that hooted wildly as soon as anyone of them began to move. Down at the water's edge there lay piles of disgusting seaweed that smelled bad all the way up to the base camp they established in the shelter of a stone fence, some wind-washed gray sheds together with a number of newly tarred boats which looked like little decorative viking ships drawn up on land. The road had suddenly just ended on the sandy beach and there they stopped. Some old ladies with kerchiefs on had indeed driven up a herd of lean cows and heifers toward the farms above the shore meadows, but otherwise they had been completely alone; with the exception of the boy of course, who at regu-lar intervals came trotting by, stared at the car a while and then disappeared. He was there now again. But when he saw the fine gentlemen approach he dashed away at full speed, far out onto the beach. There he sat up on a sand dune, grabbed a straw of lyme grass and began to chew.

The spectacle could begin!

To begin with, no one wanted to be included. They said no, there was a fuss and blushing. Finally she had to get really angry. Silently, single-mindedly and resolutely she carried all the towels and sheets down to the beach, lugged them all the way down to the seaweed piles at the water's edge. There she spread out everything before the others' astonished eyes and jumped a few times very effectively on the textiles.

"Put the camera where you can include everything in a really good picture!"

Ludvig looked around lost.

"There perhaps?"

He pointed around in general terms. Hans Jörgen moved the tripod and fixed it.

When Asta Nielsen got her clothes off, it turned out that she had a thin, thin silk swimsuit underneath, skin colored, latticed by the most exquisite embroidered edging, a fabric so fine that she seemed neither dressed nor undressed. Her arms naked, blindingly white, surrounded by sun.

"Hurry up now. I don't want to freeze to death."

She stopped speaking and looked pensively away along the beach.

"Besides, Hans-Jörgen, bring that little voyeur here and teach him how to shoot your picture machine."

All but violently he dragged the little shaking boy to the camera. He pressed a shiny dollar into his sweaty fist and showed him how the shutter worked.

They arranged things, with the sea at the same time as an ancient observer and an appropriately surging background. But it took some time before she was really satisfied with them. She moved around, barked:

"Well, are you ever going to get finished? The whole time you boys claim that we are on the way to making film history, the first naked scene in Danish film with both men and women. For god's sake get ready!"

She passed her hand over her stomach and waist, curtsied with one hip.

"The princess of course is the exception; she is divine, no mortal can see her without clothes. But you, Ludvig, you pretend to be so fine with your little old man's voice that you can just as well keep your shorts on, then the illusion of the maid will be almost complete. Look here, there you have my hat!"

"Hans-Jörgen! Now you must summon up your courage. I hope you understand what the role demands of a true Odysseus."

He was freezing from sweat, dripping from the cold; alternately, at the same time. Obstinately he stared straight into the lens so as not to see.

"And then there is little miss Tone. Come on, no fuss. Swish!"

Hard and resolute the divine one pulled up the zipper, pulled the dress off the girl and crumpled it up into a ball that she threw up high, high into the air, with a laugh so radiant that all the lapwings and sea-pies and redshanks became silent.

It had been a hurry in the morning for little sweet miss Tone, so great a hurry that she had absolutely nothing else underneath than the very most wonderful soft white flesh!

Not until late in the afternoon, several hours after the remarkable company had disappeared with a stream of blue exhaust gas behind itself, did the boy from Austers dare to go home. Still later, in the evening, some women were seen out in the water, with rolled-up skirts. They were rinsing the sheets and towels. On all of them the word Pernille was embroidered, skillfully stitched in high relief. Still far into the 1980's there were people on the farms who remembered the story about the fine sheets. At Östmans they even claimed that one of the towels in the hall absolutely for certain came from that remarkable beach adventure.

Be that as it may.

Little miss Tone, however, is still not out of the saga.

The controlling and controlled society demands a lot from its tools and lackeys. It does not suffice just to go around disguised. Disguises can be pulled off. For the one exercising the power this can create problems. The very prerequisite for power is known to everyone: war on the conditions of the powers, with one important limitation – just enough war, limited conflicts.

This proposition is universal, just as valid for the smaller family quarrel as for huge devastating world conflagrations. All control is based on information. Controllers and informants, therefore, have at all times dressed up in different disguises. The art of changing shape and form at the right moment has, as a matter of fact, been completely decisive for these mercenaries to be able to satisfactorily carry out their mandates.

There is no reason to take offense at this, talk about system errors or blame poorly educated programmers. The system is quite simply such as it is.

The rainbow is an excellent example of the beauty in this process, this relationship between heaven and earth, gods and men, the powers' double root system. Before, she was called Iris. She wore thin silk through which the sun broke so blindingly that you could be inveigled into believing that she wasn't running anyone else's errand at all but just shining by herself. She is, however, easy to recognize from behind. The wings appear at once as small growths at the bottom edges of the shoulder blades.

However, Hermes is more difficult to unmask. Many like to wear a broad-brimmed hat. And the difference between today's exclusive jogging shoes and winged sandals only experts, these collaborators of the powers, can investigate.

Human knowledge has its limitations. No doubt we will never learn how to find out his real contribution to the obscure affair about Penelope's infidelity or even the degree of intimateness between them.

Morality is one thing. To moralize is something entirely different.

Especially if you want to go under the name of Odysseus.

The shades pulled down. The door crack toward the hall so narrow that the light isn't enough to read by. The strain is felt in the eyes, and now he can't do it anymore. He lays the book on the floor alongside the bed, on a worn out rag rug. Already lying there is the Elementary School Reading Book, a workbook on the geography of Sweden, the pencil-case, the ruler. Now the light goes out. The outer door downstairs slams shut. It becomes completely dark around him. Blackout outside. So quiet that the sound from dad's squeaking ski boots can be heard through the closed padded window. A squeaking from the garden gate.

Alone now, his brother doesn't really count. The bed is a secure island in the night's ocean. He draws up the covers over his face, with wide open eyes. No difference in the darkness, very uniform. The cave is filled by his own warmth. Then he pulls the covers down with a quick movement. The coolness of the room washes his face. He pulls them up again, enlarges the hole, raises the roof with his arms. You can't lift too high. Then the night will stream in. He breathes with open mouth, calm and regular, with all his senses open. It is a question of surviving at any cost.

The breaths are his camp fire.

Spring is coming was the title of the chapter he had just read. Tomorrow he is going to be a tailor. It is about time. His clothing must look terrible. But does it really matter. Are they ever going to find him on his desolate island. Perhaps he will remain always. Is he himself going to find other islands? The remarkable string of words rings in his head: ferte opem misero Robinsonio. There it is in any case, carved on the tree trunk with the flint knife, so that all will be able to understand. So you have to learn Latin to be certain of being saved. Have to ask the teacher tomorrow when they're going to begin learning that language. Otherwise, how are you going to have a chance of being saved from strange islands. Ferte opem misero Hansjör-genio, just think how much better that sounds.

He stuck out the tip of his nose to get some fresh air, turned on his side; the cave collapsed. It was cold in the room. He stuck out his whole head, pulled up the covers around his neck. A clear padding outside in the upstairs hall could be heard, the door was pushed open.

"Is it you, Fredde?"

"Yeah. I'm afraid."

"Have you been reading on the sly again?"

"Quiet. Can't you hear?"

However you exerted yourself your ears were just filled by the weak murmur of silence. The covers were pulled back and the bed filled with your brother's sweaty body.

"There's something in the house, downstairs. Besides, I heard how the gate slammed."

"Then mama has probably come home."

"She was going to come with papa."

"But he left just now. It was dead certainly him you heard. You better take off now. You are so disgustingly warm."

Then he too heard it. Something was moving in the downstairs hall. But it could still hardly be the right war. In any case, no airplane noise had been heard.

"I think we should lie under the bed, for safety's sake."

"That's all right with me. Just lie there and freeze on the ice cold floor and get pneumonia and ..."

Now you could hear very clearly that something was rummaging about and lit a light and was coming up the steps with heavy steps. When his brother dropped down he wasn't far after. They squeezed tightly in toward the wall. He was thankful for his nightjacket. There was a draft from the cool wallpaper, the cold somehow radiated straight out into his face. He had squeezed inside of Fredde, it was after all his bed. In the weak light from the hall he saw how his brother lay with his face downward. Besides, he was holding his hands over his damp forelocks for safety's sake, as if to avoid a blow. Like you did when the gym teacher walloped you because you didn't dare jump over the awful horse. Ferte opem misero, he mumbled, for safety's sake.

"Quiet, you idiot. The Germans can hear."

Or the thieves or child murderers, they exist too, even though it was the war that was of concern.

The distinct steps approached quickly over the hall floor, the vibrations boomed into their ears, like a bombing attack. The door opened up. He glanced under his eye lids. That sight he would never have believed. The black boots. The gaiters. The gray pants. The rifle butt that banged shinily against the floor's dark pine boards.

"What kind of nonsense is this. What in the hell are you doing?"

The war bent down and looked at them. It resembled papa. He looked stern in his Home Guard uniform. You could see how angry he was under the helmet, but also something else.

"I'll be damned, now you really scared the hell out of me!"

This must have happened sometime around the beginning of the war. The winters were cold with big woodpiles around the school and vacations when the coke ran out.

At that time you were for the most part without parents, not like in real war-torn countries of course, but still; get used to being without them, even mama who otherwise was just there, everywhere and always, disappeared in the evenings, with yarn and a knitting bag. But after the soldiers got their share there was enough left for us too with interest. The Christmases were totally destroyed by soft packages, thumb mittens, prickly thick socks and sweaters, of course. Mama was a specialist at sweaters with bright, shiny gold buttons, soft light blue, half-angora garments for her little princes. During the days she was at home, of course, made oatmeal porridge in the mornings, had sandwiches spread and ready when you came rushing home for lunch, forced in an egg you didn't want, took care of the hot chocolate when school was over, before you were going out into the woods or down to the lumber yard to run around with Uffe and Ove or to the Mission School to sneak up on the seminary boys and play ping pong with Gäcke high up under the roof ridge in the huge silent house. In the evening she warmed the food papa had brought home from work. He carried it home in a big tin that dangled from the handlebars. It was divided into three compartments; gravy and potatoes at the bottom, a little piece of meat or awful bony fish and then compote or pudding as dessert. It never tasted like real food. The potatoes were mostly loose and abominable in the fat brown gravy. Some-times there were also over-cooked carrots, for that matter everything was boiled to pulp. Of course, it was a big perk and we were supposed to be so happy to get that food which was left after the directors' and engineers' lunches. Papa was an engineer. I have never understood how he could stand to eat that food twice a day, year in and year out. But it was wartime after all. Everyone had to make sacrifices. Me too. You always had to eat up exactly what was served on the plate; also white, quivering fish with bones sticking up everywhere.

Any further control over your parents' lives you didn't have at all, and obviously you tried as best as possible to avoid their attempts to civilly encroach upon your own lawless life. It was more than enough with the school's demands of regulations and silence and order and attention. In the shadow of the great war you preferably looked after yourself in the residen-tial community with its still free and extensive wild areas. Several times a year, though, you were painfully and obviously forced into the implacably continuous and painful civilization process. Mama polished her long nails, sat for hours in front of the dressing table's round mirror in the bedroom powdering herself, layer upon layer. Papa swore and cut his chin with the safety razor in the bathroom, and we had to get dressed in long pants and newly made sweaters for princes. Everyone had to hurry, otherwise we were going to get there late. Then we rushed down to the bus stop at Kvarnen and took the tram to Brogrenen where we changed to the Southern line and continued to Central road.

The huge house was enthroned high up on the hill with a view over the water in toward Stockholm. Below lay the factory's tiled quadrangles with broad, high windows and long narrow chimneys. There the beacons were manufactured, that shone over evil and good over the whole world, and gas and radio apparatus' and record players and secrets for the war and papa worked there in the laboratory. We were there one time, my brother and I, went through huge halls with machines and a bunch of old men who were looking after wheels, turning on taps, looking at instruments with pointers and figures in red and white and black. Papa had a white coat on, just like a doctor, the others gray or blue dirty overalls or jackets. Some looked like fighter pilots with big glasses right over their faces. They were cutting in iron with blue and white hissing flames. Sparks flew, jumped in all directions like late summer grasshoppers before they died on the cement floor. Then we went up a floor. Up there it was lighter and almost quiet after all the din and racket downstairs. The ones working there were dressed just like papa, in white coats, behind glass walls. They were drawing on large slanted boards. Some were soldering cords, some were just sitting and reading. There were also ladies who were writing on typewriters and smiling ingratiatingly as quickly as they caught sight of us. Farthest away in a corridor behind a closed door sat uncle Gunnar. We bowed to him. He had a gray suit on and didn't need to have on any coat. He was a director. It is to his house we are on our way.

In the hall we are helped off with our outer clothing by black-clad maids with white aprons. We also have a maid at home, Maria from Evertsberg. But she is never so nicely dressed, she mostly has on just a skirt and blouse or an ordinary flowery dress with a belt. She smells strongly from the armpits and never goes along when we go away. Before we continue into the house's high rooms, mama combs us carefully and sees to it that our legs are dead straight and that our hair is lying absolutely flat on our heads. All of that work is completely wasted because then we get to go on forever, bowing to a million black suits and crisp dresses before we are stationed in a corner together with other children dressed up beyond recognition. A few look completely desperate in suits and ties. We are the only ones who have sweaters.

"Oh, what lovely sweaters? Was it mama who knitted them?" says aunt Margareta when we hold out our hands that have become slippery from all the greeting. She is married to uncle Gunnar and the most imposing of all in a blue shimmering long dress. I like aunt Margareta much better when she has the Swedish Woman's Defense uniform on and is sitting at home with mama in the kitchen completely red in the face and laughing at something they are whispering about. Then even mama laughs. Otherwise, she is content with smiling mostly, for a long time. It is difficult to know whether she is really sad mostly or happy occasionally. Presumably it is not the idea that you are supposed to know how adults are doing. Now she is doing fine in any case. It is obvious how happy she is, for her whole face looks satisfied and the deep wrinkles above the root of her nose have disappeared.

"Come now, Anna, let's go get a drink," aunt Margareta continues and drags mama off to the big exciting table with all the sparkling crystal bottles. We ourselves sit dead silent around a huge oval table and drink juice and eat green marzipan cakes with lighthouses on or also AGA is drawn right across with sticky red cream. The roar from the adults increases while we children seriously and stubbornly toss into ourselves piece of cake after piece of cake after piece of cake. Finally, we are forced out onto the floor to dance with all the sweaty adults around the Christmas tree, but by then you are already so heavy and full of all the muck in the stomach that it is hardly possible to budge. If you're unlucky you get to hold onto some horrible girl's hand as well. The whole party is terribly unfair besides. Aunt Margareta's and uncle Gunnar's children are much younger than we are, one can hardly crawl and just shrieks, and they get to be noisy and fly around and quarrel with us and all the others and several also behave remarkably badly, but we don't dare to do anything, hardly even move. At regular intervals papa comes over to the table and glares at us with a thunderous glance as if we were some sort of unusually rotten arch villains. When everything is finally over, small hard packages are distributed which are not even to be opened on the train. We have to wait until we get home. It used to be a funny paper knife or in the best case a fountain pen with AGA on it.

The war was still going on.

But there were even worse things to endure at that time.

It was when we began with gymnastics that you discovered in earnest that there are different sorts of people, entirely different types of people. There were those who had garter belts with suspenders and those who got off. Besides, there were those who to make doubly sure wore vests with a thousand tiny buttons. I was one of these wretched creatures. Ove and Uffe from the lumber yard had long johns on in the winter and nothing at all under their shorts the rest of the year. Their life was so uncannily much simpler, the recesses after the gymnastic lessons filled with fabulous adventures while we who lived in the houses sat in a row on the benches in the locker room, like little cocky young devils, fighting with our painful garments and trying to bring some order into them. First, horrible light brown prickly long stockings were supposed to be slipped onto the legs and buttoned to the garter belt's elastic bands by means of slippery buttons. It often failed totally, the stretched bands just snapped back so that the skin smarted and burned. If you cheated or skipped the least little part in the dressing process, then the only thing that remained was to suffer through an unpleasant day with sagging stockings that finally seemed to want to spread out over your entire body.

At the end of recess the teacher used to come shamelessly into our stinking locker room, put her hands on her substantial sides and utter a hippo-like sigh. Extremely sternly and quickly she then took charge of us. The pinches you got from her in the classroom were nothing compared to what you were now treated to. The blue marks on the thighs remained for days. Eventually, you yourself were supposed to manage to fasten the vest's tiny buttons into eyes that were too small. It was like sitting in hell's back yard. As if gymnastics itself weren't punishment enough for crimes you presumably committed but in any case were not sentenced for in some court of justice. For that matter, of what use was gymnastics to the Indians? Had anyone ever heard about Deerfoot playing leapfrog over fat girl's backs, Pirate Jack on the wall bars while the whole sea stormed? The only thing that was really fun of course was forbidden, climbing all the way up to the ceiling on a rope and rope ladder; the only thing that could remotely remind you of the pirates' and Indians' meaningful lives.

In these terrible clothes you were wasted, completely in the inhuman power of the adults. The world was shamelessly unjust. The guys from the big ramshackle houses by the lumber yard down at Kyrkviken lived a completely free life in or without underpants, we who lived in separate houses in Hersby were stuck in our tight compulsory garter belts. It was a question of getting free, the whole time.

Besides, there were several ways to dress up small boys. Mama's matter-of-fact way, quick, practiced, without a pinch; she could do it with her eyes blinded by morning slumber when you were supposed to be off to school. But sometimes it was Maria who helped out. She was soft and warm from sleep and mostly laughed while her fingers fumbled everywhere in a ticklish and annoying way.

"Come and sit down on the old girl's knee," she said.

Her father was at Långholmen and there was an entirely different smell about her than mama. No old scent or that from the perfumes on the dressing table in the bedroom. Different. Like in the forest, under the trees, from the tufts in the marsh where freedom began.

The milk was driven around to the homes by horse and wagon. In the evening you put the milk jug out at the gate, sparkling clean, newly washed, cool. In the mornings the clatter was heard at a long distance, the hooves dully tramping in the road gravel; smacking, whoaing, sometimes the crack from a whiplash. During the summer the sour milk ripened in the bowls in a row in the kitchen window. The milk was thick and fat. Often there were thick clumps in the glass that made it yechy to drink. It was better suited for the morning porridge and the fruit compote desserts. But you could also do without porridge and cream, it was more than good enough with sandwiches and rolls with the juice or the hot chocolate during the winter. Next after school, food was freedom's enemy number one. Meal times developed into grim rituals of force during which the untamed ones were supposed to be civilized, tamed, domesticated, habituated with the discipline of the adult world. The weapons that were used in this battle between freedom and coercion, control and freely growing life, were apparently monotonously mild and harmless: silverware and napkins, words and tones of voice, pauses, silences; appetizers, main courses, desserts.

"Well, and what have you done in school this week?"

"The usual, of course."

Papa pours beer into the glass, lets the foam sink, takes a gulp.

"And what is the usual then?"

Fredde doesn't answer, thoroughly calmly stuffs his fork into his mouth. There is an awful gnashing of his teeth.

"Do you always have to eat that way?"

A lengthy glance from mama. "This is the way it is done!"

She cuts up the world's smallest piece of the sinewy roast veal. There is a grating a hundred times worse from her plate, but that noise sort of doesn't count.

"At least watch your mother when she is speaking to you."

I look too, for safety's sake.

Mother puts the fork between her shining red lips and somehow sucks the bite off. The only thing that is heard is an insignificant ripple of saliva. She wipes herself off with the stiff napkin that becomes all smeary with lipstick.

"Now it's your turn, Hans Jörgen!"

"I didn't gnash my teeth."

"No one said you did."

"Okay. Besides I've already finished eating."

Papa cuts up a new huge, much too thick slice of the Sunday roast.

"No thanks, I don't want any more, I'm already stuffed."

"Here you are. Eat it up now and show that you too know how to!"

"I didn't ask for anymore."

"Do as father says."

"Anyways you eat far too little for your age."

I feel clearly the kick from Fredde under the table. He is just stuffing the last bite into his disgusting trap. The gnashing is greater than from any unoiled saw down at the lumberyard, but no one seems to care about that any more. All attention is directed at me. I look around the table. There is papa's face with beer foam on the upper lip. His tongue moves quickly over it. There is still some left.

"Well," he says and wipes it off with the back of his hand.

How can this sort of thing just happen? It begins with Fredde answering impudently to a question from papa and ends with me having to cram a half a dead calf into myself!

"Please, Hans Jörgen, don't make trouble, you know so well how it'll end."

Yes, I know how it ends, we all know how it ends. On the steps up to the second floor is a little niche with a shelf decorated by an old copper bowl. In it are pieces of rope of various sizes, a gift from papa's Danish brother who works in a rope factory outside of Copenhagen.

"I want dessert now," Fredde exults and exaggeratedly neatly and properly puts down his knife and fork on the right sides of the plate, licked clean. He hasn't finished eating at all, there are piles of awful gravy and overcooked potatoes left. Mama looks down at her knees and wipes them with her napkin as if that were more important just now than anything else.

I give myself plenty of time, first fill my glass with milk, drink half of it to grease my mouth which has become very dry and then take a last look at the remains of the hairy moo-cow. I see clearly that it is nodding at me, actually blinking encouragingly with its hazy cow eyes. Then I stuff it in, without bothering to cut it up into a bunch of well-behaved small pieces. That would just bring about completely unnecessary and meaningless suffering for the poor dumb animal, by a cruel fate placed on our Sunday table. I clearly feel her damp thankful muzzle nudging somewhere in the hollow of the stomach. By filling the rest of my oral cavity with the milk that remained in the glass it becomes totally impossible to move anything in my entire mouth. I cement my lips shut the best I can. At the same time I can feel clearly how it begins to spill out and run down my chin. There is still war in the world. We should be thankful, those of us who have something to eat, think about and never forget all the unfortunate starving children.

I would rather remember the whole shiny calves of summer.

Papa has already gotten up from the table. The rest of us remain sitting.

There were also other things from Denmark in the house. Some pictures. Haystacks on hilly soft landscapes. A road bordered by trees; dark purple trunks, broad blue shadows over the grass, orange sun-spots. One painting showed grandfather, a powerful figure with silver hair; another papa when young. Once he too had been a boy like all the others, like on the picture, in a green suit with red necktie nonchalantly wound around his neck. One hand on the door handle of a cabinet full of secrets, the other deeply and securely shoved down in his pocket. Above the cabinet stuffed birds, on the wall behind the desk a cross. Open books. And the horse. The Danish horse. Nowadays it was on the staircase up to the second floor, on the shelf at the bend where it turned around for the second time. Everything that had to do with Denmark as a matter of fact was on that staircase, a constant reminder of something you never talked about. On the wall hung etchings and drawings, a town gate, deer, a brook meandering under tall beeches. A Denmark that didn't exist. Yet, there was a blond boy with a relaxed manner and a serious smile on the picture, the one who once built the horse for his father.

Somewhere on the road the boy had irrevocably disappeared, been transformed into an ordinary Sunday dinner papa. I wonder whether he in spite of everything hadn't hidden himself in one of the horse's secret compartments. There were old-fashioned tin soldiers in the small drawers, several that needed repair or repainting; some were completely broken and maimed. Once the Danish horse had been white. That could be seen clearly on the picture above the sofa in the big room. Once papa must also have laughed and played, but had been painted fast into a picture. Perhaps it was for that reason he never wanted to talk about Denmark.

When nobody else was at home, Hans Jörgen used to sit for a long while and stare at that picture. Putting on the green hunting jacket was easy, it was more difficult with the kerchief; the knot under the chin was so indistinctly painted. The blond cut fringe he himself had, the pouting lips too, the eyebrows that were hardly visible. But his eyes were very black and inaccessible, just pupils. Just as black as the crucifix on the wall above the picture's desk. To be sure it could be seen that something was hanging there, but the artist must have been careless, there were only a couple of quick light brown coarse brush strokes. So much on that picture seemed to be unexecuted, a sketch, something on the way that was never really finished.

The cabinet door was shut, closely guarded by the boy's hand. He himself readily wanted to go up to the picture and open it, but never dared to turn the handle enough. Or also someone came home and the picture became just a picture again and he disappeared quickly from the dark room with the high curtains in front of the windows, up to the adventure books and lessons or out if it was still light enough and his homework done.

One morning the milk didn't come as it was supposed to. We were on our way home during the breakfast break and distinctly detected the smell of smoke. But it wasn't the usual somewhat biting or sour smell like from an open stove or piles of leaves; no, the wind drove something thick, sickly, sweet far into our wide-open nostrils, almost nauseating. We took off the rest of the day.

Death was everywhere. That's exactly the way war had to look and smell, real war, that's the way it hissed in the ruins after the bombing attacks while the fire extinguishing was going on and the survivors were clumsily rooting around fallen beams and under collapsed walls. The only thing that was missing was human bodies. But it was good enough with what there was; the stench of singed meat, shafts of bone sticking up out of the horses crushed beyond recognition; blue, pink, violet viscera that in some way belonged to non-existent charred calves, our calves, summer vacation's calves, the meadow's and forest edge's scampering calves. There were parts of us that also died there, something incomprehensible that happened. We who otherwise always had so unnecessarily much to say to each other, knew well how to mix reality with words, create terror and deadly fiends whenever it was necessary, we suddenly became completely silent. We were surrounded by cold, it drifted into the forbidding smoke, clung fast, silenced us. There was nothing to say. Our otherwise so secure group of guys dissolved into individual absolute solitudes.

The whole cow barn with all the animals was gone, the stall too; the storage barn with the tools burned out, just a smoking charred shell left. The only thing untouched was the old parish storehouse with the tar-black shutters and the iron spigot high up under the ridge of the gable. the Falun red took on an ever stranger color in the afternoon sun. The shadows that fell over the elder bushes dripped soot; the grass too blackened. As if something that didn't at all belong there flowed out over everything, and in what was running there was also the stench and the silent voices and our own wordless terror that we were not able to nor dared show others; therefore, each and every one of us by himself poked among the remains.

Up at the storehouse sat Ejnar's papa crying. It was almost worse than all the other gruesome things. Worse, because you were so unused to seeing adults cry. He had his pilsner alongside of the stepladder. He always had a pilsner nearby, a half-empty brown or green bottle; when he drove the milk around too. He was completely ashen white in the face, the fat oval without contours, dissolved, as if he was on the verge of turning inside out. Ejnar stood alongside and felt ashamed. Yet we stood there and stared, a tightly-closed reassembled bunch of boys after the solitudes on the border of the dangerous, the wanderers with sooty staffs, little old men with recaptured cocksure faces in the common confidence that Ejnar never was part of. Behind the masks long dreams were supposed to rage full of death's grimace, wide-open numb lips over yellow rows of teeth, burst eyes, a tail without a body; the viscously flowing light sitting fast like thick sweat in your pajama jacket. When you woke up damp and warm, the darkness had the color of blood and your pulse thumped outside your body, in the ghastly outside that you could never really escape from since this outside was at the same time inside of you, floating between the dream's space, in corridors where nothing, absolutely nothing could be watched over or be controlled.

They stood there a long time, without moving, legs freezing, for the summer had to be retained as long as possible, even though just as shorts far into October. The first one who said anything was Ejnar. He bent down over a sugar tin.

"You have to help me," he said. "Otherwise he will kill them too."

He gathered up two kittens and held them out.

"What do you mean kill?"

"Throw them into the wall there."

He pointed at the storehouse's coarse logs and we saw. Now he was sobbing too, just like his papa. The blood stains showed distinctly in the slanting hard light, actually just as a little darker red against the already sun-reddened boards. There was somehow nothing more to say, nothing other to do than to walk home along the world's longest and saddest roads while the sun tried to show off one last time and gilded the last leaves high up among the maples. As if it had been any autumn day whatsoever and nothing, absolutely nothing had happened.

Behind every trip there are motives. For Telemachos it is a question of gathering information now that can become decisive for his own life, guide decisions with consequences just as far into the future as they can influence history itself. To obtain factual information about his father's wandering around, however, is not the most important purpose of the trip. As a matter of fact, it is completely subordinate to the overall goal, the education of a young hero, capable entirely by his own power of filling the same role that his father had played at home and according to rumors, partly unconfirmed, continued to appear in even far away from his home island's barren infields and steep cliffs.

To become his father's real son and spiritual heir he was thus forced in a way and against his own will to repeat that one's exploits, show courage at sea as well as search out foreign people and distant lands, cities with strange customs, souls and temperaments. It is a question of literally imitating the absent one so as to complete his journey and then again be a son, father to new sons, new heroes; himself the third.

I say this intentionally in a way, for the trip is at the same time a unique teaching, a completely unparalleled opportunity for education. Nothing, you see, hinders the son from becoming a coward, in the end utterly cowardly taking the life of his own father in order thereby to take over the hero's magnificent role, all the grazing herds, the ships and the gifts from friends. Camouflaging your motives well is indeed no bad lesson; practicing disguises, feigning life. All of this is inscribed right through the words in every story, also in the one true one that is in progress and encompasses everything, without mercy or compassion.

In the eyes there is fire, the glance is straight; he makes a show of being cool, a bit reserved, but underneath can be glimpsed the entire time vivacity, pliancy. You cannot avoid noticing the fine smile, the simple and unobtrusive words that convince long before you are able to find anything to object to. Wisdom seals the lips, like a seal. But who is the father, who the son?

An entirely different matter it is to travel together.

The war ground to a halt at the French-German border. They had cut out and colored English and American miniature flags and pasted then onto pins. Patton and Eisenhower were clearly printed with India ink on lead-colored paper helmets. A flatter headgear represented Montgomery's beret. At the beginning of autumn everything went at breakneck speed. Brussels, Antwerp and Liège were taken in a week. On the other side of the map Stalin, surrounded by red banners, was moving quickly over the Baltic. The Finns had quit fighting together with the Germans. From that area they had removed all the flags. Swastikas still marked Oslo and Copenhagen. As soon as a new war map was printed in Svenska Dagbladet, they cut it out and corrected their big National Geographic Magazine map. It was hanging on the wall in the upstairs hall between their rooms. Already at the invasion of Normandy they placed a picture of Hitler on his back right over Berlin and drew a large skull and crossbones over him. Yet, you could still hear him on the radio, between crackling and military marches on the medium wave band. There you could also listen to Churchill. Over London they fastened a fat cigar that they had gotten from grandfather. Two voices and yet so remarkably different. Although you hardly understood a word, you understood immediately who was evil, who good.

The Spitfires had fixed runways, one on the kitchen table and one in Fredrik's room. Besides, there was an exceedingly secret airfield down in the cellar, near the coal bin. It was used under extraordinary conditions. From there you could also fly directly out into the yard through the cellar door. The fighting activities had, however, decreased considerably during the autumn since Fredde had begun in junior high school and mostly went around in a ridiculous cap with a shiny visor trying to look big. Besides, no one wanted to be German after the invasion. The Messerschmidt was put aside. He flew mostly alone, long dangerous raids deep in over enemy territory, the desk in papa's workroom, silent reconnaissance missions over the sheets on Maria's bed in the maid's room, in among the dresses in mama's dark closet.

In the course of time he had created a superb set of motor sounds, a linguistic arsenal full of signals that were produced through long drawn-out exhalations, vibrations of the soft palate, lip action, in various combinations all according to the different types of expeditions. Within the family there were various opinions about the necessity of these long drawn-out noisy disturbances. Therefore, it was immensely important to be able to adapt both the number of revolutions and the exhaust rattle to prevailing conditions, papa's newspaper reading after dinner, mama's never ending sweater-knitting, his brother's alleged homework.

He hung almost still for a while at a low RPM idle in front of the map and moved a red flag all the way to the Danube. Actually, the plane had needed to be transformed to an autogiro for that sort of trick, but necessity knows no laws, least of all during wartime conditions. The situation was as so often tense after dinner. Papa had just read aloud from Aftonbladet that the Ukrainians had gotten all the way to Budapest. But that wasn't where the war was supposed to be decided, on the eastern front by the red army. That part of Europe didn't count anyhow. It was at the Rhine the decision was supposed to occur. But there most of the needles stood still even if he had placed an Eisenhower helmet, which really should have been Patton's, at Aachen. From there to the river there was still a good bit left. He was just going to fly there to get a good idea of the situation at that tough front sector for himself, for you could still never really rely on the radio's and the newspapers' reports, when Fredrik came dashing up the stairs with the usual old noise around himself.

"Did you turn the horse?"

Fredde leaned against the banister with his hand. He actually dived steeply down under a suddenly emerging Messerschmidt squadron and still succeeded in landing on the top step.

"I didn't touch anything."

"Has anyone seen the horse," his brother shouted down, "I've got to have those old tin soldier legs. We're going to make an experiment."

In three dangerous steps he jumped down the steps. The whole house shook. Indignant voices were heard downstairs and then the rattle from the outside door after a final curse. Hans Jörgen flew slowly down toward the kitchen with damped motors. In the living room the sofa lamps were already lit. Papa wasn't to be seen. Mama sat in the easy chair. Her face was as usual. Always so perfect, completely clean, without a wrinkle around her large sorrowful eyes. Yet, she was smiling at him, although it was clearly apparent from the hollow above her nose how mad she really was, so angry that maybe she was really planning to tell papa.

"Why did he get so awfully mad?"

"Don't know. Come here please! Since you are still here you can just as well see whether the thumb hole came out right."

The mittens were always most beautiful before they were done. Then all that soft woolliness was still there, soft against the skin. Later they became for some unfathomable reason more and more prickly the closer they were to being done.

"Does mama know where the horse is?"

"Papa has taken it along to work. Why do you ask?"

He shrugged his shoulders and got loose from her cool hands.

"He's going to fix it. Did you really eat up the roll?"

Half of it was still in his pocket. It was a matter of putting aside supplies, always having reserve victuals on hand, especially under such extraordinary conditions as world war and family life. He pushed the start button. All the horsepower got going without the least misfire. The plane lifted from the sewing table's well-polished temporary airstrip, settled into a wide left turn past the high cabinet, elegantly dodged the velvet draperies toward the hall. He adjusted the trim and elevators and then gave it full throttle. Violently clattering, he flew up the steps and landed in the empty niche where the horse used to stand. Then he took a huge leap over the five lowest steps and landed on the hall floor without breaking either his feet or his wrists, tossed on his cap and gray jacket and dashed out after his brother and friends. What kind of experiment?

When director Kineman returned from the Berlin visit young Hans Jör-gen had the horse ready. It was really a little wonder. But then he too had devoted large portions of the summer vacation to the work. Besides, he had rebuilt an old camera, changed lenses in the optical system, polished some glass and produced photos that greatly astounded all who saw them. The horse seemed to be at least as tall as the house and the huge tall decid-uous trees it was placed between. Pure unadulterated magic! In one of the pictures he had placed his brothers and sisters between the legs under the horse's belly, one two three and so on, all seven, with Erik, the littlest, in big sister Else's arms. Mother of course hadn't wanted to be included. She was on another picture, with the horse in her arms, pressed against the black dress' effervescent white ruffles.

Several days a week Toresen took him in from the big summer house by the sea to his workshop near the studio in Birkeröd. What did he care about sun and swimming and icy juice on silver trays, chocolate macaroons, candied cookies and all sorts of things, carried into the yard by the ser-vants in the kitchen. The convertible top was down, the wind tousled in his reddish-blond adolescent mane. His eyes took on an extra shine from the apparent wind, from the desire and happiness, expectation before the day's work. It even happened that he sang. This very late roll from a breaking voice was drowned out, though, by the Ford's merciful noise.

It was peaceful in the atelier during the summer. Everyone was out-side on exteriors and filming. Mostly he got to work in peace. Toresen, who combined work as a carpenter and set-maker with the assignment as the family's chauffeur and handyman, was of course always ready with advice and suggestions, knew where the tools were and could show how to use them. But the horse was his own work, entirely his own. He loved the smell from the shavings on the floor, the scent of oil and released electricity that filled the whole room with future when the lathe got going, the sound from the place where the airy details in the belly's light architecture were hammered out. The warm soldering iron against the palm of the hand. Smoking sandpaper dust in the streaks of sunshine from the open window above the workbench. Outside all the birds of summer were brawling. Outside the sun was sparkling like hell in the little round lake. Outside the wind came from the distant sea through the beeches' high masses of leaves. What did he care about that? With his lips narrow from concentration he prebored holes for the screws, greased them in so that the wood wouldn't crack when he cut the last careful curve with the chisel.

Who has time for summer when the future is already peeking around the corner? He was going to become an engineer, inventor; that he had decided long ago, construct the future with electricity, atoms, wave motion, optics. The film was certainly only a beginning of a fantastic development. If you could use the radio waves to spread out sound and listen to the whole world in a loudspeaker, then the next step should lead to your also being able to see it in a box of some kind. An electric mirror for reality and truth. Radio pictures. That's where the future was!

He stood for a long time with the chisel in his hand staring out the window, completely immobile, absorbed in his dream of life, the laboratory's eldorado, all of his apparatuses that were going to transform the entire world. So far away was he that he didn't at all notice Toresen's hand pressing on his shoulder.

"That's enough for today. We also need some time to shop for cheese and wine."

Toresen helped him off with his work coat. The shirt underneath was impeccably white, like the horse when it was ready, lacquered, shining.

Remarkably enough he wasn't a bit disappointed when he got a clear idea that it was never going to be used for what it had been intended for, the film trick, to illustrate the crafty man's most crafty craft. To begin with it stood on the desk. The cabinet alongside was filled with electric articles, resistors, coils, fine copper wire, cables and odd glass tubes, measuring instruments. There was a total ban on red-haired sisters even coming near that cabinet. Finally, it got so full of odds and ends that he was allowed to clean the shelves, take out all the old stuffed animals and put them above, below the ceiling. The owl, the song thrush, the squirrel and the pheasant without a head. The future constantly needed new space. Most people didn't care about it, didn't have any idea about it. Possibly they were uneasy about it. But for young Hans Jörgen Kineman the future was nothing to get uneasy about. He knew where it was. Legendary little mechanical horses belonged exclusively in old books, remote stories, unproduced films. Way inside of his head apparatuses were growing, like torrents, still indistinct images, complex wiring diagrams without visible connections. But they were there. He knew. There were secret connections. He knew it. He alone knew it.

She never figured out her father-in-law. There was something totally inaccessible behind the restless energy that never came to a halt; the sullen expression behind the pipe, constantly wandering between hands and pockets. If there wasn't sufficiently much to do or rebuild at Blue Thorp, he instead prowled around near her; popped up out of nowhere, was in the way, gave you a bad conscience without reason. Certainly the house was still his on paper, but now she was actually living there and paying substantially for it. Yet, he was obstinate in keeping his workshop in the shed with all its odd and irreplaceable and constantly lost tools. Which, moreover, mysteriously, miraculously, after a time always showed up again. And never once did he apologize to the poor archaeologists, although he was always on them, finding fault and accusing. Just like he went at Hans Jörgen. But in spite of the always turned-up sound levels between them, there was something strong that tied them together across all the difference in age, the concentrated silence when they did something together with their hands, to the boats for example; the fittings, the splicings of rope, the finish on the centerboard. She herself knew so well what it was. She brought it along from home from her own beloved, dead mother. All the practical. The insanely impractical in proving yourself practical. Everyone who knew how to exploit that weakness in her.

The bobbin came off for the eighty-first time. It would certainly have been faster to sew new curtains than to repair the old ones. There was too much play for such fine thread. Surely the eternal error in sewing sails. Now on top of that he had dug out the old Finn sails. How many times hadn't she gotten to mend them, she the practical one who hated little leaning boats? My dear friend, you who know everything, you can do it for me, huh! And then the quick kiss on the forehead.

Finally she had found the sewing machine up in the loft, with the girls. Ler and Långhalm were busy sewing sun shelters from old potato sacks, to be used at the outdoor seminar, stretched up between the pines to create the necessary extra darkness for all the explanatory overhead pictures. The ping-pong table where she was sewing was the center of the summer's intellectual activities. There preliminary reports were written, the handy computer was fed with new finds, they quarreled about scientific futilities and presumably did some screwing at times. You could have your suspicions. She really didn't understand that they could manage, how she managed. The latter, least of all. This meaningless undertaking which she again and again took charge of in earnest when he disappeared on his eternal travels. What did she want to prove with it? That life begins at forty? That it is eminently possible to remain beautiful and fit and attractive and a happy mother to the world's messiest and most ungrateful teenage son with ten thousand pals who always seemed to be precisely at their house, the summer one or the winter one, yet to continue full service, to devote yourself to friends with family lives at least as difficult as her own, never get tired, just encourage, encourage, encourage all the others; never to worry about the other Hans Jörgen, who was so often a runaway; yet never to really get space for herself, sufficient time to heal absent-mindedness, be steadily reminded about this absence through everyone else's obvious importunate presence; the father's, the son's and the holy friend's, amen; wasn't that enough?

For the final time she drove the needle down into the edge of the hem. Now everything was going as it should. Oh, these machines, as fickle as people. And then the exquisite pleasure when everything functions! To be alone. Concentrate on one thing at a time. She increased the pressure on the pedal. Actually, she loved to sew, nothing was more relaxing than when everything worked as it should, machinery, mental activity, pure and coordinated; like when the footsteps finally ease under the pines at Ulla Hau and heart, lungs and skin become one with the air, moss, sand.

The wall secretes heat. If he shuts his eyes and totally concentrates, the border between the finely piled limestone and his back dissolves. Impossible to decide where the heat is coming from, if he is in the stone or it is in him. The roughness against the skin softens up, pores open, it runs, flows, bodies change places. So far everything is fine and dandy. What is needed for a complete absorption into the stone is that the sun itself be defied. Strange signs move under his eyelids, signals from the stone that is already flowing through him. Yellow, gold, wine red; the setting for the arrival of the sun-birds changes. The actual capture, the freezing, the black arc when the stone is swallowed by the explosion and the very first man comes into existence requires nets of ice feathers. There is just one moment when everything has to last. A wing that breaks, a motionless head-sail, catabatic wind – and the catastrophe, the stone man, is a fact.

There are other possibilities of catching up with the first man, keeping the light breath that surrounds all things, the living as well as the dead. The moment has to be chosen with the same care, the place as well. Each one of the senses is powerless, linked in steadily new unions they create life. The fundamental conditions are the same. The back has to be free. A tree trunk works well, the shadow from a whitebeam. Invisibility comes from itself. Calm. The sea a copper bowl with room for all of the swallows of evening. All too seldom are all the conditions fulfilled. Besides, the breath has to be so deep, so full of all the scents of the shore grass that no roots follow along. The actual exchange is hardly noticed. Outwardly nothing at all is visible. The swallows dip their bellies in the water, scratch with their bills. The transformation begins in the lungs, first as smarting and small shouts. Moreover, the differences are small. If everything has gone right, then the melodies will suffice for a lifetime. The stone man can look around for other victims.

Every human being can do like this. Yet, he wondered whether the others really understood. It was called being lazy. Not wanting to do anything useful. Keeping away. Any further understanding was in any case not to be counted on.

The sea yelled. He blew the swallows out over the bay. They could be used several times. Between the clouds' burning lower edges and the holm's knife-sharp grimy contour the sun rolled down. It was enough that he knew where it was, that it existed, the first man. No one else needed to know, the tool people, the implement people. Not even she, the other one.

The old man who was soon going to die watched the boy in front of himself. For a long time they had sat still together, without speaking to each other. Now the sun had gone down and the shadows stopped getting longer. High, high up under the clouds the swallows were advancing, but he could no longer hear the swifts' high shrieks, just divine their hazardous exercises. He still knew so well how they sounded, the swarms of swallows over Själland's cape, the waves against the shore below high sand dunes. In a while the boy, who was sitting opposite him, with his back pressed tightly in to the high wall of limestone, would get up and help him in. He had stopped keeping his eyes shut now. Where had he been? The sweet little girl at his feet would also provide support. She held her arms around her skirt, which she had pulled down over her drawn-up legs; presumably to protect herself from mosquitos he no longer felt anything of. The old man who was going to die soon didn't want to shut his eyes. There was already enough lead in the eyelids. At any time it could melt and run out over the ground, make it quite gray. That's it. Recounted. The last summer.

What were they thinking about?

"Children, now you might help me in," said the old man who so willingly wanted to live.

With joy he felt the young strong arms around his body, their hands that briefly brushed each other behind his back. He smiled. Just as quickly they moved apart. As if they had gotten burned. Once it had been his task to give dreams life. Now it was their turn. They were also going to learn.

The small wavelength in the receiver's oscillator circuit brought about the use of clystrons , sometimes even rumbatrons. The future, the time after the war, ought to, at least commercially, mean an explosion of civil development; ships and planes for example. Reliable cathoscopes adjusted to the markets of peace, an easily readable measuring device, so practical that you didn't need to be an engineer to be able to use it; a deflection system built on a straight or spiral-shaped curved time axis; rotating antennas or why not a search beam which in some brilliant way could be gotten to sweep over the horizon or in a parallel circle to it?

For engineer Hans Jörgen Kineman it stood out, nevertheless, in the end as something obvious that an intensity-modulated electron beam, a sort of watch hand that moved at the antenna's rate of rotation, would be the right way into the future. For a long time the solution to this sub-problem had completely occupied his thoughts. The laboratory management encouraged him to continue with his speculations on radar. The lunches were taken up with intensive discussions with Dalstedt and Grankvist and young Werthén about common questions, not the least being the lack of cathode ray tubes; small, effective and above all durable. Or why not something entirely different. Fixed unbreakable conductors, an entirely new technology for controlling voltage and current, increasing power, reducing resistance. The key to the future was called control, the possibility of directing and controlling the processes. One day someone would succeed in producing cheap fluorescent screens for all the people. Then space would break open. The whole world, misery and happiness, would be lifted into every home.

Not just as sound from a radio device. No, the pictures of the world, peace's pictures, peace's world. Everything had begun so promisingly even before the war, in England and the USA. Certainly, researchers there were on the verge of solving the fundamental practical problems; the elimination of fragile glass tubes, for example. Most preferably you naturally should work with small fixed bodies, with materials that are found everywhere, crystals, silicon. Dependable. Efficient. Controllable. The engineer's dream.

In the middle of November, at the same time as the west front again and finally began to move over the boys' map, engineer Kineman was called up to the highest chief. The managing director, his brother-in-law, was even there together with an unfamiliar gentleman in a uniform who greeted him guardedly with a bow, but didn't introduce himself, didn't even shake hands.

"If I have understood correctly then the engineer is Danish."

"I have been Swedish for ten years."

"Don't misunderstand. I don't mean anything bad. I only mean that I suspect that the engineer still speaks his mother tongue fluently?"

"I try to speak Swedish, as well as I can. I have nothing to do with Denmark any more."

Director Dalén filled up the strained pause.

"Hans Jörgen, you speak quite an excellent Swedish; no one has any objections ..."

The stranger interrupted:

"It is a matter of an assignment of a little, shall we call it, special nature. You would be able to carry it out at the same time as you visit your sick father in Copenhagen."

"Is father sick?"

He looked around the table. The man opposite took up an envelope from the brief case. Gunnar and Malcolm stared hard at the shiny tabletop.

"Engineer Kineman. Because of important duties significant for the defense you have been exempt from the draft during the entire war. You have excellent testimonials from the Lidingö Home Guard. Your bosses see you as unswervingly loyal to the company and your new country. A man of just your capacity, with those qualities we are interested in. A competent engineer who can independently assess certain information which we are anxious about, information that can be obtained in occupied Denmark. It will involve a trip, a conversation. Possibly also bringing back something which we can probably for the time being call a strategically interesting product."

He handed over the letter.

"We also think that it would look good if your youngest son went along to say hello to his old grandfather. Let him take this along to his teacher tomorrow. The principal has been informed."

Gunnar cleared his throat:

"This could mean so colossally much for us, for the whole factory. For your future too, Hans Jörgen."

The man in the uniform watched him intensively, almost without blinking. Perhaps a tiny bit of irritation could be discerned in his voice when he finally broke the silence:

"Is it quite certain that you didn't receive a letter from your family in Denmark?"

It lay on the hall table when he came home. Brother Erik asked him to investigate the possibility of coming down to Birkeröd promptly. Danish authorities had been in contact with the Germans and permission could be arranged. Humanitarian grounds should be given as the reason, alternatively business. Fredrik had a violent and uncontrolled outburst at the dinner table when he found out that only Hans Jörgen was going to go along to war. That was very unpleasant, this business with your grandfather, said the assistant headmaster with an affected and prying voice. His pals showed envy by getting excited.

"You're going to shit in your pants," Ove said. "They rip up people with bayonets. Especially now that the war will soon be over. That is what is so repulsive."

It was December before they got away. Mama knitted new mittens in

Denmark's colors, red and white. Papa kissed her on the mouth although they weren't at all alone on the platform. Fredrik got very embarrassed and furious, got as far away from the family spectacle as he could and kicked a hard sooty snow pile. He actually didn't feel a bit safe in spite of the fact that papa was holding his hand hard. He let go and hugged mama once again. They didn't usually go on like that.

"That's enough," she said and instead squeezed her son tight, tight into herself. That didn't exactly make things better. He glanced over at his brother. Everything was so unfamiliar. Then he got free. Papa grasped his upper arm hard. It hurt, as usual.

"Give mama a real hug now. No nonsense."

She pulled off her glove, gave him a pat on the chin. Her soft hand smelled of salve, straightened up his cap, pushed it over his forehead, smoothed his hair, arranged the kerchief around his neck. It was raw and frostily cold at the Central Station. Mama was probably freezing in her silk stockings. She bent down over him. He turned his face away quick. No more now. He didn't really need to be kissed too. He would have preferred to run over to Fredrik and help him with the destruction of the snowdrift, but he didn't get anywhere. Papa held him there in his iron grip and lifted him up onto the train. The compartment window was frozen shut. It was almost just as cold in there. He breathed on the glass and drew patterns with his finger.

"Now wave, Hans Jörgen, the train is going. You can do that later. Hurry up now!"

He rubbed away the steam with his palm. That became a sort of waving. Mama and Fredrik disappeared to the rear. She took his hand in hers and surprisingly enough held onto it. Then it was just he and papa. He went at it really methodically, drained himself completely, filled the black pane with thin breath. His fingertips followed the face's contour, filled in the eyes, mouth, nose with the blackness from the tunnel. As the steam evaporated papa's face too developed in the reflection. Actually, he didn't look so dangerous. Actually, he could also be nice. Actually.

For it wasn't the war he was most afraid of!

The night was wet, dripping wet. The dampness collected in big heavy drops that ran along the railing. One of the ferry's floodlights was directed for a short moment against the dock, then it was put out. The darkness got thicker the closer they came to land on the other side of the sound. The huge castle was swallowed up. A rustling of coarse chains from the stem. Someone pounded against the wooden wedges that fastened the wheels against the rails. It sounded dull, muted, except when the axe missed and a bright sound of metal exploded.

The first real living German soldier showed up inside the arrival hall. Everything seemed suspiciously peaceful for it to be war. The helmets lay on the table. There too was a half-empty bottle of beer. In a smaller room inside sat the next person in a uniform. He had on a real German high peaked cap. Yet neither did he look especially warlike, he even smiled at him. On a long low bench they had to open up their luggage alongside the few other passengers' suitcases, bundles and sacks tied with rope. He counted eleven pieces in all. And then his own rucksack of course. There was a burning smell in the room from the stove. Every so often the officer stuffed in a piece of wood. Nobody was in any hurry. One after one they were called forth and had to point out their luggage and open it. It was mostly soft things, clothes, like in their suitcases. Those who had wrapped packages had to open them too. The German had a big wide face, half shaded by the visor of his cap. Therefore, you actually saw only his mouth and a couple of hairy nostrils that he picked at at regular intervals.

It was his turn. He untied the rucksack, opened up the flap and held it out. There were the schoolbooks and the extra sweater, of course. The horse that grandfather was going to get lay properly wrapped up. He looked at papa. There was a tightening around his lips. They moved against each other, inward, as if he were about to swallow them.

The strange hand moved around among his things, with glove on.

"Shall I show it to him, papa. Is that what he wants?"

The horse was like new. Shining white lacquered. Not the least seam shone around the secret tin soldier boxes in the neck. On one side of the withers was the Danish flag, on the other Sweden's.

"Es fehlt doch eine Fahne," smiled the German and lay his hand on the horse's back and patted it several times. "Schönes Pferd."

"What is he saying, papa?"

"That a flag is missing. That it would have been finer with the German flag."

While papa continued to talk German, he himself wrapped up the horse in the sweater and stuffed it down in the rucksack, tied it up properly, fixed the buckle on the leather strap's third, worn-out hole. Then he got a cracker from the German.

"Sag Danke schön," his father said and the son did as he was told. Besides, he bowed and shook hands as he had learned. The soldier stretched his arm out over the table and said Heil Hitler. The cracker mostly resembled a biscuit and had no taste, just got thick in his throat. It was simply not possible to swallow. He continued to chew all the way until they were again on the train. Then he vomited, right out onto the floor in the corridor. For no reason whatsoever. Papa held him softly around the back and rubbed his hair away from his soaking wet forehead.

"Well, well, my boy. Now nothing is dangerous any more."

He vomited one more time. Just straight out. For safety's sake. So that he became quite empty.

000

He wandered with his upper body bare, still strong, up the ravine. There was shade, but not enough to completely stop the mountain's growth. Higher up the verdure merged with thorny shrubs. There the sun was raging freely. Also, he had to pass the fields. The stones in the knapsack felt light. When he reached the crest, eagles were going to step in. Then, if not before, the burden would evaporate. He knew. He had turned back enough times down the precipice, knew the paths well, the ivy's hideout, the olive tree's weight in the valley.

Comrades ought to surround him. The warriors' return. But this time he was coming alone. There was certainly still time to grow old among the others in the ravines that run out into the lowland, where sour fumes drift and the wind dies in the trees. Presumably there were mates there who manned the merchant ships, visited the islands with tales, courted the naïvté of the listeners. The donkeys' braying was still heard all the way up, the market cries from the ferry berth.

Up there the paths divided. The wind from down on the sea cleansed the face of dust. The straps cut deeper into the shoulders. The broom flowers glistened gold the whole way down to the shore. Now ravens and gulls were hovering way below him. It was too late to turn back.

The story remains the same. The ease with which he moves on over the red dry earth can show whether we are right in our conjectures.

You are sad in the eyes, she says, you are no longer here. Another day she says that there is a yearning to get away in my body and I know that she is right. The nasty wound under the knee has healed. The pain in the chest after the blows is completely gone. I have recovered just fine, but it is certain to be a long time before I can run as before; my right leg simply seems to be a bit shorter than it was before the accident. Presumably, I too will finally – like everyone else – become an old man like that, like the old people who sit on porches in deep shade, with open leather vests and their faces invisible under the broad brims of their hats; men with lots to tell but with no young people who want to listen. Many of them are right here and I have listened carefully to them and promised myself to always remember what I heard. Nor will I forget her. I know that you will be just fine, she continues consolingly. We have used strong medicine on you, nothing else helped.

Yes, I have decided. I shall return home. Conclude this continuous story with its well-known, banally recurring ingredients: adventure, impossible love. Return to what presumably is best described with precisely the same words. Perhaps with the addition everyday, ennui? Actually, it is incomprehensible that the same life, same person, here and there, then and now, can be forced into this decrepit and scarred body.

Finish. Return. Begin again? That is, of course, what everything finally is about, the eternal beginning so as to postpone the end, the wall on the other side of the room, the cliff wall right across the valley. This eternally repeating story about how the very first man peeked out from his mother's womb and without hesitation immediately decided for life. Out there everything seems extremely beautiful under the summer sun. Someone is certainly already waiting from the beginning hunched up in the summer cabin high up in the tree where the wind goes hard and stiff between the pines' branches, and the whole earth swings together with the sea farther away. And you put your hands on my bare shoulders and I feel quite the same longing in you too. And we prepare camp for the childish bodies of our mutual fears and for the very first time the second man meets the first. But it is also the last time. More banal it certainly can't get.

Yes, surely it will be as she says, as she has repeated so many times when I woke up from a dream, that now you will soon leave me. It is not at all certain that I want to; perhaps not she either. But something else has decided in me. I shall try to explain this, if possible. A moderately scarred warrior's tragicomic account, for the eras of the real heroes are certainly irrevocably past. This has been played out in other spaces, more modern perhaps, but just in some sort of superficial meaning. For the actual adventure exists, for some impenetrable reason it is actually that way. You can never wriggle out of it, if it ever gets hold of you, you are hopelessly stuck. If this also means that the future, all other unfamiliar spaces, in all eternity are mortgaged against this single adventure, that I don't know. In that case others will have to reveal it. I only know that there isn't any so-called logic in this. No morals either, for that matter. If there are any, then I apologize already now, it is, in any case, unintentional and guaranteed harmless. For I don't want to hurt anyone, nor go around with lies. If I say that I would prefer to stay with her, then everyone knows now that I am lying. It has already been written how this is supposed to happen. That it should also chance to happen to me no powers in the world could either anticipate or prevent.

Yes, she put out my passport so that I couldn't avoid noticing it. I don't know whether she means that I should head down to the bus station without a farewell, that she doesn't want to meet me any more. Certainly the leg holds. The injury is assuredly healed just fine. For that matter, everyone here has seen through the malingerer long ago, known very well why I stayed on. Of course I will be able to continue running, even if it were simply jogging through one or another marathon. I'll never be at peace sitting on a cool porch in the shade under the afternoon's high, sand-colored cliffs, patiently listening to others' fantastic cock-and-bull stories. But before I hurry on, I'm still going to give myself time to pull up my shirt and show the little mark under the shoulder, for whoever wants to see it. And I will not care whether you burst into laughter and say right out that worse liars would have to be sought among crazy coyotes who howl through the nights around the deserts.

It was going to be the best of trips, the project The Hero's Return. The sum of life's collected experiences. In short, the filmmaker's film; well, a short film then! Everything was so carefully planned. I had even succeeded in scraping together a few bucks from the Institute for the lectures in the USA. New dream trip, Märta in the cashier's office laughed when I picked up the juicy advance and the tickets; you better take care you don't get fat if you're going to be gone so long from the lunchtime gymnasts. No problem, I countered and signed, if you work alone on a production like this, it is exclusively a question of work, hard physical work. You don't believe me? Be your own porter, chauffeur, camera assistant, electrician, sound engineer, producer, reporter, photographer – you still don't believe me? That it should be so damned difficult to get into people's thick skulls that it actually is a normal honorable job we are trying to carry out, tiring, risky, thankless, sometimes even dangerous. Not a bit glamorous. You seem to believe that we do nothing other than travel around the world taking it easy, quartered in the world's most fantastic super hotels, bathing among half-naked women in heart-shaped swimming pools, living indecent lives of luxury on sky high expense allowances eventually returning home with a pile of pictures and sound that we hastily arrange in the cutting-room with just the right amount of tricks and lies and cleverly well-adjusted texts so that we soon get a new documentary project approved, again take off to the country for a few months or to the library to study up or scout for locations before we – after a short visit to the ever dustier office module – rush down to the travel office and collect the cash for a new covert pleasure trip on the viewers' expensive license fees. Okay, where do people get everything from? The evening newspapers? The pictures of Nils Petter in Cannes?

I can agree that the conditions for once seemed tolerable, but is that something to grumble over? For someone who in spite of everything has followed the last adventurers' business for twenty-five years? To escape all the rubbish about super apex prices and specific times to pay attention to. But that the trip is OPEN, as it is called in good travel bureau Swedish, that was actually the Institute's gain, not TV's. Really only two times to watch, the March week in Texas and the May days at UCLA. In between Arizona and the conversation with Cochise. Before that Ithaca and the long since agreed-upon but constantly postponed meeting with Odysseus. Robinson on an optional West Indian island. I can agree that on paper this sounds a little too nice to be true. But – that's the way it is. Some, the gods punish right away, others it takes a long time. Travel when the Nordic winter is at its worst, return home and be nice until the Midsummer dance and then take vacation and compensatory leave! NEW TV SCANDAL EXPEDITION. That's how brutally Inger in the editing room expressed herself when I kissed her goodbye and promised her many fine pictures to cut and put together – and God help you, she threatened, if you don't write a bunch of cute postcards to me!

At home you began as usual to clean away the residues after me already long before I got going, unusually early I thought. I hate it when you travel or is it also pure, healthy envy I feel, of everything if only you are going to get to live quite by yourself – you don't look at me when you say it, continue to rub the sink although it has been sparklingly clean for a long time – but I don't want to see any traces of you as long as you are gone. Although you are always welcome home, my friend, you know that, she says in the same breath and gives me the well-known hug and the cool kiss on the cheek. For a long time we have been living with the still current arrangement between us, a remnant from our so-called open-minded youth. I don't know how we suffer from it, or more correctly, whether she too suffers; part of the agreement is that if you don't know anything, then nothing serious has happened. This was the only way out for us, for some reason we seemed to live best together; everything else was just awkward. At least that is what I try to imagine. You usually claim that the pact exists because of the downright convenience from my side. It's a long time since I made use of this unwritten letter of freedom. Undeniably it eases the conscience during circumstances that might come up on longer expeditions. There will be an occasion to return to this. In spite of everything I have never really been able to reconcile myself to the thought that she has others, or worse, others her, whatever the right expression is. Bamse of course is inevitable. He has always been around. But so has his Annastina too. This is a remarkable friendship or love. That too is part of the story.

Hans Jörgen inaugurated his brand new driver's license by driving me to the terminal. I'm going to begin strength training in earnest now so I can take over your old Finn, do you have anything against that? Excellent, I answered, keep it and I'll commandeer the Laser instead. He threw a glance at me in the rearview mirror, pretended to be distressed. You, old man, it is actually no great fun for a son to see his father age in this way, see how quickly it can go downhill. No marathon runs any more, no hardy and refreshing hanging out of the Finn. What has become of you, dad, you are as good as dead already. I know, I answered and squeezed his now strong fist goodbye. We looked a bit surprised at each other. It was probably the first time we took leave of each other in this way, a powerful handshake between grown men, as before an unusually risky expedition. He is full grown now, the little guy. Otherwise everything felt very good in the snowstorm, as it usually does when you take off, well thought-out and planned; most of the dangers even realistically foreseen and marked on the itinerary. The February snow whipped around and whirled after the Arlanda bus, like dirty yellow smoke.

The snow showers were sparse and sharply lit up by the slanting sun that, thank heaven, finally managed to get a bit up above the winter horizon's miserable lowest position.

Everything began in the greatest innocence too, far from all the mythical violence, the archetypes of farce, the recurrent everyday of tragedy. A few days' work on Korfu among frozen British spring tourists, though without getting hold of really genuine Phaeacians who knew what had really happened; even less any modern day sweet Nausicaa, willing to play ball for a few insignificant honorarium dollars on the extraordinarily filthy strip of beach where I should have washed ashore according to linguistically and geographically reliable text interpreters. Shivering and cross in the still winter-cold winds from the interior of the Balkans I gave up, had myself ferried over to the mainland. Soon Albania's rugged mountains receded in the rearview mirror. I drove the straightest route through the story to Patras and the Ithaca ferry, without stopping either at Actium or Missolonghi.

During the crossing I made contact with two cheerful American girls. We shared cheese and bread and wine and still everything was so very innocent and flirtily uneventful as it could ever be. I told a bit about my project, and they actually didn't tell a thing about themselves. Which under the effect of light inebriation made everything moderately mysterious when at dusk we swung in toward Vathi. We made plans to meet early the next morning at the cafe near the boat's berth. Already then I had decided to ask them to take part in a couple of sequences I hadn't finished with on Korfu. They seemed far from impossible. During the night even Poseidon coughed three times. Perhaps it was meant as a warning. Anyhow, the following morning I rented a taxi and we went northward on the island. The one, youngest and sweetest, was actually named Pen as in Penelope. She was a tall calf-legged coed of that wholesome sort that you can often see on educational pleasure trips through old Europe. The other one turned out on closer observation to have Scandinavian stock, Danish to be more precise. We joked about being related and upon urgent request I called her Marie Louise instead of the more California-sounding Mary Lou. Her hair was strawberry blond and certainly quite genuine. There was something melancholy in her personal charm, at once trying and almost heavy, in her fine face. She was significantly older than Pen. But that could only be seen at close quarters. In any case, I got my longed-for pictures and, it feels a little awkward to have to confess, in return they got me.

We met again in the evening. Then everything was just formal, felt silent and dumb and I actually wished the whole thing were undone. After a while we didn't have anything at all to say to each other. Finally, I decided to walk home and go to bed quite alone, took out my calling card from my wallet and wrote professor Shideler's name if they should want to get hold of me in Los Angeles a little later at the beginning of spring. For unfathomable reasons I always assume that American girls drifting around ought to be students at some wretched college in the Middle West prairie regions, alternatively but more seldom from some of the prestige universities on the east or west coast. They looked quickly at the card and then laid it down without comment on the marble counter full of breadcrumbs and smeary from olive oil.

A bit surprisingly sweet Pen placed her hand over mine and said after a moment's obstinate staring down on the plate's tough octopus remains that she actually was very distressed too over what had happened outside the cave. I don't understand what got into us, she said, can you explain? She looked appealingly at Mary Lou who was stubbornly silent and instead ruthlessly devoted herself to fixing her eyes on mine. I tried to slip away, one of my most common tricks when things begin to get too hot. This time it didn't succeed. After a while I felt completely invaded. I couldn't figure them out. One moment they were like two sisters, intimately chattering, mysteriously smiling at each other, effectively excluding the world around from every meaningful attempt at contact. In the next moment Mary Lou was transformed into an impenetrable, ominous well of the darkest brown silence; Pen to an endless source of strings of everyday phrases and general nonsense. Were they sisters or a mother with a daughter of almost the same age or quite simply a couple of ordinary lesbian California women on the road? The gods perhaps knew. I didn't need to know. I had my feet of film. That was good enough for me.

A group of loud Germans, resembling overage longhaired terrorists from the good old days, poured in and spread out ruthlessly everywhere. There was hardly room for us anymore, in any case not for me. Still, I sat there, cemented by her glance. The whole thing actually felt quite unreal.

Pen got up first.

"Hi Swede, bye Swede," she said and stretched out her hand over the table. I took it and the spell was broken. There was a terrible noise in the place, I could hardly hear what I myself said:

"Are you going along tomorrow too," I wondered paralyzed.

"I hardly think so," answered Mary Lou. "Do you have a pen?"

She leaned over the table, came quite near me. It burned. Her bodily smell almost got me to feel sick from sensual pleasure, I cannot describe it better. She wrote something quickly on the back of my card.

In the door she turned around. Somewhere outside on the dock a car must have been standing with its lights on. She was hardly visible, just an indistinct silhouette, frizzy hair and a bodily contour shining of thin gold. Perhaps she had meant to say something. But she turned at once on her heels, disappeared out into the darkness after Pen. Her pungent odor, though, remained in my sweater, even longer as a memory in the skin. I picked up the card and read: Old Danish Beauty Parlor, Santa Monica, Calif.

I too should have gone home and gone to bed. I should have gone to sleep. I was supposed to be tired. Yet I sat there, in all innocence certainly, and got tipsy; for the second evening in a row. It was quite clear that something was wrong with me. I didn't get going to Nestor until the Tyrolean terrorists had begun to yodel in complete earnest around midnight.

To the south, long before you even get close to Eumaios' hovel, the road passes from Vathi into something that quite well resembles a creek ravine, possibly suitable for the hooves of clever donkeys but absolutely not for heavily loaded, hungover stale middle-aged filmmakers. Tender patches of spring grass dotted the red earth between stout olive tree trunks. The stone walls followed along far up toward the mountain. Lazy lizards were lying there, lapping the sun and staring contemptuously at me under heavy reptile eyelids. Now and then you could hear the braying of invisible mules, tethered in the oak groves higher up, as if someone was sticking sharp knives into them at irregular intervals. Still higher up, on the bare cliffs' very highest tips, sat the sky as it should: a blue and clean-blown cap. Behind every new bend in the road the sound from the little city was dampened finally sinking away completely. Sounds of unfamiliar birds took over, the buzzing of insects. I was the first man. Everything had to be called something; the strange, different, divergent. Greek thrush, gravel finch, cloud hawk. Artichoke, stone flower, mule grass.

Already after a good thirty minutes walking stubbornly upward there was a spot to rest at. I sat down in a sun-warmed crevice between recently bloomed trees covered by white flowers with minute yellow features on the petals. It smelled sweet, a hint of apple blossom, a few drops of rugosa rose. They reminded me also of the Baltic's rugged whitebeam. Completely in accordance with the best Linnéan tradition I thus gave a name to the unknown tree after its discoverer, arber itacensis hansjurgensis. To find the right Swedish name was more difficult. Finally, I decided on Ithacan sun birch. Up in the clouds the swallows were on a hyperborean binge, but the low bleating from a goat brought me quickly back to Mediteranean realities. I emptied the beer bottle and in any case got rid of my restive thirst. The larger part of my head still felt thick and sulky, armor-coated, with narrow openings for the senses to peek out and be let in. The next day buzzing in the right ear, that has developed over the years from leaning against droning camera motors, usually grows in strength. Today was to be sure no exception. I cupped my hand to a shell. Inside it grew to a roar, eruptions and landslides in the brain's convolutions. The healthy ear picked up other sounds at the same time, distinct steps, the rustle from small stones that were spattering away from hooves, broken branches. I quickly got the camera loose from the hooks in the knapsack and got ready for shooting. But it was no age-old swineherd Eumaios that showed up in the aperture's zooming in field of vision. The eyepiece was filled by bare legs, a waving girl-woman, astride a spindly mule which she was skillfully maneuvering with her thighs and heels up over the path's treacherous pebbles.

"Good thing you're so organized that you told the people at the hotel where you were going," she said.

"Old journalistic experience. People quite simply ought to know where the rescue expeditions should be sent. It results in your never being able to work in peace. But you would also like to imagine that a terribly important telephone conversation is steadily searching for you over the whole world. That sort of thing strengthens your self-esteem enormously."

She laughed to be sure, but very dutifully. It could be seen that she wanted something. She was riding bareback except for one worn-out, coarse blanket. The miserable animal was no larger than that her long legs reached down to the ground. It almost looked as if she was supporting it. She pulled down the white terry cloth band from her forehead and let it hang as a neck-band instead. I could read parts of the pink text: Danish Beau ...

"Do you need help with anything; that for example?"

She pointed at my rucksack.

"Please."

We put it on top of the pointed mule back, between her naked thighs.

"Farther up?" she nodded.

A mere three miles south of Vathi the road was wiped out entirely, turned into the stoniest heath you could ever imagine. To the right arises a wild and quite bare peak around which birds of prey circle, resting on the thermals from the sea far below. Right in front it descends abruptly and steeply toward the ravens' cliff with the thin waterfall. I have never seriously even tried out the thought of sometime going down that way. To the east the mountain levels out to a plateau with low wind-worn shrubs and some stunted parasol pines. Dry ravines run toward the shore. The rocks there are so sharp that they cut right through the soles of your sandals. And from far, far down there the updrafts carry the roar of the surf, like mystical, reverse windfall. The islands don't even float. Everything flies, is lifted into swirls of shadows clear as glass and unmerciful light. It is an unbelievable sight. No pictures can do it justice. No words either, for that matter.

"Down there, do you see the beach?" I pointed.

She stretched herself, forced the unwilling animal a couple of additional highly dangerous steps out toward the precipice. She pressed her legs hard together around the animal's belly. It stopped with widened nostrils and the upper lip drawn up high over yellow, broken teeth.

"Are we going down too?"

"You first in any case."

She backed the animal away from the precipice and dismounted.

"Do you feel anything from the wound?"

"The wound?"

"You haven't already forgotten!"

She got close behind me and pulled up my sweater. With her fingers she rubbed lightly around the underside of the shoulder blade, stopped to the right.

"Nothing heals like the blood of the pine," she said and slipped in close to me, now with her arm around my back. Together we took some dragging, almost hesitant steps, as in an ancient ritual, up to the edge of the cliff.

"You could stay here forever, just exist, it is so beautiful. Become stone or wind or bird. Look at the black-backed gull there! What wings, what divine strength, what repose in flight!"

We turned toward each other. She kept her hands on my shoulders, I let mine carefully brush her slender hips.

"Don't you really want to come along down to the beach? Now that you have ridden all the way here?"

"My role is that of the simple messenger. Mary Lou really wants to meet you when you come to California, later this spring."

"But, it is you who are Mary Lou!"

She took hold of my hands and took them away from her body, but without letting go completely; her fingertips moved into my turned-up palms.

"You are an unusually sweet and childish old Odysseus. A person actually has to like you a bit. Therefore, I'm going to give you some good advice. If you want, you can consider it as a warning. Promise me that you will never look for us if you ever come to Santa Monica!"

She broke the contact, mounted the pitiful animal and cracked the whip carefully over its back.

"As a matter of fact I am an odious witch!"

It was dark in the evening when I returned after a long day of profitable interviews with Eumaios and Telemachus. Completely stiff, with my knees far down in the totally worn-out sandals, I tumbled into the room and dropped off right away. The morning roar of the ferry awakened me. Raw and inhumanly it roared outside the Mentor Hotel, on the way back to Patras, at low speed passing between the embankment and the little orthodox chapel on the fortification island in the middle of the bay. I wrapped a bath towel around myself and went out onto the balcony. On the quarterdeck two waving figures could be seen. I can't swear to it, but it could well have been my California girlfriends. I waved back, a bit relieved, actually.

Six hundred yards already finished. There is a golden rule on this job. You should always go out hard. In order to retain the work ethic, civilized man's worst curse, I quickly wrote out yesterday's picture and sound report. There was actually only one problem with it. One of the five rolls of exposed film was missing!

The one from Odysseus' cave. The one with the goddesses.

To be sure there are no wasted words, no meaningless movements. Everything speaks about everything. The outer movement about the inner, inner feeling through outer gesture. The words, the way of moving, every change in the body's posture reveals at once the actor as a part of a connected whole. The least fragment deals with the task of the whole. There are those who notice every sign. Not even the very finest correspondences escape them. Then there are all the others. It is a question of perspicacity or myopia. The fantasy can never become an obstacle. The imagination is only an invitation to reality. The body's fantastic changes nothing other than false reflexes. At the bottom prevail stable conditions, sharing, nearness. Earth. Words.

So far everything may seem very well. Every event a sign for another. The shard is the decisive proof. No one needs the whole pot any longer. As a matter of fact it never existed. No scientific formulas can capture this connection. The weaver weaves. The eagle attacks the flock of geese on the palace grounds. Grammar is uncompromising. Outside everything is alike. Movements, gestures, words. Inside everything is still changed.

Like that time he followed Autolychos' sons through the thicket. Their ivory dogs caught the scent, yelped. He was ready. Yet the tusk cut up the flesh, above the knee. It was an annoying mishap. He actually never wanted to talk about it. But the scratch is there. There would be more.

No one has ever said that I was supposed to be a big brooder, even less with a particular philosophical turn of mind. Yet you perhaps ought to keep in mind, that the extraordinarily slender BA exam that was given in the fifties at the University of Stockholm also contained practical philosophy, alongside of the required credits in literary history, art history, and the history of religion. My parents, relieved, were content with the poor result, all the more so as the oldest son, the family's pride and theoretically gifted person, had done exactly as mama and papa had wanted, become a lawyer and in spite of swinish and almost incomprehensibly wretched table manners had been accepted as a candidate in the State Department. In continuation I was left alone undisturbed with my cameras and tried to survive as best I could according to the extremely simple philosophy of life which at all times maintains that what happens will happen to you as well. Picture by picture. Sound after sound. In room by room.

Long lonely days here on the reservation got me to remember and be reminded. Or more correctly: the memories imposed themselves on me, without any real help from my side. Recollection is to be sure a remarkable process. For me it is always set in motion by some physical stimulus, a sort of kick-off of sensual pleasure for the memory. I am obviously not alone in this, just as little as anyone else is alone in anything.

There is a wind harp hanging on the porch, an ingenious and simple device which lives entirely on the wind from the deserts. It never repeats itself. It is made of the simplest things, bone stumps, stones, almost petrified pieces of wood that are polished by the drifting sand. There are also trivial remains of civilization: some sky blue pieces of glass, rusty pieces of tin cut out of beer cans. The sound grows from one moment to another. I don't believe it has ever fallen silent as long as I have been here. It functions like a memory machine. Sometimes there have been moments when I just wanted to scream, as if to restore a lost silence. This is entirely new to me, difficult to explain, incomprehensible. Nor can I ask someone else to understand what I myself don't get. Or can you?

I have a sound in my ear. It is quite low. Long periods can pass without my noticing it. Now, in any case, it has established a remarkable connection with the wind harp outside. There is a position where these sounds and tones quite simply cancel each other out. I become completely clear. Far back through all spaces and landscapes I hear the man's, the youth's, the boy's voices, long shreds of conversation I believed to be totally obliterated by the constant destruction of brain cells. And yet there must remain masses of dams, remote spots and gorges from where nothing arrives. But which are there. Sometimes I simply wonder whether I am anything other than a terrible fiction in someone else, a half completed icon, a fickle idea from this unknown other who at anytime whatsoever can empty me out, make me blank and empty; a dark unfinished whole. And then just begin again somewhere else with someone else, as if nothing had happened!

The first man must ever and anew give birth to himself. Over and over and over again. No one can take that from you. It is a terrible fate that you, thank heaven, share with everyone else. We are all inscribed in each other, weighted in, consecrated. The real freedom, the mysterious, incomprehensible we usually call life, it exists only for the first man; where space curves and passes over into time. But also for the second one, who is just as necessary: she who is waiting.

This is the paradoxical. What happens to the wind harp, happens to me too.

Four rings. The first one:

I got the book as a Christmas present, The Wooden Horse, but didn't read it until summer vacation. Of course my memory can be at fault, but I think that it dealt with a group of prisoners of war on the way to escaping from a Nazi prison camp through an ingenious tunnel to freedom. There is no reference library here where I can check the facts, just the wind, the desert and you naturally. The whole thing can very well have dealt with a wooden horse, my wooden horse, with my own war.

Clever Fredrik did his military service that summer. I myself had gradually begun to prepare a single-handed excavation far inside of Ulla Hau, where no one could check on what I was up to. It was almost a question of fleeing from a summer that seemed to be on the way to beating an unbreakable world record in crap. After having studied a sand mound a good many hours and filled a couple of buckets with sand I gave up. Suddenly and unexpectedly gratifying reinforcements arrived. Fredde's best buddies, on bikes, completely exhausted of course; draped with knapsacks, tent and sleeping bags. Biffen, Hasse and Bamse had a last year left before it was their turn to be ground down into soldiers. Now they were here, to surprise Fredde during his harvest leave. I had never gotten to be included in their terribly tough gang, surrounded by the shadiest rumors that circulated around the schoolyard and in the corridors during the terms. After a week's cycling from home via Kalmar and Visby, however, they didn't look a bit dangerous, tired and dirty, in a miserable state in short. I took a chance. Since at the beginning of August it was as chock-full of unnecessary relatives as usual in all conceivable houses and nooks, and, besides, my Danish grandfather was busy trying to die in peace in the shade of the oak in the courtyard, it was considered to be appropriate that the latest arrivals to the summer catastrophe pitch camp a ways from the actual civilization, in the forest inside the sand dunes. I went along, leeched onto them. It actually looked like I was at last going to get a couple of well-deserved days away from all social control, before Fredde arrived. The first day to be sure a no doubt seriously meant but far too lame attempt was made while waiting for his arrival to get the muscular group of youths to help pour the slab and get up the framework for the extra house that ever since then has been called Blue Thorp, although to my knowledge there has never been the least bit of blue on the shack in question. However, I informed the gang about summer vacation's unwritten rules and my special interpretation of them. Already by the second day we were free. They seemed a bit impressed by my firm action. Actually, I was simply lucky. I was finally going to have fun with the real guys, get rid of the Skåne cousins and the year's chance companions, whose presence mostly led to tremendous catastrophes; at least for me. I suddenly felt like an elevated and almost equal member of the company of youths, enviable owner of a quart of booze as well as a worn-out pile of Pinup magazines far down in one cycle pannier.

Quite near the parasol pines by my old wooden hut the sand is firm and damp under the sun-dried surface, perfect to work in. Together we continued my interrupted undertaking. We worked resolutely downward, strengthened by tiny spots of booze from the cap, dug on, inch by inch toward the middle of the earth, filling buckets with gradually heavier, browner and wetter sand. It reached to the knees, it reached to the stomach, it reached finally to the chins of some of us. Naturally, the others got tired after a lousy hour and instead rushed down to the shore to swim. I remained alone, had no desire at all to go along. The sweat dried, my pulse went down in revolutions. I climbed up on the platform, my dilapidated wooden ship between heaven and earth, settled down on the edge. The wind stiff, cool against the chin. You could see powerful geese on the bay, off shore. They could have it, the lazy bastards, the disloyal deserters; the ice cold water was just right for them. Tomorrow, I could easily arrange hard labor for the whole bunch, at the building site.

I stretched out on my back with my legs dangling in the air, closed my eyes. My shoulders hurt but the pain was dissolved quickly by the sun's heat from the boards that fused into my body. The sway of the limbs became part of me. It could be felt how the wings were growing out, the needles transformed into feathers. I was flying; I glanced under my eyelids, upward, toward the bubbling cumulus clouds. Soon I was going to join the whirl of buzzards up there, faithful late summer comrades.

"Hiho, is anyone there?"

I rolled around and carried out a nearly perfect belly landing, dangerously close to the precipice. It was Astrid. With her toes she poked a fine sprinkle of sand down into my arduously dug hole.

"What are you doing?"

"Digging as you can see."

"You're really crazy. How old are you actually?"

Old enough for her in any case. And then my thoughts began to spin on. This was perhaps the right occasion for the final attack, the possibility of repaying her for all the ignominies; nothing shrinks as fast as summers in August. But before I even managed to begin to seriously fantasize, reality climbed up and sat down beside me, unpleasantly close, surrounded by that confusing, provocative scent that she was always radiating toward me with the sole intention of paralyzing. I was immediately stuck with my chin pressed hard against the outside of the deck. The skin stretched over her shinbone, smooth, almost a blue-black brown. Little, pitifully little light downy hairs glittered above her knees. Without cause something began to grow in me with furious speed. I struggled against it for all I was worth so as not to be lifted right up into the air, a pathetic and slight youthful body balancing above the world's hithertofore longest and slimmest manly organ. I didn't dare, couldn't budge.

"Up here you could actually live perfectly, if you just arranged things a bit. Shall we do it? That would really be nice."

For the moment, appropriate Pinup sequences drew past in a rapid cavalcade. Large pendulous breasts, funny poses with bulging behinds surrounded by garters and odd panties, plump soft stomachs that mostly ended toward the bottom in smoothed-out retouches instead of attractively depicting the delightfully hairy monster that once and for all was going to make an end of an almost unpleasantly tragic, unnaturally lengthy male chastity. As quick as lightning I sat up, at the same time as I turned around. In that way I ended up with my back toward her, discretely spared from all too irritating curious eyes. I pulled up my knees and huddled up. Cold sweat poured over my entire body. Soon that disgusting little snout was certainly going to sniff its way out of the flapping legs of my gym pants.

"Please help me with the tie, I think it's coming loose?"

The catastrophic period was by no means past. You could already hear the bellow from Fredde's abominable buddies. It was just a question of seconds before everything would be painfully over. I fumbled as if possessed with the knot behind her back. Finally, there remained only one reasonable way out. Death.

I threw myself over the edge, landed askew but still succeeded under excruciating pain on the world's worst sprained ankle in crawling down into the protective hole. In novels, prisoners of war dig fantastic passages to freedom and peace. With furious frenzy I tried the same thing. With a very rotten conscience they were going to find me again, the whole time faithfully toiling for them, while they were just devoting themselves to taking it easy with swimming and warm booze. It was tight down there, sticky wet with the ground water, almost impossible to manoeuver the shovel. And nothing became immediately easier when her damn tie pants followed along down into the pit and furthermore got tangled in everything!

I caught a glimpse of her behind the big guys. They lined up around the edge, with disgusting grins. She was still sitting unconcerned and calm up in the tree, with her arms demurely crossed over her small white breasts. I definitely remember how she slowly shook her head, before the tears made it totally impossible to see anything anymore. The shame was total.

At that time I of course didn't understand how terribly impressed Bamse and the others were by Fredde's very advanced little brother. That summer was lined with unusually many reverse triumphs. Possibly because it was the absolutely last summer. Anyhow, it is almost improbable what disgusting things a youth at that time had to go through on the way to becoming a grown man. If that process is ever over.

Four rings. The second one:

Bamse and I sauntered over Norrtull street to Ogo for a sandwich. The same year Parker died. I had a public mourning for several weeks and played my old 78 rpm down to gravel where several fantastic runs drowned out, finally being obliterated completely. I have heard the same old tracks now again, the classical recordings, repeat after repeat, variation on variation, digitally remastered, laser-read. But it isn't my Parker, can never become the desperate Orpheus who burst reality and spoke to me through surface noise, for the first time really let me get a feeling of what life is about, the space it's played in. He ripped up the world and made it all at once more understandable and incomprehensible for at least an innocent guy from the suburbs. Others dug Bunk Johnson or roared in chorus in the Royal Tennis Hall while Armstrong clowned around on the stage and drowned handkerchiefs with sweat and swayed back and forth and grinned and the entire idiotic audience thought that they had to do the same thing and experienced music history. Bah.

You notice how quickly I slip away, hesitate. We had just suffered through Karling's obligatory lesson of slides about the transformation of English gardens in Scandinavia. After lunch Oscar R was waiting with his futuristic French 18th century architecture. At that time you still were properly educated. We strolled as usual over to Ogo for the obligatory shrimp sandwich, a cup of coffee, a dry cinnamon bun and a drop of Loranga. A later era's intelligentsia crowded in everywhere, new associate professors and professors and authors, Espmark, Jonsson, Ekner, Berefelt, Orre, Tranströmer. They were sitting in groups, clique after clique, or alone, with BLM's reviews opened up. You were sitting on a sofa by the window. You sat there under the mirror, at an already overfilled corner table. Bamse immediately went over there and we moved in close. At that time you wore your hair artfully braided in a little hard pigtail, fastened high atop your head with shimmering metal pins. This is Hans Jörgen, Bamse said. You looked at me with a smile, with your eyes boldly wide open, eyes that I dodged, and I trudged around the outer edges of your face, carefully gazing into the bold corners of your eyebrows, broad lips, small yellowish shells on your ears where blond tufts of hair ran a riot outside the braid's strict bonds. I know, you said, we've actually met before. Do you possibly remember a summer girl from Skåne?

Third ring:

The wave hit brutally from behind. It broke much earlier than estimated, rolled in diagonally from the stern and immediately filled Frilla to the brim. I was not at all prepared. She turned over at once. The sea was choppy and uneasy after the hard, stubborn northwester of the past few days. The currents collide outside Skär and the waves change direction so quickly that a single moment's inattention can be enough. As luck would have it I was a good bit outside the reef at Kamben and the top of the mast didn't hit bottom. In good sailer language there is, however, nothing that goes by the name of a surprising gust or an unseen breaking wave. I had only myself to blame; out of training, stupidity, recklessness.

This little boy's boat was constructed according to English plans that the practical engineer papa had brought home after a buying trip. He of course built most of it himself, so that it would be correctly and accurately done. We boys possibly got to countersink and put in screws, file away unevenness on the frame, sandpaper the planks of waterproof plywood before it was varnished for the first time. It was built on the billiard table up in the attic and, of course, eventually led to an inhuman effort lugging it down all the winding staircases before we finally got the hull out onto the grass under the apple trees. But everything was perfectly calculated and computed from the beginning, the slope of the stairs and the angle of the bends; neither on the wallpaper nor the banister could the slightest scrape be seen. The transport down to Ekeviken went via truck to Värtan and then by cargo boat to Fårösund. It's a wonder that you survived all of the boyhood years' more or less unintentional capsizings in the ice-cold waters of the summer vacation. At that time no one had heard of life jackets or wet suits. The inflated inner tube from a car tire would have to be enough. I don't really know how many times the sea god got it.

Frilla had lain for many years and looked miserable way inside Folke's barn, under layers of straw, drifts of flour dust and tattered cobwebs. The mast and boom were hanging properly with sheets and halyards under the rafters. I conveyed her down to the shore with the same happy intoxication as if I were still a fifteen-year-old instead of maturely filling the role of moderately steady and already slightly flabby twenty-seven-year-old father of a small child. Annastina and Bamse were down for the usual ritual vacation visit with us. Together with Astrid they were excavating some old house foundation at Hau. I kept myself away most of the time, a fine old bad summer habit that I reluctantly wanted to get rid of. Extremely amused, hunched up and crouching in the shelter of the stone fence and wrapped to the bursting point in bathrobes and towels they observed my sudden activity. I rigged her up and set her into the water. She leaked a little at the centerboard box, miraculously enough after all the years in the dry barn, floated high and light and you could really notice how she vibrated with joy when I hoisted up the old yellowed cotton shreds. Of course, they had mildewed a bit and shrunk in the sail bag, assuredly you could see significant creases from age along the leech rope, and under no circumstances was it possible to stretch the main to the end of the boom, but so what; it was still my own beloved Frilla who after all the years again lay where she should, past her prime but still magnificent, the swan of my heart, used to obeying the slightest motion from the helmsman's experienced hand. I looked out over the bay. It was blowing way too much, and it had certainly been a thousand years since I last boarded her with the fifteen-year-old's superior skills. Bits of ice in the wind and squalls were spreading out like black and blue fans over the bay's crisp water. Cobalt and gold where the seaweed belts on the bottom didn't darken the surface with brownish violet steaks. Rapid cloud shadows rushing between clear green patches of crystal. Let me have the little boy, I shouted ashore and Bamse waded hesitantly out with him and solidly held onto the boat so that it wouldn't overturn while I carefully lowered Hans-Jörgen into the cockpit. The yelling, however, immediately assumed such obvious proportions of child abuse that I just had to hand him back to nice uncle Björne. Papa is dumb, he cried. Bamse is nice. Yes, Bamse is nice, likes to come and visit from this year's summer excavation at the old viking harbor at Hau Grönus. That is never any trouble for him, on the contrary, he loves to allow himself to be taken possession of really thoroughly by all of us. The girls also came down to the edge of the shore, shivering and freezing to death, Annastina triumphantly sticking out her seven-month stomach. I'd be glad to take care of little Hans-Jörgen, she said, we can enjoy the sun behind the fence at Blue Thorp so you can freeze your butts off together out at Norsta. She tried to sound really cheerful and convincing and generous and friendly, just like it should be when dear old buddies and relatives are together. It would probably be nice for you to feel really free a moment; not be encumbered by me and my stomach. She didn't mean one word of what she said. Bamse at once put one of his hairy arms around Astrid's naked back. With the other he swung up a three-year-old howling with joy onto his shoulder. As soon as we have filled the bicycle baskets with grub, then we'll come out to you. If you don't listen to reason, of course, and come with us instead of going out with that. He nodded toward Frilla. What unparalleled impudence both toward her and me! I rolled up my pants as far as they would go and pulled on the worn-out greasy Icelandic sweater over my shirt. Wave to Odysseus, Astrid said without a trace of a smile, very solemn; look at what a clever papa you have.

I regretted it long before I got her outside the first sandbank and it got deep enough to get the centerboard in. I held her up against the wind and scrambled aboard under the fluttering rig. The waves were whirling around quite nastily. I put on the life jacket. It was tight, but at least gave a bit of protection against the icy wind. A sudden falling gust right outside of Håpuhällen tried at once to overturn us. I felt like an ungainly big baby in a nutshell. At the last moment I got my feet in under the slings and hung out. She straightened out and bore up. I adjusted the sheets and with some difficulty got her level on the back of a wave so that she lifted almost at once. The trails of wake were wiped out. We were flying at fifteen second-meters. Then the gust died out and I could throw myself aboard, for the wind was coming at full speed from an entirely different direction. I let go of the foresail sheet and let the main run out. We drifted away. The old knowhow was indeed still there! I turned around. Bamse was already on his way up the path between the shore meadows. He was juggling the little chap, glanced at me quickly. Presumably they were gathering a lovely bouquet of effervescent wild chervil, blue thistle and radiant hawkweeds, strongly smelling dame's violet. Pastoral idyll vs. the strategy of sulky loneliness. I went upwind and pulled down the foresail. Eolus was really not in his very best mood, mostly just sarcastic and fickle. Tailwinds from shore the whole way out toward Änden. With one sail she responds poorly when spoken to. Therefore, things went to hell too as quick as lightning when the wave took us.

A water-filled sailing dinghy of wood doesn't sink, nor does it float very well, sits up in the water surface, dives down under the waves, comes up again with tremendous speed if the wind gets hold of the rig and tosses her around on the other side. You calmly grab hold of the centerboard and raise her up, let the wind shake the water out of the wet sails and continue as if nothing had happened. A normal capsizing is no catastrophe, you should be able to right her in a couple of seconds. But Frilla was lacking floating tanks. When we were small we used to fill her as I said with well pumped-up inner tubes. The centerboard was made of a strong but light metal alloy. I had forgotten to fasten it. It dove like Poseidon's trident toward the bottom. There were no inflated tubes aboard. She filled up time after time with water, it was completely impossible to get her on the right tack. To be sure, she came up with the rickety mast between the shroud and heavy soaking wet main, but went down again at once. The foresail broke loose and floated away, a white nymph-like veil. The paddle drifted away. The loose sheets played around my legs like octopus arms, got twisted around and wanted to drag me down when she again toppled over. Time after time the whole of her came over me, but not at all in the way I wanted to have it; I wanted to have her calm under me, wanted to have calm waves, a calm heart that wasn't beating so damned unpleasantly. Strangely enough I didn't feel a bit frozen. I was lucid and cold and at the same time so hot that I was literally sweating in the water, as if the work with her was pumping wave after wave of warm life through my body, all the way out into my extremely numb limbs. I had no special desire to die. We drifted farther with the current, she and I, but not at all in toward the shore where the waves were going, but parallel to them, out beyond the outermost tongue of land. The top of the mast banged on the bottom several times but without getting stuck or breaking off. Calmly I tried to survey the situation, held on to her hull, felt lighter. It was just a question of time before I got my wings and rose like a black-backed gull toward the heaven's blue slope. Otherwise, the trip would probably end in the Baltic, with a subsequent protracted camp sojourn on Siberia's northeastern tundra. It was beginning to be time to make something good out of life. No doubt he was already screwing her with the hot passion of his heart and cock, rolling around between the dunes. Annastina, dull, honest, reliable Annastina was certainly going to be an excellent mother and wife to all of them after the mildly moving funeral ceremony was over and done with at a suitable sea cemetery. Together they would establish a completely irresponsible republic of the senses and of bliss, while I was standing among the angels and staring and you would be grinding out more and more chil-dren in the most generous of large families and the worms would get sick at the mere thought of the contents of my slimy coffin.

I remember that I never in my entire life felt so strong and happy, yes, even elated when I kicked you in the side and took off, cleaving the fire, the sound and the fury that came ever closer but mostly from behind when Berra turned off the motor and Bamse stretched down his hand, as if I was going to need help from someone to get up. I raised myself, time after time, but was still just hanging onto the railing with broken wings that Berra tried to pry loose. I fought against them, of course, wanted to fly on, but they won in the end. What beautiful blue lips you have. Have you done enough splashing to and fro do you think? Perhaps you might even want to help for a moment instead of playing water elephant. Jealously she held onto me, embraced me, finally she let me go.

You weighed a ton out there, you know, said Bamse later after emergency treatment with internal whiskey and external sauna. It was damn nasty to see; as if you really didn't want to come up at all!

Can we get the boat now, I wondered.

Fourth ring:

There is a squeak in the window lift when I wind up the side window. All glass is filled with frozen breath. Outside it is very cold. I let the motor idle a while. The fan tosses around the tiny bit of heat left in the coupe. It is over an hour since you walked into the house, a long time since the light went out upstairs. Possibly a candle has been lit; there is a weak yellow, intimate fluttering in the curtain. You should just drive the car here. As usual he got drunk at our house yesterday evening. The agony of divorce, you said. He will never get divorced. We all know that. But you are so kind. Put the car keys above the left front-tire and take the bus home. It doesn't take more than half an hour. You do it after school. I'll never ask about this. I don't want to know anything. When you come down into the illuminated gate, I'll go back to work. Now it is completely dark upstairs. It is cold. You are tarrying. I am freezing. It has been a long time. It is now. It is always.

Many, way too many, seem to think that old stories mainly consist of harmless nonsense. That is, of course, due to the fact that they don't notice how we even today are everywhere surrounded by immense cyclopses and cannibalistic Laestrygones. Still they wait for the right hero. That will take time. They have all that in the world at their disposal, can wait for millennia if needed or strike in the next second, assault the ship from high cliffs with huge boulders. Ultimately it is a question of the importance and the duty of being prepared at any given moment to step in with all your strength, to blind everything in the way of one-eyed monsters, whatever they must be called or call themselves. It always begins in the same way. The innocent adventurer or, more commonly, a scarred hero surrounded by a bunch of comrades of the same feather sees smoke at a long distance from a chimney or the reflection of a flaming fire in the cave. Naturally, only women and children and dumb animals are at home. You settle down and await the man of the house, his silently stealthy or braggingly noisy return from the field or from among the herds of cattle. Meanwhile, there are a lot of fun things to do, romp about with the women and make new children, grill young lambs, pour down beer and wine, make a mess. Yet the end is always the same. The hero escapes, usually alone, with the greater part of his life intact; possibly additional scars have come about, traces of all the boulders that rained down on him. Realism is meticulous. Exact details about harbor entrance and the best way to anchor the ship; amazingly precise instructions about how the expedition ought to be equipped to be a success. Even the roads far into the country or up the mountains are thoroughly described, how smooth they have become from all the timber that is dragged down from the high forests, or muddy from too much donkey tramping. This happens always and everywhere. No one can avoid it, not even in distant countries shrouded by clouds and fog, where the sun almost never breaks through to bring light to miserable and mortal beings.

Gus Larson once bore a respected and well-known name back in Sweden. Already when he was very young, armed with an arsenal of well-articulated arguments from old-fashioned heavies like Boström and Hägerström, he was a popular and intelligent adversary in wide circles in the Swedish public debate; especially during the beginning of the sixties. But when Lagercrantz and his promising boys began to take over, in order eventually to completely invade Dagens Nyheter with ever stricter vicar's son's moralisms and a dead straight schoolmaster know-it-all tone of voice, then there was no longer a place for him in his ungrateful fatherland, which actually can only tolerate one debate or one ideology at a time in the newspaper columns. Increasingly embittered he left us for good. In his baggage he took along a couple of pretty well-received new simplistic poetry collections together with the treatise on The Liberal Mystique that had been praised by Expressen and Svenska Dagbladet, but that had been considered totally incomprehensible by most other level-headed reviewers. Having just reached thirty he headed on to the great freedoms in the west. In peace and quiet he left to native revolutionary revisionism the task of working on with Swedish society's cementation under the guiding stars so heartily detested by him, conformism, constancy, consensus, control.

As a naive young filmmaker I actually still believed in the possibility of combining the lens' sober objectivity with the eye's humane softness. It had to be possible to bring about a sort of magic realism of the fantasy that would get all people to realize that it wasn't at all too late on the earth. It was merely a question of creating a world of people for people instead of the present one of war and more and more silent springs. We too had gotten something new to work with, a domestic television worthy of the name, and outside the barracks on A1 there was a whole world to describe with our cameras. Young intellectuals no longer needed to become incomprehensible poets or unread novel writers. You could become a filmmaker or TV producer. With our glimpses and views, our fresh insight, our unclouded pupils, we were going to get the scales to fall from everyone's eyes. Together we were going to teach all of us to see. Holy silliness, it might seem, today when we sit with the results in hand. For, probably it is that way, that only on the edge of reality, in space's very outermost crannies, can you begin to suspect and perceive the presence of change, of time. But not as a fateful threat from an ossified history, rather as the promise of movement, birth; the eternity where even death itself is embraced as something growing and good. The film strip returns, though always from another and surprising direction than what you expect; well-known and new, space of white summers, flowering winters' green bells.

With a philosophy of life of that sort you survive well and long, like a latter-day Don Quixote, without needing to attach too much importance to all the know-all and pompous ass Sancho Panzas. Life is where it is with all morbid actions and absurd pranks, that's that. Earlier meetings with the Uppsalian child prodigy professor Gustav Larsson, alias now transformed beyond recognition into an honorary professor at the University of Texas, Austin, TX, USA, have, moreover, every time reinforced my over the years ever more steadfast conviction that for man there exists no nemesis divina, only a very uncomplicated nemesis humana. Though I by no means want to claim hereby that this fate should be one bit more mild than the divine variant.

Thus, he now lives in the apparently best of worlds. The jet streams that cross the continent toward the east over green hills always carry along the world's most powerful weather systems. The cloudbursts are colossal. Texan thunderstorms make a summer storm over Västervåla seem like a puny fart. Nothing in the whole world can be a more garish scarlet red than the Mexican pepper he now chews raw with his steaks without batting an eyelash.

Nor is anything more beautiful than his latest wife, Cindy.

The magnificent house on Thirteenth street is adorned with two floor high Ionic columns. Inside the facade the tidiness is meticulous. In his earlier home absolute chaos prevailed. Here there is only room for clinical luxury, pleasure and tranquility. From earlier visits I remember the dogs, huge mastiffs on the living room's worn-out sofas; growing piles of dirty laundry waiting for new wives after the old worn-out ones; lengthy divorce proceedings; troops of his own or possibly others' children who were marching around with huge mountains of ice cream through all the rooms; long forgotten peanut butter sandwiches on top of an early and rare Kant edition; ancient Underwood typewriters with half-finished lesson plans about the household gods Baudelaire, Rilke, Kierkegaard, Nietzsche.

Kierkegaard in Texas perhaps sounds like a bad joke. As a matter of fact the university officials on the very highest level were compelled into a discreet intervention and discontinuance of overly well-visited courses which by some circles, within an otherwise unusually liberal College of Liberal Arts, were seriously seen as undermining basic Texan moral concepts. In an apparently logically inviolable and metaphysically more than satisfying way, you see, adjunct professor Gus Larson turned the already beforehand seriously compromised and morally suspicious Dane topsy turvy. Thereby, he showed batch after batch of innocent but grateful students an entirely different way of life; one that leads from narrow-minded fundamentalist piety over a Cartesian-softened ethics to a definitively hedonistic aesthetic stage in which man completely and fully can allow all the phases of existence simultaneously to be characterized by all the senses' innocent and thereby angelically pure pleasures.

Kant is still around of course. Now in a complete and annotated edition surrounded by equally complete Leibnitz and Spinoza editions in the newly built, consummately tidy work room where an intimately humming hard disk under a computer of the latest generation is possibly gossiping about current intellectual activities. The dogs have been banished to an elegantly timbered garden alongside the garage; the grass takes care of itself in that the sprinkler system which is buried in the ground automatically measures the moisture in the ground and waters only when it really needs it. With the help of competent and well-remunerated civil lawyers all earlier children have been sent back to their respective mothers or placed at appropriate colleges to take care of themselves. In the new house there is quite simply no longer room for any Chris or Benjamin or Alex or Sigri or Sandy.

Everything had been set up to receive a new little Larson.

No costs had been too high when it concerned the professor's new life. Cindy took care of everything. No longer any unnecessarily fatiguing brain work. The earnings from her fortune probably covered more than the total budgets of seven large depopulated towns in Bergslagen. Gus Larson had from the beginning learned to love all the unphilosophical and banal commonplaces of the Texan everyday. Now there was nothing to keep him from these. Now he was going to concentrate full time and devote himself to becoming father to Cindy's first child, the heir, the prince. No unnecessary teaching before the whole thing had been settled. Cindy's papa, who was in the university administration, arranged for a leave of absence without any difficulty. It was already into the second year. But it seemed as if Gus Larson was straining at the task.

This most recent tragic development in a dear old sparring partner's life I hadn't the least idea about. John W told me about it in the car. He met me at Robert Mueller Airport wearing the usual shorts, T-shirt and five-gallon hat. American Airlines was hours late, almost midnight at my arrival. While I listened, I was fighting desparately against an absolutely too early death, brought on by an acute lack of sleep after the non-stop trip Athens-New York-Dallas-Austin. Yet I knew all too well what was ahead. When we turned up the steep hill from Lamar into eleventh street the inevitable came:

"The rules of the house are the usual ones. I'll wake you at four o'clock. The guys are looking forward to running with you. You're in good shape, I hope. We'll start at five, as usual. Welcome to Texas!"

Among human virtues ever since Homer's days hospitality has been one of the finest. Wherever happy Odysseus has been during his, to put it mildly, eventful life there were always friends whose homes he could rest in on the ever longer and circuitous road home. In peace and quiet he healed scratches or larger wounds, got fed or got rid of persistent rolls of fat around the belly.

"You look hideous," said John W, "but do not despair. Just give us a couple of mornings and we're going to get you back in good old form."

Jet-lagged and groggy with sleep I thus tried to place on my legs everything that remained of a stale, drowsy body. Punctually at quarter to five Billy and Terry and John P walked into the kitchen, intimate running companions for more than fifteen years. The host on the spot was devoting himself to violent sit-ups accompanied by diverse bodily sounds, while the guest, wild-eyed, was hanging on to a piping hot, steaming, guaranteed healthy cup of decaffeinated coffee. Wisely enough, the newly arrived realized at once that the whole group was going to be pronounced guilty of aggravated and unpremeditated manslaughter if I was forced to go along on a number of miles of dawn running up the improbable slopes of the Texas hills. The professors' common sense and my pitiful condition brought me as luck would have it a day's respite. With cogent arguments even John W's sympathy for life was slowly awakened: the state of Texas' appalling prisons for example; after the most recent budget cuts, the conditions there probably still had to be regarded as considerably worse than at the state's prestigious university. He took pity at last, indistinctly muttering something about pithless vikings. Half the day I sat with heavy feelings of guilt sunk down in the hot tub in the garden, a huge wooden barrel in the shade of the pecan trees. Ferocious streams of water kneaded my body into voluptuous innocence. I tried to keep my head high and cool above the foaming, steaming surface. The squirrels on the block were chattering irritatedly around nuts still hanging. In vain I tried to collect my thoughts for the coming lecture.

The following morning though there was no pardon. There is no reason to lament about old untrained limbs or the remarkable circumstance that the hills around Austin without a doubt increase as the years pass; the slopes become more ruthless, fabulous precipices that at least in the false light of dawn only seem to go upward. Facts kick fairly. No darkness in the world can protect stupidity from its rightful punishment. I have been there before, many times. I knew what awaited. Afterwards only the performance in Waggener Hall, room 211 remained. I intended to take a dreadful and dazzling intellectual revenge.

"There is a chronic historical short-sightedness in man. No one however able an optician has succeeded in correcting this. Even our supertechnological epoch's most alert and critical observers suffer from this defect; authors, artists, musicians. Most of them turn a blind eye to this of course. The same thing is also valid for simpler figures, the fraternity I myself belong to, the riffraff from the mass media. During this short hour with simple examples from my remote and innocent homeland I wanted to show what also happens in the most protected existence, where the most disgustingly stinking dailies still for the most part shine with their absence. You have been able to ascertain with your own eyes that in practice nevertheless nothing separates us. We like to consider ourselves as knights of the order of the shiny lens. But today there is a larger aperture that no one any longer seems able to cope with, a more mighty Cyclops than the one Odysseus once simply stood up to. I fear that it exists within us, has taken a seat there without our even having noticed it; invisible filters have burned themselves into our consciousness. Self-censorship, resignation, lack of courage to stand up for our beliefs, simple normal fear; there are other suitable expressions for this. Yet, I will refuse to the very last to believe that things are this way. That would imply a total abandonment of the most beautiful of ideas, the one that you over here especially try to embrace as the fundamental one: that all people are created equal. One of these master ideas that unfortunately is forgotten all the more often in face of pressure or threats from all the faceless, impersonal forces that hide behind showy slogans like post-industrialism, information society, telecracy; I don't know what sort of dumb thing it is called that is on the verge of crowding us out farther into the desolate marshy grounds of the definitive control society. Besides, who has asked for these masses of uninteresting so-called data they constantly force on us. Who wants the myths demystified, the legends picked to pieces into tiny basic structures? There has to be an end to this dividing up of ourselves into pieces, sufficiently digital to feed ravenous little microchips that don't give a shit as to what they take in, just change life and things to electronic vomit. A reality we can never really recognize ourselves in. Nature, I say! Man, whoops! Presumably this is the very point in this subtle game with ourselves. The actual basic philosophy behind what is going on seems in any case to be that society today consists of everyone's war against everyone else, then there remains in the end your own interest as the only reliable motivation for man. What kind of man? In these here regions you used to claim earlier that the only good Indian was a dead Indian. Things have turned out the way you wanted them. My country, right or wrong! The end justifies the means! We all know what kind of ideas lie behind fascism.

It has been said that there is nothing more dangerous than a man with a single idea, even if it is the only one he has. We are all created equal. We are all created unequal. With merely two ideas we can be saved!

Odysseus succeeded in blinding his Cyclops. Okay. But he actually left many more on the beach. They have grown up. Over the years they have in no way become more beautiful to stare in the face. Take a look yourselves!"

I stopped there. The digital numbers were ticking green. I ejected the last cassette and gathered up the notes, looked furtively out over the auditorium. The audience consisted of two classes of commandeered communications students together with some polite teachers and students from the little valiant Scandinavian department. Everyone looked quite bewildered. That last deviation from the subject wasn't in the manuscript. I have no idea as to where it came from or why. Obviously, they expected something more that could sound like a conclusion to my miserably prepared lecture on Myth and Media: Recent Developments in Swedish Television. After a painful eternity of silence there was finally a scraping of uncertain chair legs. I quickly distributed a pile of brochures that the information service in New York had sent down and handed over the two cassettes, a magnificent donation from Swedish Television AB to the University of Texas' School of Communication. The still obviously confused assistant professor of European Studies answered cleverly by inviting me to lunch at the faculty club. A gumbo pot of the very best southern state brand was offered. It consisted of a spicy, thick dark brown mixture of the sort in which the pioneers from the borderland used to stuff down everything that could be chewed at all; old beaver tails, lean raccoon thighs, rattlesnake pieces. With this, steamed rice was served, warm muffins together with thick browned pieces of ham, well-smoked and heavily salted; as well as black-eyed peas and a sweet-sour preserve as an exotically tasty offset. The meal was washed down with a bottle of ice-cold Texas Sauvignon Rouge, vintage '85, from the university's own vineyard Llano Estacado. Euphorically stuffed, I trudged out into the mild spring afternoon. The enormous university area was filled to the breaking point with resting students who were going from one course or classroom to another. The redbud trees were blooming and cocky black birds were blustering in the tallest oaks. Damp wind from the south carried with it the promise of still unvisited virgin islands in the Caribbean. I already saw the scoop in front of me, the classical moment, immortalized by my camera: Odysseus throws out a coarse fist to press the other one's just as weather-scarred fist and mumbles into the microphone: Robinson Crusoe, I presume.

That life which is beyond the reach of the absent traveler but presumably going on as usual, but which moves in other directions, for example in distant native countries on the other side of the globe, has a remarkable ability of showing up on the least expected occasion and making itself felt with all force. A telephone conversation from a wife who cheerfully reports that she for the zillionth time has withdrawn her dissertation, but that otherwise everything is fine, the summer congress under control and everyone is fine and says hello. What do you mean everyone? A normal professor from UCLA calls up and reports that a mountain of pamphlets about Swedish cultural life have arrived from the Swedish information service, as well as several video cassettes from Sweden. Besides, a lady stopped in and wanted to know whether a Mr. Kineman was really on his way to Los Angeles and when in that case he was expected to arrive. A lady? A letter arrives from an employer who keeps track of his own extremely carefully, even when scattered abroad. It contains a pithily short questionnaire where you have to put an X in one of three squares: 1) I plan to quit the company; 2) I have already quit the company; 3) I do not intend to quit my tenured position at the company. In the event that you against all sound judgment persist in choosing alternative three there is the possibility of underlining one of two alternatives: A) Resignation with six months' reduced salary, including vacation; B) Labor court. The latter alternative would mean immediate release from service on the grounds of refusal to work, alternatively lengthy difficulties in cooperating with the bosses. While waiting for a juridical test, salary is payable for the time being with the C-deduction, i.e. no salary at all.

Since we have lived with this sort of personnel treatment the past ten years I did as we usually do, filled in all conceivable crosses and underlined in good measure where it was prescribed. Possibly this reminder from the personnel department seemed somewhat more brutal in tone than in earlier years. As the loyal civil servant, faithful to the company, that I had always been, I mailed the reply at once, with the usual greeting to the vice-president Sam Nilsson and his personnel director, dear Mrs. B. Bödelin, now clearly the only ones with permanent positions and super fat salaries who after years of analysis and economic catastrophes were going to continue to work with a much more restricted Swedish television.

Why did it concern me? I had valid and open plane tickets, was the lucky owner of an American Express card good for three years into the future, drawn on the company but in my name, ditto a Hertz card for rental cars, I lived cheaply on the expense allowance and old friends, camera and other equipment were functioning excellently; in short, I didn't feel especially threatened. In Texas there remained only the obligatory meeting with my old friend Gus, to see what had become of him at this new stage on life's path. Thereafter a quick jet stride via Miami down to the Virgin Islands' white beaches, rustling palm leaves and the tourist brochures' sparkling emerald sea.

The now aged and thoroughly worn-out tennis club at the intersection of North Lamar and Twenty-fourth Street has over the years been witness to many odd rallies. That Swedish tennis reached world fame with Björn Borg did not come as any great surprise to the local Austin pros. They had already understood that sooner or later something really big had to happen with the sport in Sweden. In the middle of the sixties, you see, Gus Larson appeared daily down at the courts. With scientific preciosity he polished his serve against nylon nets designed especially for that purpose, that effectively caught the balls and conveniently rolled them back to the frenetic, indefatigable hard hitting professor. Sometimes doubles matches were arranged with partners who were just as flabbergasted every time. Gus Larson's game, you see, lived entirely on a single stroke, this remarkable and awkwardly produced serve; that is to say the few times it actually didn't go out. Then, in return it was guaranteed to be unplayable. Together with some capable partners, who alone had to make all the other shots that occurred in a doubles match, this meant a number of initially surprising successes in certain smaller university tournaments. Together with the all too well attended Kierkegaard lectures this quickly gave him a name within the College of Liberal Arts. In the end though his totally exhausted partners couldn't handle this strength-wasting game. He wore out one after the other.

Because of a constitutional defect in coordination with the server, in the actual attachment between the right arm's rounded musculature and the otherwise lean, leathery well-trained upper body, the ball, you see, took a totally unexpected path every time, that is to say most of them, when he didn't get them in. To get in the way of this extension of his considerable brute force could mean mortal danger. Since both a number of opponents and completely innocent spectators urgently had to be conveyed by ambulance to Brackenridge hospital for treatment of all conceivable injuries, from smaller superficial contusions to serious internal bleeding, it was absolutely impossible for him to find new, willing doubles pairs as opponents. Of course, there could never be a question of singles, since his repertory only consisted of this one, in a double sense, deadly shot. One bitter day in the middle of the seventies he hit his last serve. A bright spring sky reflected in all the little blooming bluebonnets on the ground. Birds of prey and Mexican swallows were headed north in unchecked processions. An old raccoon wandered circumspectly along Shoal Creek. All of nature seemed to draw a breath. The ball is supposed to have gone like a spear right through the somewhat rusty protective net around court 3, with still undiminished speed, physical laws notwithstanding, passed the increasing afternoon traffic on North Lamar finally breaking the picture window in a house more than two hundred yards away, on the other side of the park.

It surprised me thus that he had arranged a meeting precisely at Caswell Tennis Center, his old club. I became even more surprised when I caught sight of him busy being playfully outplayed by a slim young woman in a cherry-colored warm-up. He was playing with his back to me. I stopped in the bar and ordered a beer, watched the two players furtively. The well-trained arms and bent sinewy legs from before had over the years changed into something that mostly resembled spindly limbs, temporarily fastened to the still magnificently proportioned torso with loosely attached trunk. The beautiful head, however, was the same; now grayish white curly locks topped his high, masculine lumpy forehead in a Roman caesar-like fashion.

His partner moved over the court like a ballet dancer. Long, straight hair fluttered like a curtain over her face when she lithely bent down and clear as a bell returned a backhand. It had a violent topspin, dropped down precisely on the other side of the net and died on the spot. It looked amazingly simple. Gus made an equally pathetic as well as lame attempt to reach it.

"You're not overworking yourself, darling?"

I tossed down the last golden yellow gulp of Pabst and stepped out of my hideout.

"Hello there," I shouted, "it's been a while."

"Well look, there you are, silly old man: so nice that you could come."

The bear hug was the same hearty one as before. The woman looked at me curiously, possibly suspiciously. With a twitch she threw back her nut-brown hair from her face, brushed it away from the temples. There was something of the Jane Fonda penchant toward thinness about her appearance, the pronounced lines around her mouth perhaps reminiscent, the intensively searching glance that I in vain tried both to meet and dodge away from in Gus' iron grip; there was obviously still a good deal of dangerous strength left in that body. A quick smile passed by. There absolutely was something I recognized in her!

He let go of me.

"May I introduce my new wife to you. What do you think?"

I fumbled out some appropriate phrases.

"I'm going to take the opportunity and leave you gentlemen to yourselves a moment. You must have a lot to talk about. Just don't tire yourself out too much, darling. You know what is waiting."

Her lips brushed his fluffy unshaven cheek. With an icy, jingling smile she nodded at me, handed over the racket and balls.

"You can certainly see from my clothing that I had no idea that we were going to play tennis. Besides, I thought that you had packed it in long ago."

He looked at me, as if he was in doubt or was sorry for something that had already been irrevocably started.

"That isn't at all why I wanted to meet you," he said and was suddenly silent.

Only now did I see. Gus Larson's face was quite gray under his now eternal Texas suntan. The glance, once exuberant with intelligence, vitality and brilliance, resembled a dried-up bog; the eyes were like closed mines where the elevator shafts had long since stopped screeching and roaring.

The guy was simply scared to death!

"You understand, my present father-in-law is enormously wealthy. I had no idea about it when I first met Cindy; that sort of huge fortune is seldom seen on the outside. For me she was, to begin with, a very normal sweet coed, attractive, that cannot be denied, one of many who seek out my classes in huge numbers. Terribly intelligent, of course, otherwise I would never have taken the trouble of noticing her before it was time to give the mid-term grade. As usual my old family life piled up sky high over my poor head. I was actually on the verge of drowning in a kitchen midden of old women worn out too early, older and more expensive children, insatiably ravenous dogs. In my whole body it felt like it had been a long time since I had stood on that top of life's path where the water runs up, the rivers divide themselves and run out over the world with my gifted ideas. In pure desperation I was simply on the way to exploiting my miserable old Swedish citizenship by running home like a coward to Västmanland and there letting the social welfare authorities freely take control of what was left of my wretched life. Laugh if you want, you dirty bastard; it wasn't a bit funny, I guarantee you that.

This young lady had obviously carefully found out everything about my personal circumstances beforehand. Nevertheless, she proposed after one of my lectures. When I as indulgently as possible explained to this silly woman how impossible everything was she just dug into her backpack and handed over a paper for me to sign; power of attorney for a well-known law firm here in the city, specialists in divorces and other family law disputes. They took on the matter of straightening out all tangled personal and economic affairs together with the irregularities connected to it. Cindy was going to take care of all the costs. What could I do? I found myself in a hopeless situation. A gorgeous girl offers a new life, to take care of an old age that more repulsively every morning was staring me in the face in the bathroom mirror. Old buddy, imagine a wreak mumbling around with its brain stunted by the Alzheimer quarry, on life's very last long downhill slope. What would you have done?

She's gorgeous, isn't she. Looks rather innocently all-American, still unspoiled skin, supple over her whole body. I saw how pleased you were when you lapped up her appearance, the way she moves, like the spring wind against the current over the waves of the brook, the young puma between the boulders. You know, there are still hours when I constantly dream about being able to shape reality precisely as before as poetry instead of misrepresenting it as philosophy, although everything of course is appearance and phenomenon and unfortunately nothing else. As a matter of fact she is a spiteful rattlesnake child. Behind the seductive sweetness of her tongue the substance consists only of paralysis, degradation, final death. Yet, I love that creature rashly! Can you understand? But she still keeps me at a distance, never allows me to get close. Strength, she says, You're supposed to be full to the bursting point when the moment comes! I'm incessantly spilling over. The whole thing is extraordinarily disgusting.

I'm telling you this solely because you are a faithful old friend, decent enough to say hello when you pass by here; in spite of the fact that we, thank God, don't have very much in common, or perhaps just for that reason. But we live in the same danger zones, you and I, never forget that. We are people, not gods, whatever we think. My woman is a muse from the abyss. I wouldn't even wish my worst enemy to fall into the hands of something like that. She has made me completely dry. I haven't thought a single independent thought since I landed in her net. Can you imagine a worse fate for a liberal philosopher!

Still I could be wrong, blinded by something that exists only in my miscarried imagination. Perhaps everything is quite in order, she is a young and innocent girl who loathes the mere smell of tired old men? Or the daughter who is using me as a tool for a loathsome revenge against her own father? As you can understand he and I are the same age. Otherwise everything sets us apart. He is one of these unknown Texas billionaires who never makes a fuss about himself outwardly, who makes dear Reagan's buddies over in Orange County seem like recently graduated, diapered brokers at the provincial stock market in Stockholm. His economic empire he inherited from his father and grandfather and he has only needed to build onto it as growth hurried on. How? The whole thing is a stroke of genius. By producing all of the nation's work clothing under thousands of different labels and brand names, carefully adapted to everything from high technology to low service. The factories spit out everything you can conceivably need between eight and five or during nightly uncomfortable work periods; the uniforms of sleep, the filmy delicacies of love. White coats, blue overalls, MacDonald's aprons, space suits, superconductor masks, the leisure hours' millions of jogging suits. Export over the entire world, including the third, virgin one, with its markets that have hardly been penetrated yet. This line of business is completely idiot-proof. The shares can only go in one direction, upward. The profits are invested exclusively in power. Soon the whole globe will be clad in his damned garments, without anyone noticing it. You understand that I shudder! There is something so terribly Swedish about this, so disgustingly and uniformly conformist. Everything I have sought to escape my entire life. That old man, my father-in-law! What satanic irony, that I of all people should be struck by this. But now it has to come to an end. Even I see that. You have to help me! I think there is one way out of this ...

John W has blabbed about what nonsense you're up to, this fantastically stupid film about Odysseus, Robinson and the noble Geronimo. What I can offer ought to fit you like a glove. You will get all the pictures you need, more than enough, way too many; your editing table will be spilling over. And it doesn't have to cost your one-eyed employers a red cent; you can invest all your expense allowance and hotel money on women and bourbon. From what I know you have never let yourself be corrupted by the powerful. Why should it happen now? You are a highly normal honorable Swedish civil servant, have a sufficiently developed sense for the objective and impartial, with a self-selected, extraordinarily stupid assignment on the edge of reality. If you don't look out, the myth and gods can take over completely. But why should something so bad happen to a good white man? What do you say about the following suggestion? Rearrange your filming schedule. Begin by looking right away at your dumb Apaches over in Arizona. Then fly to Saint Thomas. I'll meet you at the airport. My father-in-law has a sixty-foot sailboat lying there. During my forced leave of absence I lead a clandestine study circle on the aesthetics of revolution for him and an exclusive bunch of his closest friends. Down there among the sugar islands under the wind we are going to have a final seminar in just a week. That will lead to stage two in this ambitious project: the human ethics of imperative performance. Their good God they protect themselves; every Sunday an amen in the church and an honest handshake of the congregation's minister. Religion as power will be a later question. I assume you want to be included in the crew. Cindy has already spoken with her father. He is tickled to death about getting a prominent European intellectual as a working guest aboard. I ask you, I appeal to you; come along! There probably still has to be something left of the curious journalist in your old paws?

What do you say?"

With a certain relief I left the slapstick days in Texas behind me. It couldn't get much worse. To get to do some serious work again felt like a liberation. Well-armed with loaded cassettes and battery belt I landed in Tucson. I had a week to look for Cochise, Geronimo or Mangas Colorados. I got a nice rental car price on a Buick and immediately headed toward the blue violet Gila Mountains, past the old air base outside the city. Generation after generation of the strangest and most ancient types of planes have been arranged and left behind a little bit everywhere after a last flight, bordering runways, destroyed by cactuses and that dry, treacherously sharp desert grass you can cut your fingers on, if you aren't careful. Mile upon mile of gaping sheet metal bodies with rusty propellers and wing flaps fluttering in the desert wind on half worn-out steering cables; hundreds of chocked-up jet motors; helicopters like grotesque birds, picked apart and gutted of everything inside; empty hangars behind the barbed wire fences' warning signs that guarantee a quick and certain death in the event of trespassing; high, desolate watch towers on legs of crumbling reinforced concrete.

The only thing visibly alive were the birds of prey, a fantastic accumulation of them; heavy, ungainly jumping on the ground, supreme wing gliders as soon as they are up and have gotten sufficient lifting capacity under their broad wings. Eagles have always been here. Even when the bluecoats of the army just one hundred short years ago were carrying out the last brutal and successful pacification campaigns. Every time I come here it is with the same respect that I leave the highway and drive my present day horses into the small roads; dead straight over the desert toward mountains, that at first seem shrunk but then suddenly and surprisingly attack from straight above with red cliffs and menacing ravines; dangerously winding up and down Galiuro, Gila, White Mountain; dusty and indescribably uneven in the valleys where the shock absorbers continually hit bottom. The roads of civilization. Black River, Aravaipa Creek, Bowie, Fort Grant. The actual adventure is there for good, carved into the badly maintained sign posts at places where not too long ago they definitely reduced nature and freedom to second rank phenomena in the name of democracy, peace and holy development, amen.

The man in the tall star-adorned hat kills the Indian princess. The one freedom will be the death of the other. One set of values replaces another. While I was still in Texas, and was getting ready for the job by filming stills I had ferreted out of the fabulously well-filled hiding places of the Harry Ransom Center, it occurred to me how well this process could be illustrated by a simple sequence of pictures. Ever since the first whites began to represent the new continent in pictures, America – Hope, Freedom – has always been personified as an Indian woman. First she is a fertile and voluminous queen from the Caribbean, later a slender and virtuous daughter of Britannia. In her third stage, after independence, the gracefully natural Indian princess undergoes a slow transformation into something that most of all resembles a veiled statue of a goddess of unmistakably Greek origin before she suddenly and abruptly undergoes a brutal change of sex and changes her name: the Indian goddess America becomes Uncle Sam! Of the princess there remains today only a weak reflection, so weak that Indian candidates seldom get very far in the great competitions; a guaranteed white Miss Texas year after year wins the title of Miss USA.

For that's the way it is, the unknown and unfamiliar, different and divergent, must be fought with all force. To successfully carry out this struggle History has been created. The story, the only current one or all the stories, is on the other hand something quite different; images and myths preferably placed deep in on the forbidden shelves, if they hadn't already been evicted from the archives once and for all. For the powers that be the big problem, though, is that these stories are like clear water running down the mountain, like the winds and clouds of the air; you yourself are one! Banal, mundane, trivial, vulgar. To get some order in the world, fix family relations, flatten the powers and stride over diverse thresholds: more complicated than that it doesn't need to be. Mix, give, receive!

I got her name through the Anthropology Department in Austin. Talented girl, they said. Absolutely incomprehensible why she wanted to bury herself in the school out there in the desert. But it is clear, her professor elucidated: she is a woman of two worlds, half coyote ...

No wonder then, that it was with a certain expectation that I braked in my fast Skylark Cordillera on the clayey school yard on the edge of Fort Apache. Magpies were shivering on the telephone lines. In contrast to their completely black, jabbering Texas cousins these almost looked Scandinavianly well-known with their white specula. The air felt at the same time frozen and mild, quite light in the nostrils. Several of the parked cars still had skis and poles on the roof racks. There was still plenty of snow in the sparse pine forest under the steep slopes. Higher up, the peaks became black and blue when the clouds passed over; otherwise glittering, as if hanging by invisible threads from the blindingly white, infamously broiling sun.

The sign on the door said Principal. A thin, fairly tall girl with character-istically round metal glasses opened the door. Short clipped, intensively lustrous black hair.

"Hi. Is there anything I can help you with?"

For some unfathomable reason I had expected a significantly more substantial bit of Indian woman, of entirely different dimensions than this slender creature. She smiled friendly, hesitated with her hand on the door handle. Presumably she was waiting for me to get something sensible out. I stared past her, into the room, as if I was looking for someone totally different. It was the usual impersonal office interior; a rather messy desk, gray metal file cabinets, a round table in the same federal official style, piles of books and copies; there was also room for a little computer. What had I expected? Buffalo hides on the walls, quivers full of arrows, tomahawks, boxes of powder and newly cast bullets?

The window on the other side of the room let in a miles-wide view down over the valley and the desert beyond. Somewhere was the invisible border, the white of the snow merged with the yellow red of the sand and gravel; the remarkable mountain formations I had just driven past, where the mild gray green of the cactuses left room for the pines' powerful violet trunks with branches up high and long dark blue needles.

She noticed my hesitation.

"Are you possibly that Swede who was going to come here and interview dead Indians?"

I nodded in the affirmative.

"First, I ought to meet the principal at the school here ..."

She interrupted before I finished what I had to say, pointed at the envelope I had with me from her old colleague over in the cattle-driving west.

"For me, I assume. She is, you see, me!"

I handed it over.

"I have an idea," she continued. "To be honest, I actually don't have any time at all for you now. But I can recommend a little motel down there."

She signaled with her hand at some unspecified point behind my back.

It's not the idea that you are to try to look for big signs with plumes or Geronimo in blazing neon. Ask in the store and they'll show you. I'll come by this afternoon when I'm done here. Okay?"

Quick, effective. Her eyes so dark that the pupils imperceptibly merged with the iris. Still the same friendly, but alas so ironical smile directed at the half-paralyzed white man.

"Okay! See you later. Bye."

The door closed again, right in my face, with a slight bang.

I drove down toward the so-called settlement's so-called center. Mostly gray shacks with corrugated metal roofs; otherwise wood and half-finished concrete houses in an unhappy mixture.

I should have been prepared for everything. I found myself in the most genuine Indian country. No wonder that I felt a bit jittery. What else could I have expected than brutal treatment. Two cultures meeting. Ambush and assault are somehow quite common in the area. Yet, I was completely defenseless, was totally surprised when the attack came on the downhill. It came from an entirely unforeseen direction, from within, from deep within, from home! The sight of the Indian school marm, with slender hips, blue jeans with fly, the checked shirt rolled up to the elbows – it was you! You are standing in the kitchen and picking up after the meal. Hans-Jörgen is hanging in the window looking at the trams that brake and squeak out of and into the car barns, instead of concentrating on the Second Reader that lies open on the kitchen table's blue and white checked wax cloth. I got the fellowship, you say, the school has promised me half time for the fall. Nice, huh? Can't I at least get a hug, congratulations! No, just sulk, as usual. You don't want to be the least bit proud of your gifted wife, a little happy. And then I get a wet kiss, a real dishwater kiss, right on the mouth and feel how happy you are when you hug me hard, hard, but I myself am stiff as a pin; no, worse, as a hollow, empty branch so brittle that it would break in two if you held onto it a single ounce harder. Graduate fellow, you!

Who can explain what is happening? Who can afterwards distinguish between what happened and what really happened?

During the February holiday we were as usual up in Vemdalen with Björn and Annastina and the kiddies. We relieved each other in various formations so that at least part of the time you could feel really free in the mountains. Their daughters were still in the pulka age. So every day some of us got to sacrifice ourselves and play draft horse and juice comforter and apple pealer and frostbitten finger rubber and God knows what. The avant garde liberated during the winter was playing around on the peaks while the presumably toughest wagon train ever beheld in the Härjedal mountains swarmed on into the long valleys. It was even possible to drag along the sulky, so-called darlings. The real test of manly self-control and verbal restraint was provided to me by Hans-Jörgen's so-called skiing skill, day after day, trip after trip, hill after hill, level ground after level ground. He already considered himself at a very tender age to be a born downhill racer, and later times have certainly proven him correct on that point; though I saw in front of me rather a worthy successor to Sixten Jernberg or the new young find Wassberg. Above all, for economic reasons, that is willingly to be admitted. In an unpleasant vision of the future I already saw myself ruined by a series of incessantly out-grown top-of-the-line skis and bindings, sharp outfits and lift cards at usurious prices; trips to Åre and the Alps. These early-developed opposite opinions between father and son led to constant and dramatic conflicts that echoed between the mountains; broken skis after very unnecessary excursions on the side of marked trails or suitable little hills; badly twisted feet and sprained ankles that on closer inspection, however, never wanted to swell up the way Hemmet's ski instruction book so excellently describes in gruesome pictures.

It happened to be Annastina's and my slave shift. To be exposed to her over the years ever more detailed rubbish about absolutely nothing can drive even the most petrified Härjedal troll to erosion's brink of madness. By mobilizing my stoically constitutional forbearance in face of most of life's disgusting things I seemed to survive this exceptionally whining and messy day too. The rosy little sourpusses sulked in the pulka and Hans-Jörgen loitered to the maximum in the tracks since he had broken his legs on several occasions. The climax occurred after a rest for hot chocolate and oranges. In an almost unique way he succeeded in falling clumsily down. In the middle of level ground, on top of his poles, so miraculously that both of them broke! I'll never forget his happy astonishment over the exploit. Papa, he said at the same time as he pulled toward himself one of mine, Gustav Vasa did just fine with only one pole, I will probably survive too. I calmly and cruelly pointed out that it was a question of freedom fighters being chased by King Christian's sheriffs and soldiers or by honorable men from Dalecarlia, an entirely different matter to have to deal with a fucking pissed-off father who had had more than enough of his son's gangster-like manners. My dear boys, don't quarrel now, came a squeak out of Annastina's pink anorak, you're scaring the girls. Just look, their eyes are already quite full of frozen little tears. Poor, poor little dears. Of course, we had to stop for a great consoling scene before the skis clattered on homeward accompanied by howling head winds, prickly flakes of frost and never-ending chatter.

The people who were free for the day caught up with us after three hours of happiness on the sunshine peaks and sparkling downhill runs. Generously, Björn offered to take over for me. Since the day was totally shot and it wasn't especially far home, I let them go on ahead to start a fire in the sauna and begin to get the food ready. They went on quickly; the one sunburned and freckled and fine-looking, with her hair stuffed into the Russian cap; the other with white hoar-frost streaks between the fashionable sidepieces of his reflective glasses, his ears and the ridiculous newly-grown sideburns.

"What a day!" Annastina burst out ambiguously when we tramped into the living room soaking wet, delayed at least an hour by a sudden thaw and hurricanes. The fire was already burning down.

"Is the sauna hot?"

"We'll have to light it again. We have actually been concentrating on waiting for you."

You poured out hot spiced wine into the stone mugs and handed it over.

"Bamse and I have just had it great; haven't we? He has absolutely convinced me now. No one thought he would have any success with that, huh? Skoal, slowpokes!"

He had on a brown and white, broad-striped robe with a drawstring tied in a samurai-like way around his muscular waist. He gave his wife a quick bear hug and she snuggled happily in his armpits and giggled and said that now we had to hurry into the sauna so that we didn't all get a chill; off with the clothing, kids! And you sat there huddled up in the corner of the sofa in their 18th century home moved here from the city and overloaded with gadgets to the point of plague. Your hair was loose over your shoulders, tiny little drops of sweat over your upper lip, boldly fresh and happy. At a long distance your unmistakable odors could be perceived. Under that idiotic tunic you had absolutely nothing on. But you closed your eyes.

"Relax. We're going to have a nice calm evening together. Bamse and I have already managed to prepare a bunch of goodies in the kitchen."

As usual, when appropriate, you visualized the dream about the innocent one; wide open, as if nothing bad in the whole world could happen to you. It wasn't especially difficult to imagine the warmth in your pussy, the warm juices still in circulation; the blood still pulsing long afterwards.

There was a knock on the door. I jumped up from the bed. Out there in the night stood a thin little girl. Black as coal, short glossy hair, round metal-rimmed glasses. She almost disappeared into the huge padded jacket.

"Can I help with anything?"

Laughed and stuffed the glasses down into one of the pockets.

"Now I don't need them anymore today; besides I feel too much like a principal in them."

Handed me a strong hand.

"So I am Na-Si-Ka. And who are you?"

Now I know that I am on the way home, a few weeks, delayed one eternity or another; does it really matter? For there is again a breathing in me, around me. This early in the morning the heat is turned up. Even on apparently windless days the air masses are always moving. It must have something to do with pressure changes between the crystalline cliffs right outside here and the eroded areas down in the lowland. It could also depend on my imagination that the wind harp is humming, on the wind draft after a released memory or puffs from my soul. Recently a bird thumped hard against the porch ceiling. It fell down in front of my feet, right through the harp's musical mechanism. It isn't big, about like a thrush; perhaps a little smaller, its body actually reminds me a little of the tree creeper at home. It is still breathing. The shock emptied its intestines onto the wooden floor. When I move my fingernail forward, it lifts its head, puts it a little aslant and looks at me. Coal-black eyes. The bill quite crushed. And I see how it stops breathing, collapses. It is gray, in all nuances of gray, except for the head that breaks into brown and the tail. At the very tip shines a quarter inch wide border of sun gold. I cup my hand over it and give it the name Gray Sun. When I come back with the shovel to bury it, it is gone. But I can't see any of the cats. The defecation is already dry, a shriveled contracting streak in the sun. Wonders happen?

Toward the end grandfather became more talkative and livelier than ever. You should remember to tell this sometime to your fathers when they get really old, for they don't have any idea about this, he said to us kids. We sat at his feet in the prickly limestone gravel on the ground under the oaks. He screwed up his kind hippopotamus eyes under the yellowed tropical helmet. Tomorrow we shall work on my time as a ship owner, talk about my huge fortune; you see, I amassed it with the help of two tramp steamers that plied the trade to the old Danish West Indian islands. But just melted away in the twenties' Berlin when the talkie came. You don't believe me, I can see it on you! he laughed and then everything ended in an ominous cough with a bunch of phlegm out of the corner of his mouth while we helped him in. Tomorrow, he said, tomorrow you're going to get to hear a real adventure. The real adventure! And by then he had already taken us along on the most fantastic pirate stories from the heydays of the silent film, from Copenhagen to Berlin to Gotland to Hollywood and to us in the shade under the trees in the yard. The most remarkable thing of, course, was, that in spite of everything having been pure and simple lies that it still seemed very credible. I have tried to verify this. One result of all this checking is that I am now sitting here on the edge between mountains and desert in Arizona, on the way home again with a continuation of his stories that is just as probable and worthy of being taken in earnest and told to wide-eyed staring grand-children some time in another century.

The memorial hour was held in the summer church on the former Danish island in the middle of the Baltic. Then the casket was sent home to the family in Denmark, the unknown, remote.

The end of the summer is always just as hopelessly sad. This one had broken all records. I went around mostly by myself and licked my wounds. There were unusually many, both outside and in. I barely got the little house in the tree fixed. The day before the Skåne relatives headed south I was lying alone as usual on my back up there and getting an eyeful with my binoculars of the whirl of buzzards that always hang out in August high above Ulla Hau under the clouds that are cut off straight by the wind. Fully occupied by this I didn't notice anything unusual before the shadow fell over the lenses.

"We have had many long wars this summer," you say and I think I understand what you mean. There are tears at once dangerously far out in the ducts. You have on the same canary yellow, now somewhat baggy swimsuit that I saw you in on the very first day of summer. Now it is quite soiled from paint that hadn't gone away even with a good deal of turpentine; spots from my box of oil paints that only you actually used. Besides, I've hardly blown a sound on the recorder either, sailed far too little this damned summer. Yet I try to form my features into a brave, rough manly smile. It's really tight around my mouth:

"Some still survive, as is obvious."

"Can't you ever really be serious," you continue and I wonder what it would be good for actually, in a world mainly filled with catastrophes and tragedies. It must be better to keep the disguise and laugh at misery. Then you begin to loosen up the cords around your neck, those that hold up the swimsuit so that it is where it ought to be. In very slow motion it tumbled down to your waist. Now it could be easily seen that you too must have cheated, for you are an even brown almost everywhere.

Without any shame you take my hand and put it against the breast the heart is said to dwell under.

"I still think that you have been a nice summer," you say, "no, don't take your hand away, keep it there! Feel how I beat."

Then you put your other hand against my naked, still catastrophically hairless chest. You place it right in the middle above the breastbone.

"You're alive too, did you know that?"

Then I put my free hand over hers and feel through it that she is actually right. Nothing happens to me. Everything happens. It is a miracle that happens. The summer is over. There is no war any more; just two little silent children up in the tree.

A lonely place. The spirits still prevail. White. Black. Sacred. Red. They came with four colors of sand. They smoothed out the ground carefully so that they could work. Eagle feathers made it soft. They carried pollen from the tree and four kinds of earth: black, blue, yellow and then the one that glitters. It was still dark.

They built four mounds of earth and sand and seeds. They fetched water in a black clay pot that they also filled with fish. All of this happened outside of time. They watered the mounds so that they grew into a very huge mountain. Aspens lined the stream that ran down it. The bushes and trees bore fruit and berries. Finally, they chanted the mountain four times larger. Thereafter it wouldn't grow any more. The very first ones climbed up as high as they could. But it was still a ways up to the sky. The other earth could be seen through the hole. They got four colors of rays from the sun and fastened them like rope to the mountaintop. Black, blue, yellow and glittering at the four corners of the opening. From the sun rope was built the ladder on which the first human climbed up into the light, hand by hand, and saw that the sky was father but the earth mother; fruits and rain. The cliffs are the legs, the wind the breath. Dig in the sand, fill your hands with water and you will understand.

In time other mountains came into existence; the valleys were filled with water, islands and sailing ships. The thought of power is the idea of the most recent days. It comes from knowers of cities, quarters where knowledgeable helmsmen meet and share experiences. At a distance these cities resemble pimples on the mountain, between fruit trees and blooming fields. Close in, the blackened wind can be seen drifting through the ruins; fallen columns, tombstones. You can be certain that your own name is there too.

Na-Si-Ka, I listened carefully and promised myself to remember what I heard. But there are always lacunae, holes in the narrative, details left for others to fill in. I strongly doubt that the picture will ever be finished. There are many indistinct areas on the edge of the canvas, not to speak of the tentative brush strokes in the actual focal point, where fiction passes over into its own reality. Certainly, I remember, and to be sure many with me: the helmsmen, the sail setters, the old men with open leather vests and wide-brimmed hats who concealed their faces from us where they sat hunched up at their sandals and listened.

The task has always been the same. To return home at any price and bring the narrative further, either affirm what everyone already thinks they know or surprise them with odd variations which because of general irresponsibility – faulty reporting, simple misjudgments as to whether the significance of what happened has anything whatsoever to do with history – often don't at all get into the general knowledge.

The troop assembled under the cliffs, not at all far from the shacks at Cinega Ranch, where the Greyhound bus stops today. The injuries had healed, but every time I sat up I felt a tightening in the muscle attachments above the knee and a brief stab of pain where the ribs had been broken. Actually, I don't know why I went along; I have never harbored any enmity toward Cochise, rather a desire to just once meet him eye to eye, find out what drove him to these more and more brutal deeds that are ascribed to him. Everything just to get to retain parts of this god-forsaken fantastically beautiful landscape.

Pete Kitchen who showed us the best way over the mountains between Sonorita and the Santa Cruz valley decided to return home. But Cushing was just as immovable in his purpose. There was too much honor to gain. Such a victory and promotion to captain would come instantaneously. Just a few hours after Pete left me there as the only civilian, we discovered smoke from a grass fire in the valley and we, of course, immediately came to the conclusion that the Indians were signaling to their companions up among the mountains. Now I know better. It was Pete who wanted to warn us. He himself told that to me, how he saw at least thirty of them in our tracks. But they were in no hurry with us. In the twilight we swung around the offshoots of the Santa Cruz mountains farthest to the southwest and spent the night in the barracks there. The Mexican commandant informed us that an unidentified group of Indians was staying in the Guachua mountains, but couldn't give any information whatsoever about their number or from where they came.

Now the march to the north began. Two days later, in a canyon on the mountain's east side I discovered fresh moccasin tracks that clearly indicated the savages' presence. I reported to the lieutenant who in spite of wise objections from sergeant Mott and displeased grumbling among the privates immediately ordered us to mount after the inspection of my discovery. We rode on through the broken and rocky landscape. Everywhere there should have been grass growing the ground was burned. Black ashes, sour smoke lingered under the cliffs.

After yet a tense overnight at Alisos, out of whose dry furrows we succeeded in digging up a bit of water for the animals, we continued at dawn toward the northwest, in the first place to pitch camp at old Camp Wallen. But there the grass was still burning in a landscape blackened by ashes, and the only possibility for us was to continue toward Bear Springs in the Whetstone Mountains. A few miles farther on I found the next track, a clear imprint of a woman leading a pony, also on the way to the springs. The lieutenant gave me orders to follow the track together with sergeant Mott, as well as three privates. He himself took the rest of the troop the direct way toward the resting place.

About twelve hundred yards farther on, the track turned off into a canyon, or rather a steep creek ravine, and there we caught sight of the woman. She was walking in the sand and was very careful to make clear imprints of every footstep, so careful that she even avoided stones and rocky slabs for the sake of clarity. We understood at once that she was out to lead us into a trap, and we therefore got out of the ravine as quickly as possible, carefully leading the horses past the grazing grounds of telltale gravel. Hardly had we come up on the heights before my suspicions turned out to be correct. In the canyon that ran parallel with the one we were following – a few hundred yards farther on they ran into each other – there was quite correctly a group of fourteen Indians, ready to take care of us and cut off our retreat if we continued as planned. Since we had a good position up on the narrow plateau between the ravines I suggested to Mott that we should send one man to bring back Cushing's company, while we held the savages in check with our firepower. But at the same moment as we set off to get ready for our effort, I discovered another and significantly stronger force to the left, behind us, on the way toward us with very clear intent. The only wise thing to do was a quick retreat. We again threw ourselves up onto the horses, but at the same instant the Indians shot a round that hit Green's animal so badly that it collapsed onto its knees screaming terribly. Pierce was wounded seriously in the side, but not worse than that he succeeded in saving himself on foot to a suitable hiding place between the bushes and the cliff wall. Before Mott and I managed to aim, one of the Apaches had advanced so close to the fleeing Green that he succeeded in snatching off his hat. Miller, who we sent after Cushing, looked around and immediately tossed a couple of shots and these, together with our own, clearly got the savages to think that our whole force was on the way to surrounding them, so they stopped for a while; sufficiently long to give the two of us a chance to steal away too. However, they quickly discovered their mistake and advanced in two lines; when the first one needed to reload the other one attacked. After the first rounds they withheld their fire. Apparently they intended to capture us alive.

But Cushing was closer than we thought. First, he and Simpson and Chapman showed up and right afterward the rest of the men. I pointed out that Green wouldn't have a chance unless we attacked at once; Pierce got left there for the present. We rode toward them, eleven men, and a fresh exchange of shots ensued which drove them up among the hills. They left five dead behind, we three horses. At the same time as Cushing sent three of the men back to the baggage wagon, he ordered us forward. I never thought that soldiers knew how they should correctly handle the contacts with the Apaches, but this time I actually couldn't fail to protest. I pointed out that they were at least fifteen times as many as we, that we had to attack over the open, scorched entrance to the valley, that they lay well entrenched between the boulders on the hills. The very experienced Mott agreed with me, but the lieutenant seemed to think that the Indians were already beaten. He counted us. Eight, inclusive of Green who miraculously had succeeded in stealing away and again joined us; eight, he said, that ought to suffice.

We advanced fifteen yards. They still withheld their fire. We advanced another fifteen yards. Then a single shot was heard. It hit Simpson right in the face, the bullet went out through the back of his skull. He toppled over, but he lived. Cushing left another man to take care of him, thereby reducing our troop to six. When they discovered that we were no more, they rushed down toward us from all sides. It seemed as if each cliff, each bush was transformed into an Indian. I was probably a few yards from Cushing when I heard him say with a low voice, as if it were the intention that it not be heard: they have killed me, can anyone be so kind as to get me out of here. His glance was directed toward our frightened horses, his hands were crossed in front of his chest when he fell over. Mott shouted at me to help him, and I took hold of the lieutenant's left arm, he the right one, and we dragged him backward, accompanied also by Green who seemed quite stunned, totally vacant. The others tried to get hold of some horses.

We probably managed about ten or twelve steps before Cushing was struck again, this time in the head, and now it felt like a corpse we were dragging. Abreast of Yount, who had stopped near Simpson while he lay dying, I looked around. They were coming at us, side by side, without shooting especially much. We left Cushing alongside Simpson and decided to sell ourselves as expensively as possible. A little dismayed that we never gave up they again took cover, took a short pause, long enough to give Green and Yount a chance to get up on the horses. Kilmartin still had shots left and opened fire with such an intensity that it seemed as if reinforcements had arrived and thereby gave me and Mott the chance to mount. But both of the horses were shot from under us, two shots in the flanks of Mott's poor animal, a third hit the front leg of mine; a fourth killed private Green on the spot. Mott quickly came up on Cushing's gray gelding and shouted to me to run along under cover of him, but something again must have happened to my damned knee. In one or another way he got me up in front of himself, across the horse's back. Uninjured, both of us, we reached the baggage wagon and together with the men who had also escaped there we immediately took off. On a new horse I formed a mobile rear guard together with Fichter and Miller, and the effects of our shots were clearly that they couldn't get so close that there ever was a question of a real battle. Nor were we able to drive them away so that we dared to pick up the bodies of the fallen. When we passed the salt marsh at Rio Barbacoma, about a couple of miles above Camp Wallen, we saw them again at a distance, under the low, flat cut-off mesas. They were loudly expressing their disappointment and simply shooting a few futile shots into the air, as if they had figured we were going to take the easier and quicker and drier route on the other side of the wetland.

While the others continued, I lingered a while in spite of the others' warnings that the effect of a bullet could be lethal, even at that distance. These Indians behaved with remarkable discipline, not at all as howling and boisterous as those I was used to meeting on the reservation or in the market places. Their chief sat the whole time on his compact little brown horse, during the whole battle, which was conducted without a redundant word; yet his orders seemed never to be misunderstood, the gestures, the facial expressions, the quick language of his hands.

I think that we killed thirteen of them; in any case we left that many immobile on the burnt grass. We ourselves lost Cushing, Simpson and Green; private Pierce survived his wounds.

Four horses finished off, two wounded.

The men behaved well, especially Kilmartin, Fichter and Miller as well as Mott, of course.

The stretch we covered during these days I estimate to be at least two hundred miles.

I looked around a last time.

Closer than that I never came to Cochise.

American Airlines has a comfortable straight hop between Phoenix and San Juan. It departs only every other day, but I could actually imagine an extra day, washed by the warm emerald water after the cool week in Indian country. From Puerto Rico a propeller armada of small airlines continues on to all the smaller islands above and below the wind in the archipelago; you don't need to make a reservation. I intended to show up at the right moment; Gus Larson wasn't going to have to wait.

I turned in the rental car, which was spattered with red clay and arranged for the transport home of the exposed negatives via a shipping firm that was indeed uncertain as to where Sweden was but had heard of SAS. The service was rotten. The customs official both dumb and arrogant. With mixed emotions I saw the yellow nylon bag, full of undeveloped Indians, tossed up on a freight car with Europe scribbled indistinctly in chalk on the border. Phoenix-Stockholm, morning in Arizona, late afternoon in Sweden. I called the job. Thank God Sickan was still sitting at the editorial office switchboard; this service angel without whom no program would ever get finished. She noted all the infinite series of digits and letter codes in the airplane and freight receipt numbers. She reported from the lab that the Greece material was okay. According to the picture report though one roll was missing. That's the way it is, I lied, one of my special rolls, super-sensitive pictures. Sickan just laughed: you photographers with all your secret pictures. That no one has ever yet gotten to see!

I called the general consulate in Los Angeles and reported that I had sent my suitcase there full of bulky and excess equipment. Completely untruthfully and with the poise that distinguishes every somewhat experienced journalist I said that my dear brother, the counselor of embassy in Washington, promised that it wouldn't pose any great problem. The voice in the receiver still sounded uncertain and asked me to wait. Apparently the white lie worked. I was connected higher up in the hierarchy to Wilshire Boulevard. Oh sure, no, no problem at all. Beside there was already a package waiting for me, from the Institute. They promised to pick it up from LAX. I asked them to say hello to my brother and rushed back to the shipping firm and also managed to get the big heavy metal case with extra cassettes, unnecessary microphones and the monstrosity of a tripod sent; also squeezed in my bag of worn-out and sour smelling pants, socks and shirts.

After an hour's explosive efficiency, ready for a new stage, I embarked relieved on the DC 10; destination the tropics. In my backpack now I carried only the very most essential things: toothbrush, electric shaver, mini tape recorder, a few thin summer garments tightly squeezed together; a plastic bag of new film rolls in one fist, the camera in the other. Already before the plane took off, I consumed an extra dry martini immediately after breakfast followed by a salt-rimmed Margarita; high above all the eagles silently toasting me and the ever darker reflection in the cabin window. I actually thought I was well worth the entertainment!

After spending the night in one of Charlotte Amalie's very cheapest hotel rooms, I took a taxi out to the pre-arranged meeting at the airport. The traffic going out was dangerous, if not lethal, and it didn't exactly get any better when enormous monsters of road grading machines were totally blocking the last suddenly unpleasantly clayey and dusty bit of road. Hopelessly gloomy gray palm curtains tried to survive the thick smoke of the asphalt boilers. Occasionally the sea succeeded in gleaming, an exquisite sun-sparkling grimace between the trunks. It became all the more apparent that I was not going to get there in time, since all of the drivers in this traffic were leaning on their horns the whole time and simultaneously were going in different directions at one and the same time at each intersection. I could already clearly see in front of me Gus' infamous faint smile. Completely soaking with sweat, at least a quarter of an hour after the arrival of the agreed-upon Miami plane, I rushed into the chaotic arrival hall and dashed on to the baggage carousel that thank heaven was still delivering flowered suitcases and golf clubs. The tourist rabble were crowded around in God-awful sun bonnets and baseball caps, everywhere blue and white veined calves under pleated knee-length tennis dresses from somewhere in the past or knee-length boxer shorts from the same era. There were to be sure other things to observe, exclusive exceptions, the gods will know, equipped with long and narrow well-baked thighs, brown breasts, wild eyes under frizzy manes of hair. Authentic West Indian strains were thundering out of the loudspeakers, continually interrupted by information about departures to or arrivals from all of the classical pirate haunts, Tortola, Nevits, Saint Barth, Virgin Gorda, Antigua, Dominica and whatever they're called. I shut my eyes and allowed the memories of my childhood's very happiest hours of reading to slip out, breathed in the scent of rum and sour pipes, the very special smell of gold bars just dug up from treasure hiding places; the muzzle loaders went off, the black patch was straightened out; boarding hooks flashed under the cruel sun.

When I again looked at the baggage conveyor belt, it was empty. The sweat on my back was on the verge of freezing into ice in the air-conditioned hall that was more like a cold-storage room. I gazed in all directions. No discretely grizzled professor Gus Larson could be seen anywhere though. A quickly passing feeling of anger was just as quickly replaced by one of relief and deliverance. Sure, it would have been tempting to sail with a gang of Texas billionaires on a luxury cruiser between beautiful Caribbean islands; but my real mission in spite of everything was to bring together Misters Odysseus and Robinson Crusoe, a quite delicate task which to my knowledge no film-maker had been able to cope with before.

One of the exceptions was lingering in front of me, slender and naked.

Her body covered scantily by a bathing suit in flaming neon green cut deeply down toward the crack. Loosely draped over her shoulders a shiny silver mink cape was hanging. A thinner band of the same fur was holding up her hair whose huge quantity threatened to fill the entire arrival hall with locks when she quick as lightning turned around and fixed me with her glance. The petrifaction was, however, not worse than that I was able to take a half step back out of the very worst magic circle.

"Hi there! I didn't see when you came."

Did I really know the woman in question?

"Don't look so terrified; it's just me."

Under the complete war paint I could get a hint of Mrs. Larson's features with extreme effort. The collarbone was powdered with little shimmering metal shavings. The front of the so-called bathing suit was in the same class as the back; it was impossible to understand what was holding it up. An unobtrusive diamond sparkled in her navel. Her skin glistened, still obscenely winter-white. The way the garment was cut she could probably have used a little shaving at the bottom. She leaned forward with pouting mouth. Instinctively I held up the camera between us. She smacked her lips and smiled.

"The car is waiting. Can I carry anything for you?"

I handed over the tough plastic bag with rolls of film and sound tape. I didn't dare look in any direction. Remarkably enough no one gave a hoot about this odd couple; no applause, not the least appreciative whistling. No wild drumming from a jungle brass jazz band.

She knocked on the dark smoke-colored pane that separated us from an invisible underling up in the driver's seat. A few hundred horses got the coach moving imperceptibly. I made a careful voice test:

"I thought Gus was going to pick me up."

"Old Gus unfortunately couldn't do it. He is back in his beloved Sweden arranging a professorship."

"Impossible," was all I got out. My brain tapped the fragments of memory about all the trouble from the beginning to the lamentable end of his so-called academic career; the dissertation no one understood, the row about grades, the furious farewell article in Svenska Dagbladet about the country without education and culture.

"Nothing is impossible here, my dear. Not for papa in any case. From now on until his retirement Gus has been designated as head of his own research institute in Uppsala and titular professor for its Project Democracy. Then the university will have a free hand to do what they want with the proceeds from the donation. Considering the salaries in your country it ought to suffice for quite a few well-paid positions, isn't that so?"

I looked at her furtively, out of the corner of my eye, at a very bad angle. She answered the next question before I even managed to ask it.

"He had his chance, you understand, but not even during this recent long leave of absence did he succeed in producing anything of value. And he of course had me as his very personal assistant!"

She laughed ambiguously, bent down toward the car door pocket and picked up something that with all the holes in the edges actually had to be a computer list!

"One thing more, would you like to check the facts in this abstract? It is important so that everything will function quickly and easily. In this country we have the world's most experienced and clever divorce lawyers. An office in Austin and one in Stockholm are already in full swing taking care of Gus' and my definitive separation. Then it's your turn. The firm in Sweden incidentally has begun to prepare your divorce too!"

She handed over the document. It unfolded, over one meter long. At the top my birth number 330802-1017. Then the poor excerpt from the most recent volume of Who's Who. At the bottom, physical measurements, status of teeth, blood group, muscle type. In between there was everything, a quite complete draft of a meaty biography. Here and there underlinings or a sic! in the margin. I checked some of the sports results. Everything official was there from the fiasco at the Swedish Finn championships over twenty-five years ago to the pretty nice time at the Dallas White Rock Marathon in 1982 and last fall's Lidingölopp. Schools, references, salary development, the few controversies with judicial and tax authorities. Criticism of short films and TV programs. Even quotes from reviews of a couple of fifties poetry collections, a literary activity outside the statute of limitation long ago: "... even from such romantic drivel a more settled poetry could come in the future;" Dagens Nyheter, signed J. Edfelt. Below the address of Elfgren's divorce office on Engelbrekt's street were a series of digits completely incomprehensible to me as well as various graphically produced curves.

"The coefficient of fornification is actually ridiculously low, considering both your profession and your intimate family circumstances."

She rested her index finger with the green nail under the name in question. How much did she really know?

"Just think, there are still women who allege that there are literally swarms of attractive men. I'm not at all inclined to agree. Do you understand?"

She crumpled up the computer strip into a rustling ball and threw it at my knee.

"Papa is for the present very satisfied with this development. So now everything depends on you yourself."

An abominable mistake was on the verge of being made; wrong creature led off to ritual slaughter. Deep in my nose and throat the stench of blood and strange incense, corrosive perfumes was already making me sick. I stuck my hand in my pocket. But there was only small change and a crumpled five-dollar bill. Once, very long ago, I got from a young man, possibly God-sent, some humble gelatinous capsules to swallow when necessary. They contained powder from a magic plant that, unbeknownst to me, still today has not found its spot in the Linnéan system. The root is black, the flowers milky white. It is rare in most latitudes and besides absurdly difficult to pull up whole and undamaged from the earth, a prerequisite for the drug to work. After the most recent use I threw away what little remained of the pill. I shouldn't have done it.

On the supplement to the travel bill, under the rubric OTHER, this time I intend especially to point out the islands' grand beauty, the intricate blue interplay between the air, winds, light and water; the diver's clear-sightedness, calm sea birds resting on the back of the trade winds, the verdure's unfathomable variety. No camera, no film in the world, can record this; every picture becomes just a lousy fake receipt from the visit. No wide-angle lens is adequate to capture the horizon, no lens attachment intrusive enough in its examination of the intimacies of the flowers.

No, here entirely different depicters would be needed than a middle-aged film-maker with his senses blunted by rules and routines; curious young discoverers of the archipelago of a thousand sensualities, history's effervescing over sand banks and coral reefs; the yellow-violet, emerging ground ahead, the evasive manoeuver, trimming of the spinnaker's huge bubble. After close inspection of the feet of film taken home the administration and the chief bureaucrats will find that the long-anticipated breakdown had finally happened. The old colleague will be taken down into the archive, to devote himself until retirement to cutting up his own and others' films. An eagerly awaited lacuna in the organization arises and can be promptly filled by a new economist or a young media type specially trained by the concern for the purpose, ready to reconstruct life's strange variety within the studios' electronically covered walls instead of depicting the difficult to check, tasteless and often fantastic reality far beyond modules, office building and 08-area.

Yet, the story must take its course; the roll reach its predetermined end.

Most of them naturally came from England or the new American colonies. But surprisingly many entered from other countries, Frenchmen of course,

Dutchmen, Danes and Swedes. The turnover in personnel in the profession was high; there was always a place for prospective applicants with the right attitude. What above all tied this heterogeneous and improbable group of men together was the desire to get rich quick as well as the love-hate relationship with the sea, the ability to properly handle sailing vessels of all sorts and sizes. One or more specialists with adequate urban or agrarian background also got to be included in the quite democratic community aboard, doctors, carpenters, butchers and musicians were actually quite sought after.

Life on the land mainly consisted of hard tiring physical work and social and economic injustices. A period aboard a good pirate vessel in the Caribbean sea thus stood out for many as an attractive alternative, the absolutely quickest way to glory, success and riches; an excellent way to escape hunger, disease, early death, sadistic noblemen and autocratic gentlemen of all other imaginable types. The discipline aboard the merchant ship and the navy's vessels was for that matter so hard and tough, that a short visit aboard the pirates' floating device was experienced as, if anything, a vacation trip.

Now of course it wasn't mainly to get away from the injustices and vexations of everyday life that you headed down south to these varied places of work between still virgin islands, under mild and steady trade winds. For, to be sure, free-lancing as a pirate with adventure and pleasure of an unusual kind, liquor and women, renown, freedom and power for a group of closely knit companions was tempting; even if the life aboard wasn't always so terribly different from that at home: way too many people for the wretched space; filth, shit and vermin everywhere; rats and cockroaches in massive hordes; at least half of the crew used to die during a successful trip, from typhus and dysentery, malaria, scurvy or yellow fever – but that just meant fewer who shared the valuables – and from syphilis, of course! When you took a new prize, obviously the medicine chest of the ship doctor was what you looked for directly, there used to be a real race to his corner to appropriate the mercury that could alleviate the repulsive afflictions.

Yet the choice was never difficult when it was a question of weighing the one life style against the other, the landlubber's or the pirate's. You chose the latter. A quick, pleasure-filled, rich and for the most part extraordinarily short life. It was really only a matter of lying under the high capes and awaiting Spanish galleys, Portuguese merchant vessels filled to the brim with Brazilian riches, East Indian travelers' silk, jewels, spices and ivory. Then all you had to do was help yourself from the well-laid table; easy to find a market for the goods or exchange them for noble metals on a steadily growing market in the North American colonies, even easier to get rid of all the money in the bars and brothels in Charlotte Amalie. The Danish merchants on Saint Thomas rubbed their hands every time a shady-looking ship without a flag steered in toward the city's well-protected harbor. The pirates were lousy businessmen, really only interested in getting rid of their goods as quick as possible, painting the town red before it was again time to head away to Soper's Hole or Bitter End and begin over from the beginning.

As soon as they stepped ashore they were thus plundered and fleeced down to the skin by shrewd men, merchants from Copenhagen and Helsingör and Ålborg. Actually, the pirate's life consisted of a single long vicious circle. The one who worked hardest as usual got the least out of it. Indeed, there were many madmen among them, who spread death and destruction around themselves, fire grenades and poisoned crossbow arrows and other unpleasant things; certainly many of them also died under torment and agony well worth their unpleasant pieces of villainy. But many were courageous too, smart and sharp, not a bit worse than the pirates who today from their thrones and board rooms control the fates of states and civilizations. Under other circumstances they would certainly have displayed the same morals and respectability and dignity as these; gloriously and humanly they exploited that force they were given or took to using by their own power.

That was that. The trade winds are the same. The low pressure moves along the same routes, the ocean currents have only been insignificantly disturbed. Today there is another sort of free booter and adventurer who arrives and works for the modern day's pirate captains. There are no longer any signs of equality visible. Yet, they come here with the same consuming interest for sailing, combined with the desire to drift before steady winds under a sky spiced with sun, pointed clouds, nights prodigiously perforated with stars; between voluptuous islands that scrub themselves in gold and emerald.

Allen and Woitek met me at the marina. Their forelocks extraordinarily sun-bleached, their eyes made of blue ice, their handshakes just as steel hard as the welcoming smiles were dazzlingly white and friendly and soft. They handled my equipment as if it weighed a few grams and quickly stowed it away in the rubber dinghy among ice cubes in steamy plastic bags, cases filled with Heinekens and Becks, vegetable boxes, fruit and all other imaginable provisions for the next few days. Their English had an accent that I couldn't place. I had to ask.

"South Africa, Capetown and Durban."

Allen gave me a helping hand down from the dock. Boat niggers they are quite simply called by their employers. They come from all points of the compass, one by one or in big flocks. Many, by the way, are frozen Scandinavians who head south when the short and cool Baltic season is over and the boats are tormented under flapping tarpaulins by October's brutal storms, by April ice that never wants to break up. They know how the apples of the millionaires' eyes are to be handled, professionally and tenderly; free board and lodging in advance and decently paid. Many blond cooks have found their Prince Charming here when the boat owner has flown down in his private jet a load of significant guests or customers for some indolent days, floating with the trade winds between the islands' luxury restaurants, discreetly and suitably placed near the nights' protected anchoring spots.

Cindy wriggled out of the minimal fur cape and sat down on it. Finally, I understood what it was going to be used for! The scorching hot rubber railing, practically speaking, burned a hole in my by then extraordinarily thin, worn jeans.

"Shall we wait for Carrie?"

"She has already swum out to fix lunch for the old boys," Woitek said.

She directed her voice at me, but just as much at Allen who was still standing on the pontoon; she stared hard at him in an almost indecent way.

"You understand, Carrie is everyone's sweetheart. Divine cook, took off from her family in Santa Cruz I think. Insanely sweet and actually much too well-preserved bearing in mind her age. You better look out for her. She just became available again, isn't that right?"

Allen looked moderately amused. He loosened the end of the rope and jumped down in the prow.

"Okay, let's go," he hissed between stiff lips. Woitek just laughed and started the little six horsepower Yamaha.

There are boats and then there are boats!

Little Tone decidedly belongs to the latter type.

Actually, there is just one thing you can be convinced about when you have your sailboat lying in Charlotte Amalie's harbor and that is that however large a boat you own you can be assured that very close by there will be one even larger! If Little Tone was only next to the largest in size, then in return she was without a doubt the most beautiful. Three different colored gray stripes ran along the good sixty-foot long, snow-white hull. The single mast seemed sky high. She has competed between Los Angeles and Hawaii, in the tough Bermuda race during the winter and during the summer season between Cape Cod and Maine with great success. The lines are divine. The stem's curves and lift give a perfect angle of incidence against waves and current, the profile amidships is rather like a Finn, the water easily leaving the transom. I saw at once what a lethal competitor she had to be to anything at all that can be moved by wind over water, fish and bird through the elements, at the same time participant in and superb beyond all stiff physical laws of motion; presumably so easy to steer, that by merely lightly laying your little finger against the wheel you immediately feel the rig's rudder's and keel's trim.

An old-fashioned schooner was on the way out of the harbor basin.

A huge Norwegian-registered cruise ship spewed out the day's thousand blue haired ladies toward the city's well-set tourist traps. A middle-aged filmmaker from hyperborean regions taps his backpack contentedly with the camera and tape recorder. If there is anything that characterizes life itself, and hopefully not just what is in the middle of a story, then it is just violent changes, the swings between extremes, the center of the ocean and the periphery of the deserts or vice versa, the surprises in everyday's corner. Some have as their profession to steadily be there, even if the words and the pictures seldom suffice for trustworthy reports; the agreed-upon grammar and the golden mean fail. Yet the mission must be performed. As a matter of fact it never stops. It is only a question of stubbornly hanging on, even if one beautiful day the travel accounts have to be filled out, missing receipts accounted for or deducted from meager salaries.

I climb aboard. The rope ladder is hanging over the port side. On top of a huge ice chest in the middle of the cockpit sits a bowl with fresh fruit on a bed of sparkling ice chips. From down in the cabin men's voices can be heard, mixed with a lowly murmuring female laugh and the unmistakable hissing from a frying pan, a fine stimulating aroma from a blue cheese omelet. The introduction ceremonies are taken care of quickly and informally. We go by motor toward Buck Island and Frenchman's Cap, eat and share several bottles of red wine; set the sails. She barely perceptibly lies to leeward, neat and willing, close to the wind.

"Do you want to touch her?" P wonders.

Carrie was careful not to get too much sun in her face. She often rubbed her upper lip with the tip of her index finger, as if she wanted to massage away the annoying little wrinkles, the only thing on her magnificent body that immediately tattled of age. As soon as she was finished with the dishes and got the food and silverware put away into the meticulous order that is the very prerequisite for successful culinary work aboard a sailboat, then she used to come up on deck and sit down in the shadow of the sail. The wide brim of the white plaited hat fluttered in the apparent wind. Her strikingly light facial skin stood in glaring contrast to all of the other exquisitely sun-fried. Thin blue shadows under the eyes, a sharp green streak on the eyelids. The melancholy strain around the mouth occasionally broke up into an ironic smile or the low, bubbling laugh. She had had her job for many years. Apparently she was the steady point in an otherwise often changing crew.

For several days I collected peripheral shots around Robinson. While waiting for a suitable uninhabited island to put me ashore we made sporadic forays, watched the rays' wonderful leaps over the waves, grilled shining silver-fish in the fabulously quick dusk, lit flares in the night's primeval darkness for monsters from the bottom.

Already on the second day it got horridly hot. We anchored for the evening outside Cooper's Island. Perhaps we had consumed quite a few Painkillers and Rum Punches waiting for the main course: gratinéed red snapper with black beans and fried pygmy bananas. All deck hatches and doors were wide open to let the fading night breeze draw past the cabins and if possible refresh our shiny bodies. Still it was absolutely impossible to fall asleep. After a desperate hour I wrapped a towel around myself and pattered up on deck. Like an extra star the masthead light rocked in space. Round about lay the islands spread out like grimy silhouettes, creeping, almost ominous primeval animals with stooping backs.

Suddenly the feeling of unreality was there, a noticeable and rather frightening, border-dissolving transition; sort of as if the pieces in a chess game took over the game with newly discovered moves and previously unplayed combinations. Yet, I stood steady, as it seemed, with legs apart and both hands around the sturdy centerboard stay. The hull moved below me, a living body in the dark, vessel between space and space. I noticed how I was staggering, or more correctly, there was a staggering in me, as if I was touched by an enormously quick wing, the very frigate bird of the night. A feeling of transcendence, or is transference the right word? Finally, I located the North star, which at least gave temporary stability to the darkness, in its right place, even if Ursa Minor was located remarkably far down on the northern lower hem of the star canopy.

"Another one who can't sleep," said the darkness.

The address came from afore. I sat down alongside without saying anything. Then she spread her legs. I defended myself clumsily.

"Perhaps we shouldn't do this here."

"Do you know any better way?"

I refrained from further discussion. Afterward we lay on our backs in the damp fold of the foresail, looking at ourselves in the constellations. They were moving degree by degree toward dawn.

Sometimes things are like this: when I find myself on certain assignments there exists only one space at a time. That makes life easy, every traveler's business. Time is kept under control, obliterated or reduced at least to one or more fabulously closed moments. The performance is none the worse for that. Open doors should be avoided; they mostly just lead straight into the messy closets of memory, family, work, all the collected trivialities of history. The legendary resides on the edges of reality. Anyone whatsoever can be struck, anywhere; it is a question of being prepared. There is no reason to be ashamed of this, be struck by remorse and guilt, believe that it is unnatural in some way; rather be sad if it happens too seldom or even never.

"Can you imagine an entire life as a waitress? Daughter, wife, classy whore, call it what you want, nevertheless waitress is ultimately the right word. Finally, I have begun to help myself to the main dishes. When I want and when it suits me. Rights. Curiously, it's very tragicomic to see how terrified you guys get when life behaves in reverse. In what way do you feel threatened? By my mere presence? You hesitated, but you joined in. That does you credit. But what are you afraid of, really?"

"Considering this country's official morals I am probably rather foolhardy. I'm not afraid of anything. But I am jealous of freedom, as conscious as I am about all of its limitations. You can be one, I one for you. Still we exist solely to transgress each other. Only then can the transition to the unexpected occur. Cindy, you do understand?"

It began as a quiet giggle.

"What's so damn funny then? You try to be serious in a constructive way and then ..."

She almost choked, rolled around and buried her paroxysms of laughter in the damp crease of my armpit.

"You think I'm Cindy. Good grief! Merciful darkness! Instead of the young princess you have enjoyed her past-her-prime bridesmaid."

"Should I apologize for that?"

She got up. I glimpsed her silhouette against the Milky Way's shimmering milky band. She didn't answer. Her voice sounded quite different and very collected when she asked her counter-question:

"What are you actually doing on this boat?"

"That is really a very long story."

"I've got all the time in the world," she said, continuing at a distance, half-dispersed in space.

I told. The Zodiac circle spun. I talked all the way until the Southern Cross pushed up over the horizon and the dawn was no longer far off. I realized how much more senselessly unreal everything must seem; yet I went through everything. Life played out in an absurd mirror of distortion that anyone has the right to watch without on that account needing to get involved; any stranger can use it to recognize himself in or just nonchalantly turn his back to and scornfully go away from, if the images don't fit.

"Is Cindy supposed to be married to some sort of screwy Swedish philosophy professor in Texas? She is exactly the same free-lance tart as I am, even if she happens to be the daughter of one of the real big boys. Everyone belongs to the organization. As long as we fit, of course."

Her voice sounded somewhat bitter or possibly just tired. Undoubtedly an intonation of anxiety had arisen when she continued. The light was turned up quicker and quicker. Pale yellow curtains fluttered between the clouds where they were hanging like fleecy caps above the islands' pointed mountains.

"Just a nice friend who sent you here to us on the boat. Just wonder what he got for that? And then you are going on to Los Angeles to recapture a lost roll of film? Let me laugh."

But she didn't.

"I'm going to meet Robinson first."

"Good luck. You have been lucky, all the way here in any case. You will need more of that commodity in the future, you may be certain! I'll never stop being surprised about you innocent Europeans. You come here in big bunches to try to find vanished pastoral idylls, hopelessly fascinated by our captivating loathsome culture. Instead of looking on the islands of the Baltic or among the olive groves of the Mediterranean! If you don't watch out, then one fine day we will have all of you in our power, we will invade you totally. Look, now the sky is burning! Venus is still shining radiantly clear. Please kiss me one more time. And watch out for real stars. Then you could really get seriously burned."

She stretched out voluptuously toward dawn.

"It is getting light quickly. Do you want to help me? I have to put on a swimming suit before I jump in. There are limits to morals. It's all right to fuck, as long as it isn't seen. But nakedness, the light of day doesn't tolerate that here."

With great seriousness she turned toward me.

"If you ever find your way to the Old Danish Beauty Parlor say hello from me. There too I have served and been served. Say hello to Circe; if she wants to acknowledge her old artist name."

She dove in.

The heart has many habits. Even mine. For example the bad habit of lingering now and then, jumping over a moment and almost frightening the hell out of someone. Yet it continues, obstinately, in equal parts filled by fear and hope.

Singing rig, blue reflections, daylight. The clouds' clenched fists over the islands, a double string of beads toward the horizon. Chimneys on the cargo vessels, sails instead of cities; the whirls of the wake swallow the sun. Fine silver blows over the waves, even finer dust from space sticks to the stays. The rudder's movements gossip about oceanic forces. This sea is an upside down sky; the beaches soft as female breasts, the palms' erect leaves mouthpieces for a lost verdure that is returning. The surf milks sand out of the cliffs. The curve of the bay is powdered by crumbled wreaks. The sun-coins flow right into the skin. Wild stories balance the clouds' cotton bales. The hills bloom with the smell of birth and candles never extinguished obstruct the glades with prayers. It is morning; still fully possible to change course to familiar tracts, row toward the twilight with empty nets. The sea is more cruel than any words, any love; old bodies star-rocked through dreary nights. The passage over the sea of antiquity couldn't be more dangerous, the pilot climbing up the inclined sun-warmed sides of the vessel. All rumors of canoes have to be dismissed as unworthy.

Beyond the pier the breakers explode, shiny leaves turn into foam. Bee hives of coral, hooves during a single season, a single wind. Lazy volumes paged through by a gust, an archipelago for gods. Crushed shells below the foot, blood berries, mangroves. The light jumps, like the heroes one time, between loosely anchored islands, still adrift in the current. In the salty wind the serpents die, gold turns to ashes. The wood of the caravels sewed the world together. Now the cicadas puncture the verdure with memory. Bitter nuts, crabs, borders embroidered by foam. The alphabet devotes itself to brown studies, dark vocalic exercises between sparkling consonants.

The sea stays while the rain is sent on to distant continents; the spinning wheel telegraphs ivy green, sweet banyan trees. The keys sleep. Monarchs remember the clouds over the city, but the sound of the horses' ears, the belly's moisture, races and hazily undissolved horizons have for a long time been part of the dream of the web. Coconuts, the knowledge about metals, mints is more important than distant white cities. The dew's numismatics in a complete edition; the tongue against the sugar, ancient voices under the ground swells. Tents where naked bodies after the night's dances sought common repose. Eucalyptus trees, red spices, thin livestock; everywhere the smell of dead lemon. The slaves never landed here. They passed by, to the north, under the islands, above the wind. Bad days filled the plantations with the day's work, cold-walled earthworks, cisterns. Bare museums remain, filled with war-like tourists who look at the compasses and bible from the captain's cabin. The cruise ship logs on, knot and second-meter, above the steamy bubble pool.

The corrugated school airs the picture of an icon in a bronzed hand. The bottle of incense is filled with butterfly wings. The sea's presence lights up the childrens' faces. There is a philosophy here, black bodies in white light, white in white. Above the thighs, below the navel the doll waits for suitors. Odd shops with flowery dresses, the roar of lullabies and Rock 'n' Roll. Green estates clad in the silk of conquistadors and missionaries. The rain ends all business. Rum bottles, old boys, sacrificial deeds. It stinks of acrid urine from the ground. Dry bamboo curtains separate the villages. Every spring the skies change places, feathers are strewn over clayey islands, the automobiles are put aside. Drink a lot of tea, tan the body on the porch until you look like a hero, spoil the nights with dollars. The person who has once seen the islands surrounded by foam doesn't hesitate. Occasional mountains move the clouds; the airplane's jet streams follow over the ocean. After a time you no longer ask for change.

Emerald light under the headsail, the stem drinks noisily; the helmsman's cap heightens the expectation. Drizzle on the foredeck, aft picnic necking. The time for life merges with homesickness, familiar lips on ice-filled glasses. There are no wounds that think. Life is pain, romantic nonsense, pantheistic persecution mania. Turn it upside down, take it from behind in vulgar galleys. The heart consists partly of a common passion, partly of heart. Columbus knew, the merchant ship captains knew, the men on the loaded galleys; the ocean regattas know. You too bear this bowsprit with you. Smoking coals before the mast, laughing workers scare the shit out of you. The light here isn't at all like that from Abyssinian or Egyptian deserts, driving over dried Mediterranean islands toward Baltic seas. While you spell the story goes on. Fireworks, sweaty armpits, goatskin. Lighthouses under the sea, fires over the earth. Nocturnal crows patrol. Banjo music, undressed moon, toasts for distant comrades.

But the landscape is not complete without herons, floating right below the dawn when you weigh anchor after windless nights and realize that he had been here before you, always got home before you. Lazy grass, feeble oranges, fragile air at sunrise. You go ashore on a neglected eden where the scythes did their work long ago. Everywhere barracks, empty storehouses; lagoons, meridian altitudes. The wind stiff as always. Just your vessel immobile, stopped in the middle of the storm. Here it ought to be eternal summer for promenades and tepid wine, the return of the flutes, vague watercolors. Strong smell of marina ancestors, ancient times' happy travelers. High up on the rig hangs a hand. Old ladies go around as usual in self-confident flocks. Confused, the younger ones take over. The mood climbs inside the hotel. There are now names for all islands. The schooners and yachts still enter these waters with the greatest care. A treacherous calm embellishes the quays. Even here Cycloptic mountains grow. The one who distrusts Odysseus will never be long-lived. Flight, unprotected harbors, the creaking of a mooring cable; hyperborean visitors with snowbirds in their eyes. Harbormasters register all newly arrived people, the cargo space with sponges, jars filled with chromium. Seafarers, ship boys; salt-sweaty foreheads, smoking eyebrows. You should be able to fill travel brochures. In the evening the music passes over into blue song and soft church bells from up on the hills. A lonely woman walks down to the shore. It is not a dream. It is a dream. It has already been expressed: a rosary of islands, good pastures inside the harbor, pigeons. The arms stiff after yet another day at the helm. You can praise parks well lit by lemons, the fountain of coral on the square, the brass band. You can fear the green damp night. She strips off the leaves. Only in love can this exist, in long since sleeping diaries. Write often in the sand about particular islands, the noise from the surf where you are put ashore. Peel the onion in the moonlight, study all ceremonies with patience. Plant the cross-like border poles at the water's edge, fire off canons. Sail on with worn-out sails toward ever more pungent verdure; tell about the really old man's delights; marine fleas, sand flies. There are labels on all ships. Gulls rise up. The pelicans turn around, dive. The writer laughs.

Farther in, this sea passes over into swampy ground with tiger orchids and drooling lianas. The mushrooms rot in the fresh water gloom. Everything darker; brown reflections. Canoes. Drums.

The third day we went in alee under Virgin Gorda's high cliffs, swung at anchor so close that the stench of guano from the bird mountain at first completely paralyzed the nose. It was a strong and remarkable sensation. All the senses were affected, as in a chain reaction; the roof of the mouth dried out, the eyes got damp, the skin on the fingers felt tight, contracted and got numb. Baffled, I looked at the inside of my hands. To be sure, they were beat after all the winching and hard work with halyards and sheets. But now it simply looked as if the intricate patterns of the lifelines were on the verge of being wiped out and polished!

You didn't see much of the girls. Carrie was always busy with something especially important and never had time when I approached to get more out of her, not the least about the place in Santa Monica where I sooner or later had to end up. Cindy was transformed beyond recognition under my surprised eyes. The demonic decoy for sub-human forces became more and more like the coed she presumably was, with a solid BA in home economics, philosophy and ballet.

"Carrie has been bull-shitting as usual, you can see it on her. But I didn't squeal. Sit on the same boat, you know. It'll be really nice to get to meet you again, if there is anything left of you when the old men are done. That could take some time. But it could also go horribly fast. Over the years they have become terribly capable in this variety of treatment."

There was a serious tone of voice that apparently contradicted her melancholy smile. One eyebrow was raised while she spoke, like a warning signal. The fine net of almost childish wrinkles, that no sun can reach and burn away, could be seen clearly far inside the corners of her eyes. That is how I would prefer to remember her; the silhouette of health and sensuality, the fine hand that waved before the hatches were definitively battened.

Down below, all sorts of policy papers and textbooks were spread out. The coarse base of the mast went right through the table, all the way down to the attaching bolts in the bottom of the hull. There were hooks with ingenious stands for beer cans and bourbon glasses so that they synchronously followed the boat's movements without spilling over. Since we were lying securely alee, the swells were noticed no more than as an uncertain vertical heaving, a hanging horizontally. A couple of mini-spotlights in the ceiling of the cabin illuminated the green bridge table cloth. Little more than the hands of the seminar participants were visible; coarse, darkly haired wrists, the impressive muscular ripples of the forearms. All of them were at least as capable as sailors as they were extraordinarily successful businessmen. During these days I had been impressed time after time by their sure skills with the spinnaker bubble, the quickness at sail-setting, the strength with which they handled the winches, the professional discussion about the right course against the wind, the relationship between sheet and boom angle. In short, they handled the huge sixty-footer as if it were any old dinghy.

In some way it was symptomatic that I no longer could see their faces. As is well known real power lacks facial features.

P did the talking.

"Gentlemen, games, sport and pleasure have had their chance. I think we are beginning to get ready for the other important item on the agenda during this little trip: our steady discourse on the right way to create a better world. We will of course turn especially to our guest and extraordinary hand and hope that what you are going to hear can give you something to think about, perhaps even get you henceforth in your area and with your means to influence others by explaining the mechanisms behind our way of operating. There is only one interest for us, the future. The present, history and all the petty current politics we now have nearly full control over. We are looking forward, not without a certain satisfaction. Certainly it will make you happy to hear how your home country has been an important example for us, as something of a precursor among the nations, a pattern to the very highest degree desirable for us too. Where else in the world can you by means of a couple of telephone calls from my office in Dallas or Beverly Hills for example get a practically speaking exhaustive account of every individual's most personal circumstances via your extraordinarily detailed and reliable databases, dependable national registration and friendly civil servants at parish offices and social offices: By means of our own sophisticated software everything falls into place after a couple of very brief file linkings. Then it is just a matter of setting about and making the necessary dispositions for control and regulation of the individual in question, imperceptibly put him or her on the right track for the future. Certainly there can be obscure points, which not the least the document about yourself points out, but I assume that you can give satisfactory explanations on most of the obscurities. I hope so in any case!"

The voices were absolutely alike in the dark; impossible to distinguish who was talking or whether it even was one and the same deep voice that was moving around the table.

"We have remaining one fundamental problem to solve in this country. No, don't laugh if I say that it is the question as to how we are going to define our democracy, or to express myself more crudely, how we are going to deform it in order to get a chance to create a healthier future. Our forefathers were unfortunately far too eager when they pushed through and ratified our sacrosanct constitution in all haste; just look at all the unnecessary amendments! More feeling for revolution than thought about a sensible future. This we all have to pay for. And, therefore, we have to hurry and build a system that will justify our plans and actions without the slightest difficulty. The point of departure must be a central source of power, which has as its only goal to offer people the discrete charms that in spite of everything ought to be part of living in a democracy. A theory that shows how everything works, materially as well as spiritually, visible or invisible; in short, that the world is simply to be considered as equally many parts of a single powerful being. Alone, in all spaces and eternities, straight through all metamorphoses and surface movements it will embrace and include just this one thing, itself, us, everything, me. You can be convinced that such a system in the right hands, our hands, your hands, will be immensely attractive and generous; not the least for democracy's disloyal population masses. It will bring out the very best in people, the ability to fantasize, poetry, music; also the vulgarly popular cultural manifestations of our day, porn and rock. Nothing bad about something genuinely desired, naively experienced. You yourself seem to be an excellent example of what I consider to be this new type of man together with whom we, who have the power, are in the process of creating the final community state!"

A coarse hand lay still on top of the abstract from 330802-1017. It was absolutely impossible to decide whether those immobile hands on the table belonged to one and the same figure made invisible by the cabin's darkness. Something, though, got me to offer resistance with all my strength to the very inveigling tone of voice.

"Okay. Let us willingly call what I am talking about democracy. Let us finally once and for all define the concept, give it the necessary stability. That sort of thing will create pride in the people who live under its banners and enthusiastic slogans, get their feeble brains to be vitalized; the muscles will grow from the pure desire to create happiness for everyone together. This is important, this primary illusion of co-creativity may under no circumstances be destroyed. That would mean catastrophe for the controlled development of mankind's real state of happiness. Justice, what is just, must always stand at the center. You will have to forgive me if I return one more time to the impressive and, for the rest of the world, model work that is carried out in your native land. I hardly need to mention to you that it is our regular study leader until quite recently, your excellent countryman Gus Larson in the Diaspora, who has given us this marvelous information about

Sweden. Nowhere have they obviously gotten further in regard to the creation of a homogeneous society, a simple and comfortable existence without real tensions. Such a state is deserving of a successful society and vice versa; a state that has the citizens so completely in its hand and has come so far in true democratic standardization through a brilliant education system and the information media can be nothing but envied and congratulated. Unfortunately, here in the USA we have a long way to go before we will be able to point to comparable progress. We are really looking forward to acquiring with your help additional knowledge about what sort of factors in Sweden have lead to such spectacular results, not the least in regard to the most difficult of democratic tours de force: for the few to control the many. Is this a result of history or climate? Of biological components? Or is it simply phenomenal control of the emotions that has lead to this splendid progress? As you notice we are interested in your society. But, in the end, for us it is above all a question of the individual, the unique personality. How are you going to be able to control the heterogeneous in you? Homogeneous people or heterogeneous, that is the question."

Some of the gentlemen suggested a pause up on deck or down in the sea; but not for me. I was able to have a beer in peace and quiet, digest and think through what I had heard so that later on I could supply the debate with relevant and suitable material. No sooner had they disappeared up on deck than I began to check. Yeah, I had my mini tape recorder and the omni-directional mike was still hanging there in the gray tape under the tabletop. On top were crowded at least ten different kinds of beer, from Mexican Dos Equis to Canadian Labatts, via exclusive micro-breweries like Boulder or Sierra Nevada, good tasting products brewed on a base of crystal clear water from Rocky Mountain springs. Yet, I chose a worthy Carlsberg. The Danish connection? In which case the taste felt familiar and secure. I stretched out on one of the hammocks surrounded by the stench of guano, nauseatingly strong in the southern darkness, I was reminded of dear Gus' last words to me: there is probably something left of honorably curious journalist in your old paws!

207

"Yes, now we are ready to continue the meeting. Let me then begin in a little different way through the following assertion: one of our sub-goals is probably best characterized as the triumph of the vulgar. You fight futilely in the name of so-called good taste against soap operas, rock music, simple but nourishing hamburgers without wanting to understand that the battle was hopelessly lost long ago. Popularity has been looking after itself for decades, even quite admirably, without our needing to be concerned or involved in that development one bit. In any case, we no longer need to invest in bad taste. As respectable donors we can instead devote ourselves to decorating museums and concert halls with our refined taste. As long as howling savages of all ages – and the gods shall know that a good many of them are very middle-aged now – continue to sacrifice to their great Pan, then we have both him and his short-sighted worshippers under control. In the noise from drums and steel guitars, the din of synths and amplifiers poetry doesn't thrive for very long, only shabby attacks and primitive burps get anywhere, totally harmless provocations. That is as it should be. We can take it easy. In the long run it will serve our higher purpose. As long as a uniform din drowns out mental activity and the ideas resemble each other to the point of confusion, we have no reason whatsoever to complain or interfere. Noble savages and nature-loving Indians are the best thing for us. We should save as many as we can. Therefore, it is so important to encourage this increasing interest in old-fashioned folk groups. For our purpose nothing is cheaper than to concentrate on bigger and bigger donations to new professorships in folklore, sponsorship of expeditions into well-known jungles. Loud representatives of the silicon and superconductor people are already beginning to fear the competition. Obviously, they can feel completely at ease. We will never leave them in the lurch. Better opium for the intelligentsia than new ingenious data doesn't exist. Even quicker they will swallow our attractively packaged software. Primitivism and artificial intelligence, excellent! It is difficult to conceive of a happier marriage. And while all this is going on and developing along carefully pre-programmed paths, we will work on, steadily and without any great fuss. If contrary to expectation someone should become too curious as to what we are really up to, we can always offer a pleasant junket. How about the West Indies, for example!"

"Seriously speaking, to be sure we still have a good ways left to the goal: man controlled down to the last detail. Lots of problems remain to be solved, all the difficult irrational factors, unnecessary mawkishness, earthly love in all of its forms, innocent as well as perverted. As far as thoughts and ideas are concerned we undeniably have the development under good control. With love it is more difficult; poetry, art, all pernicious images such as you and Gus love to spread widely and broadly around. In the long run people just like you, in spite of your mutually totally different ideas on most questions, become extraordinarily dangerous for our activity, which ultimately will lead to a society built on intelligence and reason, without interference from the heart's capricious convulsions and emotion-filled anarchy. I hate these intellectuals, their constant treachery and rabid faithlessness, just as much as I loathe the artists' irresponsible bohemianism. I get nauseated by this so-called democratic order that is the result of their irresponsible activity. Visionaries and reactionaries, foul-smelling excrement on history's rapidly growing garbage pile, that's what they are."

"Dear guest, dear friends, it has been a long and hard-working day. As usual far too much talk from my side. But there will be more days we hope, so that you can get to know us all properly and we you! I really hope that from this sitting you haven't gotten the impression of us that we are any sort of strange inhumans. In that case you are wrong. It would be a coarse distortion of our purpose. But not even we have inexhaustible resources. In the long run it will be far too uneconomical to let something so important as life be controlled by crude instincts and poorly controlled impulses. According to sound economic theory every commodity finds its correct price, a process that unfortunately often tends to take an enormously long time. Here and now we are in the same room. The boat may seem large, but it shrinks. The cabin is already over-full. And it will not hold some of us, neither you nor me, if really competent, refined men don't take over. Out there lie the islands of paradise, Robinson's workplace. We should never forget that it was he who seriously began the cleanup work. If in the right spirit we don't lead his creation on, only the jungle will remain for all of us, the drums, the canoes in the dark, the dangerous eyes of darkness. Who would dare to meet them?"

"I've done my best, accomplished a bit on the way. Under my work clothes and uniforms there is already beating a much more homogeneous heart. I and my collaborators will reach our goal, you can rest assured of that. You are cordially welcome into our circle. I'll leave a paper here on the table; call it a contract if you want. I personally guarantee that he who signs will not be left without a share. No one should need to be disappointed. Have a good night!"

The spotlights in the ceiling went out. The discreet air-conditioning was turned off, the hatches opened to the skylight. Footsteps dissolved into the night. Every corner in the cabin was filled with warm darkness saturated with moisture. I followed along. The lanterns too were extinguished. The only light came from constellations and dying supernovas. Somewhere the black holes were busy with their invisible and definitive cleaning work. There was a glow from down on the bottom of the sea, if it wasn't weak reflections from the Milky Way's distant electricity that were rocking on the water's surface. Aft, the rubber dinghy was being manned with low-voiced laughter that immediately drowned into a gurgling roar. As the motor noise gradually sank away the weak sounds from the shore restaurants again grew, reggae on the other side of the sound. Between the stars' powder and the sea's breathing a sooty black strip of coast could be dimly seen, the harbor lights; the lighthouse glow from the pier at Spanish Town.

The powers were already in full swing. She was waiting on the foredeck, as she usually was, close to the bulging plastic bubble of the spinnaker hatch. I stretched out alongside. Her body was still warm, her nipples hot between my fingertips. She lay much too still, the poor cadaver. Who was she of all his versatile secretaries, always ready to play that role that was demanded of them; well-paid, guaranteed homogeneous, self-sacrificing prostitutes of the powers. But I didn't intend to let myself be duped so easily. Under no circumstances did I intend to spend the rest of my life in some federal prison in south Texas. I immediately winched up the anchor, let us drift a while, ride with the weak current. Only when Little Tone's keel began to touch bottom quite substantially did I realize how close to the island we were lying. I filled my backpack with the cans of exposed film, tied a plastic bag tight, tight around the mini tape recorder and sound tapes, hung the bag around my neck and pulled on my backpack, slid along the aft ladder down into the warm surf. In queen Caribbean's billows you float high and easy. On my back I headed in toward the beach with the backpack like a swimming bladder on top of my stomach, my left arm like a beating fin on the water surface, my feet like powerful propellers. The camera I held in my right mitt, stretched up as well as possible toward the stars above. I hit bottom almost at once and waded ashore with phosphorescent whirls around my legs.

Poseidon could kiss his sticky ass!

On the Atlantic side, outside of Virgin Gorda, The Dogs were washing their paws in turquoise. This they have done ever since their discovery during Columbus' second expedition. The name they got later, when pirates and freebooters controlled the sound and all islands both above and below the wind. They lie very far out, where Francis Drake Channel meets the open ocean. Extremely seldom do sailors steer there of their own free will. At a distance, from the crow's nest or deck, they look almost consummately inhospitable; small insignificant spots of sand under steep slopes, scorched vegetation of salt-parched thorny bushes and stiff cactuses.

Finally dawn arrived. More and more quickly it rose from North Sound and flamed in a stack of clouds above Biras Hill. The chance of any skipper getting the opportunity to make for and anchor below Eastern Seal Dog seemed, to say the least, minimal. In that case, what a surprise it would have been to run across a Swedish filmmaker there who had just finished a fairly long filming trip.

A good sea mile farther to the southwest George the Dog was swimming together with The Big Dog and The Cockroach in the weak morning current. There was a white foam around the muzzles where the broad surf is pressed in toward the cliffs' sharp teeth and wheezing throat. I took off my wet clothing and spread it out on slabs of rock that were quickly warmed up by the ever fiercer sunshine. Between a couple of substantial boulders I set up a piece of drift wood as a mast for my T-shirt. The camera looked completely okay, at least upon cursory visual inspection. No salt water splashed into the film cassettes. I didn't bother to check the other equipment. Indeed, the service department had to have something to do after our business trips too.

I climbed up as high as I could on the back of Seal Dog. Actually, the whole island consists of a single lopsided pyramid-shaped cliff. From up there Western Seal Dog seemed significantly more inviting, at least for somewhat longer visits under the trade winds. It lay several hundred yards away, connected to my island by a coral reef and the sandbank Little Tone bumped into during the night. Over there you could see verdant trees and shady bushes in the shadow of the windward side. But since my island faced the channel, I stayed there. When I climbed down the steep slope, I discovered a nice hollow that well deserved the name grotto. It could be a temporary residence while waiting for a rescue that probably had to occur as soon as the afternoon stream of ocean racers got thicker between the islands. With my hand I shielded my eyes against the sun's glitter in the southeast and looked out around the horizon; in vain I tried to catch sight of Little Tone's characteristic hull and sky-high rig. To the Rockefeller establishment straight south in Little Dix Bay there were at least three nautical miles. The old men certainly had made their way there after the exercises of the previous evening for a light supper with rum and Coca-Cola and wild calypso on the porch under the palms; it was certainly there that Woitek and Allen took her after they noticed that the sacrificial victim was missing on board. I actually forgot to check in relation to the North Star what course they were steering with the quiet diesel motor at a discreet, thumping, low rpm. Their foremost task was, of course, to avoid Little Tone's getting damaged; perhaps it was their only task. You often make the tools of the powers significantly more dangerous and inhuman than they as a matter of fact are, into the tallest mythical heroes of some sort of evil, the satanic idols of the darkness, when as a matter of fact they are just as much victims as the people they are appointed to guard or liquidate. But I had had enough wits in my skull and succeeded in avoiding a summary trial on the after-deck, the plank or the pathetic swinging from the front yardarm to the ridicule of passing frigate birds and swarms of curious flying fish.

I stretched out on my back awaiting a resolution. For the time being I couldn't do anything other than congratulate myself at having been born in history's hithertofore best as well as most humane of centuries. In any case, pirates no longer put dogs ashore on tiny islands where they in peace and quiet can get thin and run wild and sharpen their teeth while waiting for some passing captain Blackbeard to throw them a meal of difficult comrades or other savory malefactors to chew on.

Farther to the north night meets day. The shepherds drive the flocks homeward and call to the amber gatherers. There is an answer from the shores. Large ships take in supplies of bread as well as roots from up on the mountain. The passengers are gathered under trees that have just gotten their leaves. Many come with salmon frozen into blocks of snow or swimming in crowds beyond the high tides. They reluctantly talk about the sea, rather shut themselves in, in cabins where their eyes water from sour smoke. The presence of sail-makers and smiths stresses the longing that has driven them together. Nothing is more precisely known about their destination. The pilots are silent. The boatmen and experienced people do not willingly leave the harbor area. They shut in different stories in jars, seal them with wax and seals of silver. The arrival of the swallows and the cackling of snipes adds to the disquiet. There is untruthful mumbling about skirmishes and raids, rebellious gangs of youths who desecrate, blood sacrifice.

The tar burner works calmly on. He knows that no departure is possible before the tar pile has been emptied. The upkeep of the fire and the signs from the clouds speak the same language. Only when the liquid is clearer than the water of the mountain brooks can the time-consuming procedure begin. First they smear the oars. Rudder and mast need up to seven rubbings. The actual hull is covered with elk skin. The seals bark from the outer rocks. The launching and loading usually go amazingly quickly. No smoke, no mysteries, no hysterical scenes.

The actual drawing of lots takes place under a mood of almost cool objectivity. The one chosen usually gets several years to mature. It is always someone else who carries out the actual trip. Relatives who still remember do not like to converse about anything other than this time at sea. Some think that the procedure can be modernized without further ado and fitted to the demands of a new age. Those more closely affected remain silent. They know that careful study would show splices in the planking no asphalt can caulk. The exact point of time is difficult to determine. It is therefore wisest not to be alarmed. The temperature of the waves is in no way decisive. There are some who wait an entire lifetime, munch on oranges, make floating belts of cork, never leave their rooms.

Most travel in shallow water, without sails, until the sea freezes.

With reality thoroughly inventoried the only thing remaining is to invent dreams. The realities of the imagination are also worth taking very seriously. Actually, there are no borders between different spaces; they move into and out of each other in the same way as non-existent time imperceptibly moves on. If you are still young and beautiful, and, nota bene, these are factors that don't have anything at all to do with so-called age, then you only have to do as in the folk-tales when things begin really to go to hell: gather up your goods and head out into the world.

Naturally, what usually always happens in stories of this kind happened, the same old banal story about the boss and his much too pretty, much too young appetizing secretary. Long before director Kineman again got his pants back onto his suspenders and little sweet miss Tone had pulled her dress down from her narrow white waist, the two of them knew what had happened: he had become so perplexed and surprised by the strength when he came, and, moreover, it had been so delightfully beautiful, that he had totally forgotten to pull out before it was too late. Miss Tone realized from the first moment that she had succeeded 100% in her intent. Certain things you virtually feel from the beginning. Several months later there was a neatly growing fetus in its rightful place down in her stomach. Soon it would just be a question of time before the scandal would be revealed to everyone, including sweet dumb Hans Jörgen, who of course for the longest time imagined that nothing at all had really happened.

She carefully prepared the next step. She became an assiduous visitor to Copenhagen's many libraries. She absolutely devoured everything she could come across in the way of travel books and novels. From the travel bureaus she ordered brochures, she clipped newspaper articles and collected postcards, took home all of the office's diverse printed matter that director Kineman glanced through with a furious mien and later just tossed all of it into the waste basket with a disdainful snort: ach, that Hollywood is absolutely nothing for us; no, little Tone, it's really here in Denmark that we're going to make a star out of you!

One fine day she strode quite frankly into Hans Jörgen Kineman's room without even bothering to knock on the door. Without a word she handed over the paper from doctor Svendsen, pulled up her dress all the way to her breasts and stuck out her stomach a little extra. Already then she thought she knew everything, more than everything that would be needed for her coming life in the entire earth's new common mythical fantastic capital of moving pictures and celluloid strips. It lay in the middle of the most beautiful of all landscapes. There were snow-covered mountains and infernal deserts beyond, but verdant valleys too, rushing toward the ocean like before a meeting with an ardent lover. All the wonderful names: Santa Ana, San Bernardino, Ventura, Sierra Nevada, Santa Monica, San Gabriel, Mount San Jacinto , Mojave, Santa Barbara! The eternal summer, the flowers, the trees the cactuses. She was going to learn all of their correct names; the dry sunshine, the mild sunshine, the damp sunshine like a beauty cream against the cheeks; the light over the deserts, absolutely diaphanous over the mountains so that all distances were nullified. But also the catastrophes, rainfall that moves over the earth like soaking wet sheets and that when the mountains wring them out, fill the ravines with lethally gurgling torrents and tear with it everything that tries to check its ravagings; the hot wind that is heated up far in over Utah's distant desert regions and then just becomes more excruciating the closer it gets, finally like a terrible sirocco sweeps past Santa Ana and dries out everything, makes people crazy with desire or makes them desire to die.

Everything was still of course only words and mysterious names for her. She tasted them between her indescribably well-made-up lips, let them out into the room like exotic birds. Some time, soon, all of this was going to become reality for her, her senses would spill over from trees and flowers and bird song, soon everything would take shape for her, words become things, lights and shadows; she was going to sense the smells, pass over the sand, taste the sun-warmed grapes, listen to the surf, coalesce with the very softest sunshine.

Over and over again she repeated the strange words, like a conjuring magic rigmarole, all while she was writing letters or trying to get telephone conversations through to disobliging bank directors who were becoming more unwilling to give deferments on overdue loans. Chaparral, eucalyptus, sycamore she hummed while her fingers ran over the keys; buckeye, dogwood, ponderosa pine, deer horn cactus. Her vividly painted nails flew like flights of birds over the keyboard. All the flowers. She shut her eyes and already saw unending poppies, mile after mile of a thousand nuances of sunny gold and orange. The tall, swaying mustard of the plains shining like lemon or the breast of a canary. She is dancing barefoot along the beaches between purple ice ferns, fragile abronia and blue larkspur. Wild roses garland the cliffs, she knows that, light red mallows in the canyon that leads up from her grotto by the ocean. An intoxicatingly strong smell of wild lily, honeydew and honeysuckle there too. And after the warm rain shower, at the foot of green rolling hills: the air full of wild mint's drifting fumes.

She breathed in deeply, shut her eyes, clattered on without any longer caring a bit about what sort of unimportant letters she was writing. Soon, soon everything would yet become reality for her and the germ of a star that rested under her heart. For director Kineman the only thing that remained was to solve the practical problems. Thank god he still had a good deal of contacts within the shipping industry. Young Mr. Kineman cried when she left. As a farewell gift she got a funny little horse he had made entirely by himself, with a long neck, lacquered in the shining colors of the Danish flag. So sweet of him, and so big he had become! He got a pat on the cheek.

Before the winter weather completely blocked Öresund, the steamship Charlotte Amalie left Copenhagen, headed through the Kattegatt on out toward the North Sea, bumped into a drift ice floe and puffed thick black smoke toward the Bohuslän skerry. The cargo space was filled with meat for New York and contraband for the banana republics in the Gulf of Mexico; dynamite, canons and rifles for bandits, revolutionaries and dictators. The few paying passengers took their meals at the captain's table, obviously enchanted with the sweet girl who was serving them over the Atlantic.

In truth, many were the youths who at that time just like her headed over the ocean and then continued right across the continent on the snorting trains of the Southern Pacific or Santa Fe toward the Pacific Ocean, to provide material for the dreams of all of us. They could be named Victor or Greta or Tone. All were going to dress the sky with stars; some great, others small, a few almost invisible to the bare eye.

It was raining, gray and unpleasant, a rain that moreover only seemed to get heavier as the Boeing gradually descended over Pasadena and in a soft curve aligned itself with the runway. Wet streaks streamed outside the windows. I dried away the mist and looked at the checked pattern between the broad traffic lines on the freeways. It must have rained a lot, for you could see real running water in both the San Gabriel River and in the Los Angeles River which had been transformed into a concrete dike. As usual the senses failed; the farther down the plane came the quicker the realities were met, the plane's and the ground's, and as usual I could do nothing, stretched tight in the rapidly shrinking interval. My body tingles during bad weather landings, and I imagined that we came in much too low over Sepulveda Boulevard. The cars in the northbound lanes were sitting absolutely still or they were moving too. Besides, does it play any role at all for the story if I continue to hypercorrectly and truthfully describe the landing at LAX in this way? Naturally not. Obviously. Everything is indivisible and goes on constantly in one and the same place; it is like the actual kernel in life's complicated aesthetics, and thus it is differentiated from art's more primitive. The beautiful only appears here and there, as chance and lucky accident, fast frozen and immovable, surrounded by unhealthy halos, cheering sections and high priests. The possibility of getting to take part in the unique is limited to your own life, and, as is well known, it has an unpleasant capacity to shrink. Trivial experiences are evidently unjustly winnowed away from history to the benefit of the simply and solely spectacular. It is of course not so simple. Everything is there and spreading out, every experience is obviously one time but yet has always been experienced by others or will be; the hard thud on the landing strip, the rain drops that are reformulated, the braking engines, howling wheels, spanking sails below foreign coasts. Once we came to Troy with Agamemnon. Achilles stayed and many with him. I traveled on. To Los Angeles for example. Every little event refers backward and forward in a way that both mortgages history and crams the future full of sorrow and pride and honor, ridicule and defeat. At every arrival it turns out that the myth and the story already have been there with instructions and rules agreed upon ahead of time. It is more difficult to sneak past the queue or find other loopholes. One piece of luggage resembles another to the point of confusion. If you get the wrong suitcase, no great damage has occurred, the contents still no surprise. These circumstances mean, though, that every serious conversation about basic human freedoms and virgin undiscovered soils in the long run will be all the more ridiculous.

In the end everything is still a question of distance and nearness, at the same time, in space's assembling points; the very accidental work of art you are where you stand and walk and long to be discovered by someone else. Experience and intimacy indicate only one thing: the surprising extent of what is still possible, the non-existent interval between legendary and probable, where everything happens and you yourself finally become visible, take shape.

Anyhow, I rented a sky blue Camaro at the weekend price, stuffed the rest of my now quite worse for the wear equipment into the back seat and headed for a very special place between Venice and Santa Monica, where Pacific Avenue imperceptibly merges into Main Street. Around the clock an anything but encouraging neon sign is lit against the eternal stream of cars: No Vacancy. Whale's Wheel has been in all of my days a halfway decent, in plain language halfway indecent, but fully respectable and cheap motel at El Camino Real. Independent of bankruptcies and inflation the price of a room since the first time I came here at the end of the sixties has remained at eighteen dollars, plus the local tax current just now. Right across the street lies a fairly small police station which results in your being able to sleep quite securely, even if it is now often noisy in the adjoining room and there are plenty of loud, rapidly accelerating cars coming out of the parking lot. The area dilapidated and marginal, a heavily trafficked refuge for junkies and prostitutes. Thus, they looked at me with justified distrust and demanded payment in advance in spite of the fact that I had both an American Express card and my passport. The latter possibly looked a bit suspicious, still damp after the swimming tours in the Caribbean, the ink having run and the stamps rather indistinct. Nor did my reflection look especially confidence inspiring; sparse, reddish gray stubble, scaled-off forehead under flat gray wisps of hair, peeling nose between reddish eyeballs.

"I am coming straight from a deserted island in the West Indies where I met Robinson Crusoe."

I tried to sound credible since it actually happened to be true.

"No kidding," the person replied without condescending to give me even a hint of a smile. The man behind the glass window pushed out the key and returned quickly to the beer can and the baseball game on the TV screen.

I tossed my clothes into the laundromat alongside the empty, winter-filthy pool. There were still nasty cactus prickers in my arms and legs, and I tried to pull them out as well as possible before I showered away the rest of the Caribbean salt deposits.

Then it was high time to call up UCLA and announce my arrival. Doctor Dagny Shideler herself answered.

"Did you all have a nice trip," she wondered in the marvelous common Nordic dialect that distinguishes American academics with Scandinavian language and literature as a curious specialty.

"It has been hard-working and interesting," I lied truthfully.

"We were already beginning to get a little uneasy. It has happened before that foreign lecturers have been strangely prevented from coming or have simply disappeared. Our continent is clearly very full of all kinds of temptations and pitfalls, not the least for hyperborean innocents who have come so far."

A few ominous seconds of silence filled the receiver.

"I hope you realize that the lecture is at three o'clock this afternoon?"

I hemmed and hawed feigning agreement.

"You were a success in Texas."

"There are so many friendly cowboys there."

"We have posters up over the whole campus. The videotapes from the Swedish Institute are here on the table. And a bunch of richly colored propaganda material from the consulate. Is there anything else you need?"

"If so that would probably be me."

Her laugh was short and effective, as usual. Then her voice changed pitch, became significantly softer.

"Some letters came for you too. From your job, I presume. The family probably. And then one with an exciting aroma with Attn: on the envelope. Probably the same woman who has been continually calling here and asking for you. Most recently yesterday she made sure that this letter had actually arrived. She asked me also to convey to you that she had something from Ithaca that you certainly wanted by all means to have. Were you on Ithaca too?"

"I promise to tell you when we see each other."

"Bye bye, my boy!"

The cold sweat was creeping over my whole body. Two hours left! In two hours I would be standing at the lectern. With all my clothes out there in the machine going through the long wash cycle! I succeeded in pulling out my jogging pants and the T-shirt from Saint Thomas and wrung them out the best I could. On the way to Westwood I stopped at a new giant shopping mall in Santa Monica and used plastic for a gray suit with discreet silver threads woven into the material, complimented it with a salmon pink shirt together with a matching discreetly turquoise-colored tie. The show must go on.

"Today it is above all film and its slave under the triumphal chariot, television, that is managing the legacy after Baudelaire: his satanism is identical with the negatives of social conditions. World-weariness gives up and goes over to the enemy – the world! Reality takes over art. Nowhere can this be seen more clearly than in film. I have tried to point out how Baudelaire from the ground up shaped both Bergman and Buñuel. Television, however, can never follow up their grandiose pioneering work since modernism in its earliest theoretical formulations, Baudelaire's criticism of the salons, is colored by an exaggerated fatalism; the intimate relations of the new with death, with the city. Television is just naive and innocent compared with other experienced muses, prefers to devote itself to nature, false Rousseauism, bird-watching with telephoto lenses. But this protest against the city is so obviously reactionary. Critical art always has to be merged into what it opposes, criticizes. Therefore, Baudelaire had to forbid every nature image, and, therefore, film fails every time it seeks to deny him. Now perhaps you understand why I showed these pretty pictures, produced by Swedish television as a service to the public and thereafter distributed over the world by the state propaganda institute for the spreading of true pictures of Sweden. We are a very little country consisting mainly of molting wounded birds and elk hunters dressed in neon-red vests so as not to shoot each other to death. At the same time as film denies the city in favor of nature it is wasted, judged to fail artistically. Presumably it is here and now, without our even knowing about it, that a great new era is in the process of being born, in the Valley of the Dolls where Dallas' skyscrapers grow toward space and the Dynasties flourish; how unappetizing the mere thought of all this kitsch must seem to a chastened European. Messy witch-hunts and charges of decadence belong there, it strikes every really new art form, has done so in all ages, holds for all genres.

Everything new is a product of history. Baudelaire's poetry nothing other than the first really well reasoned passengers to our era, our art, film; the scenario of the promised society of goods and things. Sure, some still dream about the cranes' trumpets through the morning mist, about gray seals and black-backed gulls, I do it too; about heather tufts between violet pine trunks, a quiet picnic with basket and liquor and spiced cheese, monosyllabic feelings mumbled out of the beard, a glass of milk and a sandwich after intercourse. I have shown you these happy pictures from my exotic native land. Certainly, it is not the denial of silent realities that gets art to talk. The camera and tape recorder have become modern art's only sensible tools. You are the camera. And the obvious consequence, if you want to remain a human being, that your pictures should never tolerate anything that smacks in the least of harmless compromise. I conjecture that the same thing is true even for other art forms, poetry, painting, music. In this advanced company I now in conclusion ought to express myself in German; that would sound best, a proper North Central European and convincing. Thus: all true art's modernity, not the least film's and television's, lies in its mimetic relation to a petrified and alienated reality. Never let yourselves be captured by it. Thank you!"

I obviously compressed the point toward the end. There was both laughter and sporadic applause from the audience. Presumably it was because of my bad German.

"That shit talk about crane and elk burger always hits home over here," professor Shideler smiled with sincere spite and handed over the various letters. We sat in her puny office, and I breathed a sigh of relief after the lecture. She poured out some Bäska Droppar from a familiar liquor monopoly bottle, a dear souvenir from P. C. Jersild and Tomas Tranströmer who recently passed by on their acclaimed annual USA tour. You never really get away from your origins.

"Was there too much Adorno and Benjamin," I wondered.

"Just the right amount. Very impressive. Exquisite, actually. Acknowledgement or effect. You hit the precisely correct tone. My students in any case looked completely confused, and that is the best grade in this sort of connection. Skoal!"

The telephone interrupted. It gave me time to look through the letters. Astrid reported that the snow had finally melted, that Hans-Jörgen had smashed the car up a little, the she was going to organize a responsible section during the summer's archeological conference at Gamle Hamn, that she as usual hadn't had time to miss me but was still wondering whether and when I intended to come home. The envelope from Swedish Television contained a totally uninteresting compilation from the personnel division of attractive jobs outside the company they had applied for for me during my absence. The third envelope contained a ticket to that evening's premiere of "The Last Word Is Never Spoken" with a following champagne buffet at Spett's on Seventh Street. An obvious scent of wild spices and damp earth quickly filled the whole room. Dagny Shideler put down the receiver and sniffed interested.

"It's funny with smells; at once so mysterious and obscene, completely impossible to interpret. Many of our best structuralists have been driven to or rather over the edge of insanity in futile attempts to understand what they actually stand for. Yet it's such a simple matter."

She looked at me amused. The slightly preoccupied smile endowed her experienced face with a maenadic character, which at once though was split by millions of contemporary laugh wrinkles.

"To capture the aromas! In truth a mission for the most prosaic of artistic callings, that of the filmmaker. Or?"

Still another matchless laugh blew me out of my chair.

I don't want to say that I expected anything other than the usual old nagging play about the lousy relationships of the bourgeois in everyday life, thrashed over in a thousand variations ever since Aristophanes wrote down the actual original manuscript. All the way from the opening scene's simple "You're not working yourself to death, dear" to the final line's pathetic "Darling, I'm alive" over such profound remarks as "Darling, you think way too much about yourself" or "We, you and I, everyone, lover, have to talk much more to each other" as well as "If you don't give all you have, dear, the world will go under with you" applause from the festively-dressed premiere audience stormed down over embarrassed actors who had all the more trouble getting the play to hang together all the way to the stupid end of the spectacle.

In this manner it dealt with the copywriter who works his way through heart attacks and fits of apoplexy to a new life behind still larger desks with significantly more computers and telephones than in the first act's first scene. Everything took place behind a fine-meshed net which at the same time functioned as a curtain and as decor with the large table at the center, sometimes transformed into a sick bed or operating table, sometimes into a bar with appurtenant piano or into the ice rink at Rockefeller Center. Laser projections superseded one another on the fish net. The climax heightened almost catastrophically during the wheel chair ballet with the naked nurses, immediately thereafter reaching a culmination after the final lines: a single spotlight directed at the real sick bed, that the whole time has been standing in an out-of-the-way place on the stage as a prop. The supposed extra who has been lying completely dead still during the whole performance, got up out of the bed. Supported by a fully clothed, absolutely authentic medical orderly he tottered up to the net that was finally raised to the strains of Mahler's resurrection symphony!

The standing ovation never wanted to end.

The man in question was none other than the real person around whom the so-called play revolved. This performance about his life was the third stage in a carefully planned immortalization of him and which according to the program had already found expression in a feature-length film, a prize-winning TV documentary about "Life's Indomitable Courage" and in the fall an autobiography was going to follow as the main selection of the Book-of-the-Month Club.

To begin with, I assumed that Mary Lou or Pen or why not both of them were participating as dancers in the light-footed nurses' ballet. Now and then I thought I could identify a familiar movement, a gesture, a few quick steps. I soon gave up the game of recognition. Everyone's faces were identically made-up, presumably to better represent the eternal female; besides they were all equally undressed in short, short white jackets over skin-colored body stockings with nipples painted on gaudily and genital hair in the form of different colored tousled yarn balls sewn on.

The curtain calls thundered on in spite of the fact that the lights were finally turned up. I resumed my inspection, first of the women in the audience. The enthusiasm still showed no limits. I turned around. Methodically, I watched the closest sections of the half-circle shaped auditorium built up by steps. The closest ladies seemed far too broken up by emotion and, accordingly, completely unrecognizable under freely floating jewelry. A few looked at me angrily, presumably because I was so rudely turning my back to the center of ecstasy, the artistic marvel that had just begun to be played out on the stage: the principal actor carried forth on his strong healthy arms the sick reality. This one in his turn waved wildly to the audience with his healthy arm and finally asked for silence by raising the atrophied arm. After a short moment's expectant murmuring it became freakily silent. He was carrying a black book in one hand, possibly a bible.

A woman emancipated herself from the confusion on the stage. She carried out a microphone to the paralyzed man.

I immediately recognized her. There was no doubt about it. Frizzy nut-brown hair. The posture. The voice!

"We all know how important this day is for Ross. It is just as important for all of us. The last word as always will be yours. Ross!"

Of course, you had to believe your own ears and eyes, the usually trustworthy testimony of the senses. But the whole situation was so completely improbably tasteless. It resembled more and more the salvation meetings at Villa Japan where you'd sneak in as a little boy when it was Good Friday and there was still nothing to do for several days while waiting for our holy cinema temple to begin operating again with the matinee on Easter Monday. But not only the yearning for the seats where we worshipped Errol Flynn and Olivia de Havilland got us to go there and seat ourselves in the half darkness. You had to resort to every conceivable ruse to survive, be resurrected, not totally die in the flower of your youth because of the dismal excesses of the Easter weekend, unfortunately filled more by unappetizingly runny soft-boiled eggs or meaningless visits to relatives than by delicious marzipan chickens and tasty sweets.

It felt the same as then. The bursting point came ever closer. Finally, it was no longer possible to restrain yourself. Choking from laughter up in the half-dark gallery we stuffed our mouths full of handkerchiefs so that we almost suffocated in order to prevent the worst outbreaks of guffawing face to face with the sanctimonious eyes of the preacher and the growling hush-hushing of the old ladies.

With greatest difficulty the hero pressed out his hissing testament:

"I love you all. Take care."

The auditorium exploded! In the following tumult there was not a sporting chance of getting down to Pen. In any case, I bravely tried to fight my way forward to the stage without for a second losing sight of her with my eyes. My progress was stopped abruptly by brusque punches, dealt out by a tuxedo-clad gentleman whose wife's long sweeping skirt happened to get twisted around my vehement advance with the result that I tore off her cloth sheet all the way down to the bare blue-veined legs. Some laughed hysterically. Sunk down on the nearest seat I felt strongly like going along with it.

Culture assumes different expressions everywhere. That is presumably the very meaning of it. For that matter, all art doesn't necessarily need to be especially splendid or significant to be effective according to aesthetic categories well-known for centuries, whether they be ancient Aristotelian or more familiar Kantian. Shouts of joy, rhythmically rattling thunders of applause. The air shall be cleansed, chaos conjured up. The masses moved. Comedies have happy endings; Hollywood was a neighbor to both chaos and God.

Like madmen, all the people were rushing from the salad bar's greenery and early-ripening vegetables to the juicy pieces of meat on the spit, between iced platters of smoked salmon and oysters and abalone, pressing warm onion-impregnated pieces of bread into one hand at the same time as they were picking up strawberries from the creamy cakes with the other. Most strange to watch yet was the supreme way in which the drinks were managed: a thousand hands literally flew between sparkling champagne bottles and over trays where empty glasses continually were exchanged for newly poured bubbly-filled ones. A thousand lips expressed themselves around the fragile edges of the champagne glasses in a whirling dance along the buffet table's constantly reborn piles of delicious proteins and magnificent carbohydrates. Sweaty upper lips, creamy corners of mouths, dripping chins, greasy finger tips, liquid eye shadow, widened nostrils, puttied-up pores, butterfly smiles, raptorial birds' cheeks, fish eyes. I swept around a couple of mad revolutions before I finally succeeded in grabbing an edge of the table and clinging fast in the protection of a pillar shaped like an elephant leg.

A thousand and one nights. Babylon. The thieves of Bagdad. Byzantium. Hansel and Gretel. Little Red Riding Hood. Puss in Boots. The Mark of Zorro. The Black Pirate. Playboy. Hustler. Out there in our field. Flowering season. Suddenly and inexplicably a homesickness lump in my throat. I wasn't beginning to seriously get old?

"Lost perhaps?"

"Hope not. Waiting for someone."

"For my part, I hope I never get found again."

"Then we can keep each other company for a while."

He laughed noisily and friendly. It felt really relaxing to join in. Very un-American-like he stretched out his fist and introduced himself. Emery. I realized at once why he wanted to go and hide himself; he was supposed to write about the terrible performance for tomorrow's Los Angeles Times. Not without reason he looked quite distressed at the thought of this, supported his chin on his intertwined fingers while he watched the wild crowd with amused circumspection. In some way he didn't seem to belong here. Middle-aged, just like me. His eyes pale green, candid and open under his eyebrows, his reading glasses were hanging halfway down on a straight nose; his ears were small and alert, his tongue well whetted between close white teeth. His chin and cheeks covered by a thin beard. His neck was long and narrow and sinewy. There couldn't be room for an ounce of excess fat on the rest of his well-trained body, which was concealed by a well-cut, powder blue and certainly expensively tailored suit. I felt like a clown in my idiotic attire. Briefly I explained why I looked the way I did.

After he calmed down, his voice got back the mild stress that the funny accent gave his speech.

"That explains things. Wondered just what you were doing down here. You came to the right place without knowing it. I escaped too. Judging from your attire I thought you belonged with the fine folks upstairs instead of with the congenial riffraff down here."

He gestured up toward the ceiling. It consisted of thick glass and narrow steel beams. You looked right up into the floor above. Shoes were observable and whirling legs that disappeared into ambiguous bodily obscurity.

He explained the situation. At every premiere it is very important that the right audience is invited in so that the right laughs come where they should, as well as the sobs and cries. The correct reaction almost always affects the wretched critics who populate the newspapers' theater pages. The producers stop at nothing to assure their products' success. The target group this time was people in advertising with heart conditions but still surviving. Since the lousy drama was played out in New York, they had chartered a jumbo jet from there and flown in three hundred and fifty persons from the big bureaus on Madison Avenue. Presumably, most of them knew personally the main person and were besides no doubt in one form or another involved in dumping money into this very artistic project.

"You don't believe me? Just wait until you meet my wife. You see it is she who is behind this special arrangement. She will be here soon. Sooner or later she begins to look for me to take me up to heaven from all the sweet guys and dolls, the stage hands and make-up women, congenial underlings from the TV studios, the extras and the gossip columnists who still haven't qualified for the upper floor."

I looked around. It had calmed down significantly; it was possible to survey the happy blend. People were chatting in groups or strolling around one by one, sitting at the bars or around small tables and checking each other out. Same sort of people as at home. The new culture-bearers, in jeans and cast-off curtains; broad-shouldered, narrow-hipped social climbers, agelessly youthful and ancient.

He swept up his glass and grabbed a couple of new ones from a passing tray, handed a third to me.

"I see. You're an old European. On the way home. To what, if I may ask? I myself remained. Just like Odysseus' companion. Perhaps you remember that there was one who chose rather to stay as a pig with Circe than return to a lousy stone castle close to home. I'm doing just fine. Can even imagine dying here. Why explode in Oxford or Paris, put to bed in Lacan and Lyotard and Bakhtin and Bataille? Yet, I will never manage to make head or tail of the damn civilization process going on here. It would take a new Rabelais for that, at the very least. Or art like this shit we saw this evening. Was it so damn bad, by the way? You have to think about your future! Skoal!"

He was staring hard at something behind my back. A strong smell of spices was mixed with all the bodily vapors. I didn't need to look around to know who it was.

"Could just imagine that you two out of everyone here would find each other!"

A hat as big as a mill wheel adorned her head.

We got up politely, looked first at each other with a certain wonderment, then at her quite intensively.

"Darling, you see, this is that nice Swede who showed us around on Ithaca. Did I actually forget to tell you about him?"

I had arrived.

She stretched out a chamois-gloved hand to be kissed.

The intermediate position is missing, both the inner one and the outer one; the only thing remaining was to weave the pastorals into the big cities. Most of those involved seemed rich and powerless. The choice consisted either of remaining a hero or burying yourself below the earth. The possibility of developing into a wholesome and generally accepted insect seemed absurdly remote. No one had time any more to pursue the country's temptations or monotonous hymns to nature. People who went around in work clothing and hummed lacked the self-expanding dynamo that was required in the new metropolises. Simplest would be to go up into pure energy. Fast cars already reach mystical speeds. No one any longer seriously tried to stop the development. Many foundered under the press of aesthetic categories, others because of brilliant intentions that burst. Earlier on didn't exist. Mythomaniacs didn't bother. Grateful dead returned from romanticism and flooded the block with intimate peeps. Everyone touchingly agreed. Rock's backbeat wasn't at all remote from Don Juan's hip-swaying aria, the music the only thing that gave a remote understanding of what was going on. Yet the terminals were filled with the ashes from bored travelers. The dream of returning matured into a realistic possibility. Chairmen of boards changed places on a scale of almost tragic intensity. Many maintained openly that only exaggerations lead to necessary worldly wisdom. Two hundred years' steady romanticism didn't modify the world order. Drugged with technological sexuality anyone could go out on heroic charter trips. Repeated composting liberated holy figures who after a time voluntarily left with the divine accuracy of dreams.

No one can be surprised if under such conditions you began to claim that all knowledge issued from old women, shepherds or retired assassins. But even skillful surgeons, joint caulkers and good veterinarians were sought after. In a grove, a bold expedition found eggplants and love apples. However, many who sampled bittersweet honey far too early died slightly irritated. Some children attained their own freedom and flung themselves out into life to the horror of the big cities. Civil authorities increased control, military units were allowed to use dry death. Hardly anyone dared believe that the transcendental order was shaken.

Far out on the edge of the cliff lay the old baseball field, surrounded by a high net that once caught the really long home runs and prevented the balls from being transformed into birds, carried by updrafts from the precipice out over the ocean. A wheelless Lone Star Truck was resting on rusty axles in the grass; here, but no farther. I drove on along Paseo del Mar and parked on the side of the road on the hard dusty clay, right at the place she had suggested; quite close to the sign that pointed toward Royal Palm Beach. Walk down to the shore, it is so pretty there, she said. That was the only instruction I got. Now I was here. Early joggers and morning cyclists in gaudy costumes streamed by. It had been a long time since I had gotten some decent exercise myself. I was seized by a sudden and strong desire to give up the whole damn undertaking, join their happily jabbering groups and just disappear from the assignment. But it felt like something important was close at hand. The air was sweeping up from the ocean, temptingly sour, almost smarting in the nostrils. I did as she had said, walked down the steep hill to the beach that was still whiling in deep morning shadow. The slope was very steep. It really caused my calf muscles to stretch. Halfway down a police car passed with rolled-down side windows. Hi, I said and smiled benignly as I had learned you should do to American policemen. I looked just as innocent as I actually was, and, indeed, one of the mountains of muscle leaned out, stuck his thumb in the air and answered: pretty weather, real nice!

A last serpentine curve flattened out the road toward salt-parched palms, barely surviving, jammed in between the cracked pavement of the parking places, old tank traps from the last world war, fallen rocks and the coarse dirty brown strip of sand. Some cars were parked between the trunks. Outside a rusty house trailer some sport fishermen were getting their long supple rods ready. An older couple was rooting around in garbage cans and looking between the rocks for beer cans that they stuffed down into huge plastic bags. Keep California Clean beamed from their neat college sweat-shirts in pink letters. The old folks' legs were so thin that they were rattling in their shorts. I was afraid that they were going to fall over at any moment.

So this is where you came on the right occasion, to the wild, fashion-able swimming pool far out in the sea, below Palo Verde's green hills where steep cliffs met the surf, where you saw whales go by and the sea otters still heedlessly playing and tumbling with slim, happy human bodies in the shiny seaweed. Those two could very well have been around at that time. The coast in any case was the same.

Oily and shiny the sea stretched all the way out to Santa Catalina. Icy blue and unreal, the island floated on the horizon. Zones of wind watered the surface where the clouds were not reflected. Some early sailboats defied the morning calm. A long, low oil tanker rumbled in toward Long Beach, beyond Point Fermin. Halfway toward the point I again met the police car. After having accomplished a round of patrolling along the strip of beach it braked in front of me! Not one single time earlier had it stopped to chase away all the cars illegally parked over night, certainly filled to the roof with illegal Mexican immigrants or criminally under-age copulating lovers, want-ed mafia members and counter-revolutionaries from Nicaragua. I strolled on as if nothing had happened. I shouldn't have done that! The car backed up even with me with squealing tires and a short siren howl. For safety's sake I stopped.

"Stranger here?"

I nodded. Dark curly hair swarmed on the beefy forearm that was hanging down along the door. Entirely without cause, my heart rate began to increase. His dark sunglasses reflected my presence, dwarfed and de-formed, like in the funny house; although it wasn't a bit funny. You should always appear well mannered toward unknown American policemen, even at the most insignificant traffic offense.

"From Sweden," I explained, as if it were some sort of extenuating circumstance. My pulse increased.

His colleague leaned forward from the wheel and stared with a grin. Since both were still sitting there in the car, my crime if any could hardly be of the more serious sort. I got my courage up.

"Sir, have I done anything illegal?"

He snorted.

"Pal, you have just won a beer from me. We bet that only a complete idiot or foreigner would park his car up there and walk down to the shore of his own free will; the hill doesn't exactly get less nasty when you are going to go up again, I guess?"

I glanced up at the deep blue sky above the cliff. Large sea birds were hovering on broad wings. Still higher up a jet plane on the way to Asia was drawing white streams between high cirrus clouds.

"By way of thanks I'm going to offer you a lift up. Then you can drive your car down and avoid the uphill slope."

Both of them grinned in a friendly way. I thanked them for their friendliness and quickly allowed my heart to resume its normal place in my chest cavity. After a while they stopped again and talked with a jogger on the way down to the beach together with a couple of huge dogs on long leashes.

I continued out toward the point. Everything was exactly as she had described it: the asphalt road turned into a walkway that finally became a path between eroded fallen-down sandstone rocks. All the way out, a narrow sand spot with the remains of coals and ashes after a camp fire of gathered drift wood; a little up under the steep slope the cave could be dimly seen, partly hidden behind a low cactus curtain. Still higher up between the overhanging crumbling cliffs sharp bushes as shiny as leather and stout climbing plants were fighting for space for branches and dangling aerial roots.

The flat rocks gently slipped down into the sea, the one below the other. The reflections from the bedrock and the sky colored the water surface in gold and lilac. The sunlight began to blind. I shut my eyes, listened, smelled, peered, shut my eyes again. Time doesn't exist, I thought, as usual with a certain emphasis. So much in my life has been based on just that possibly unreasonable thought. Only space, growing, shifting terrains, movement, directions. Everything can be produced from everything; a tone, an aroma, an isolated word, the moment houses the entire reality.

Time doesn't exist, just the space of the senses.

You will understand, just see to it that you are in place; so it was said.

I sat down on a large rock. The beer can gatherers passed. Through the morning silence could be heard the light hollow sound or rather the rattle of aluminum in their well-filled transparent bags that they were dragging after themselves up the steep ravine. It is expensive to get old in the land of eternal youth. A dollar is a dollar is always a dollar. And a bag full of beer cans is in the end quite a few beautiful dollars for a poor retiree.

The sport fishermen were in no hurry. Slowly, extremely carefully so as not to slip, and with their buckets full of bait, they were moving along the cliffs which were slippery from seaweed. Farthest out at the edge of the cliff the group dispersed. They took up their stations, one after one, in places that seemed to be theirs for centuries. The long rods were swaying like antennas ready to receive a message from every charged gust of wind, every sign from the depths.

The jogger came much closer. She was no longer running, was rather dancing ahead like some of Botticelli's minor figures. It was a young girl who was holding her dogs on shorter leashes to get by me down to the little snippet of sand. I swung my legs away and let her pass. She immediately let the animals loose. They rolled around happily in the sand, fought with huge paws in the air, playfully growling they bit at each other with gargantuan jaws. I noticed that she gave me a quick glance after a few more playful pirouettes between the dogs. Finally they calmed down with gentle strokes and soft words, were put on their leashes again and she fastened the leather straps around her thigh. After yet another check in my direction she pulled out a blazing yellow grapefruit from her waist pouch and began to peel it. But nor for herself! Segment after segment was tossed to the beasts. Clear juice dripped along their black-lobed lips.

With a weak thrill along my spine I realized who she was. The messenger. The dogs were the sign; everything so idiotically simple to understand. Great Danes. Grand Danois. The thin wreath of smell when she passed, weaker than that of mature goddesses, of course, but unmistakably the same. Something indefinitely pungent was floating in the air between us; which actually didn't at all fit with the preconceived notion you can have about the smell from half-grown up girls quickly coming into flower.

Partly sunk down in the ocean the fishermen stood like statues, ultra rapidly swinging their rods, fishing lines, hooks. The girl took a couple of quick steps toward me, the dogs followed along; one on each side. Still, there was nothing frightening about the situation. It was somehow obvious that she handed over a thick envelope:

"So you who are uncle Hans Jörgen."

She spoke almost perfect Danish! First she smiled when she saw my surprise but immediately put her hand in front of her mouth to hide the smile, as if she were embarrassed because of it and it actually didn't have any business being on her face, just there and just then. She bit hard on one of her fingers presumably to ward off an approaching laugh. Did I look so damn funny? With her other hand she pushed away little curly nut-brown wisps of hair that were continually falling down over her eyes. Frankly and openly she looked at me, without for a second taking her eyes off mine; without the slightest fear, of course, with those bodyguards.

Then her hand fell down. The seriousness could again be seen around her transparent lips. She took hold of the dogs' leashes and jerked. The muscles tightened under the skin on their narrow backs; one lifted its front paw and began to scratch in the sand. Out of the corner of one eye I glimpsed the lines of the sport fishermen, out of the other how the old couple was dragging themselves out of the ravine through the baseball field's broken wire fence. Reality at least seemed to be partly in place.

The little girl was dressed in cherry-colored jogging pants and a deeply cut T-shirt on which glowed OLD DANISH BEAUTY PARLOR in faded red. From absolutely nowhere a butterfly came and sat down on a fluttering trinket on her throat. But it immediately wobbled on in the breeze up toward the rock wall's flowers. She lifted her face, followed its flight. Now the smile was again there, broad mouth, narrow lips, thin eyebrows; remarkably deep wrinkles at the corners of her mouth gave character and a semblance of experience to an otherwise quite everyday face. Possibly she had put on a thin layer of rouge between her cheekbones and ears. Her lips were brown under the thin skin.

I got up and stepped forward with outstretched hand and boldly kept it extended even though the dogs immediately began to growl and their tails move with short, energetic jerks. She retreated so that she ended up behind her bodyguards. One hand held the dogs short, the other dug into the jogger's pouch and produced from nowhere a little camera. She squinted with her right eye and snapped it off. "That was it."

My sweaty hands found my pockets.

"And I am supposed to be your uncle?"

Her face tightened up.

"Your name is Hans Jörgen, isn't it? If not, I beg your apology a thousand times."

She paused and loosened the leashes from her thigh. Almost sternly she continued:

"Otherwise, I must ask to get back the letter. At once."

The dogs had very free lines now, sniffed and moved gravely toward me, like a movable emblem from the god-filled Baroque epoch.

"You can be calm, very calm. Little girl, certainly I am your real uncle.

Hans Jörgen Kineman. The one and only. And you?"

"Malou."

Attn: HJ; written with round jerky letters. I moved the thick envelope up to my nose. It was from there the smell was coming; not at all from the girl who now suddenly, without a word of departure, began to jog back the same way she came. I considered rushing after her, but the dogs were again loose. Besides, the police car had returned, parked at idle on the beach ramp under the dusty palms. She stopped and chatted, patted the dogs who whimpered friendly, jumped up against the car doors and licked the officers' arms.

With my back to the sun-warmed cliff I opened the letter. It contained two things: a videotape and a couple of pages in small print. The cassette's label was made in a stylistically pure, somewhat old-fashioned typographic design: The First Man. The protective case of black plastic looked new and unused. I turned it over. On the backside a shiny silver piece of paper was glued on. In embossed letters, like on a credit card, could be seen a multi-digit code number as well as the text printed in small letters Official Proof of Entry to the Old Danish Beauty Parlor. The numbers got me to flinch a bit. My own social security number!

Something with a familiar scent vibrated in the distinctive aroma from the envelope, but what: I sniffed several times before the smell was completely drowned out by a gust filled with the sweet strong stench of seaweed. Salty beads of sweat in the fold under the breasts? Baby shit, bulging pussy? Spicy shore meadows? No, fresher, like after a sourish morning dip or from newly scrubbed skin in the hollow of the back; sun-dried braids in wisps over the shoulders, dewy grass in the crotch.

I read:

Dear stranger and half-cousin. I at least owe you an explanation and an apology, at the very least. It was unforgivable to steal the roll of film. I still don't understand what sort of Dionysian delirium got you to take us in that way. You yourself know best, that certain pictures can never be developed, sequences of events and spaces that no one would even understand the meaning of. For that simple reason, that the apparent reality which was seemingly exposed, in all of its infamous sharpness, simply belongs among the great thoughts that frame the world, over and over and over again. Our professions have as their only task to gather the sparks of light that are left over from the illusory world we all share, smouldering in the mirror shards around us; you as a camera, I as the object of your pleasure, your desire – the eternal star of truth.

If I told you my correct name, you would still never believe me or otherwise you would blush so sweetly and embarrassed that you would still only want to die or explode in another way from rage. For your pictures of me would certainly have made you a famous man. Or at least wealthy!

That's the way it is. Recently a star succeeded – I don't exaggerate when I say that the star was in the order of magnitude of the supernovas – in tearing herself loose from all the heavenly mass-medial attention, the un-abashed fiddling of the erect telephoto lenses. She ran away to some islands she had always wanted to visit. But what happens to her aboard the ferry between Patras and Ithaca? Yes, her best friend and boy-crazy companion comes along dragging a fresh sacrifice victim, a winter-white middle-aged intellectual type of undoubtedly Nordic origin, without the least difficulty picked up outside the boat's garlic-reeking third class restaurant. To be sure, I love that girl – everyone does, but there I could actually have killed her on the spot. Some the gods punish right away. And she has really had to work hard to straighten out this affair, which could have become as painful as possible, for all involved. Sorry mostly, of course, for the thin-haired type who fell into our hands. On closer inspection he turned out to be a very ordinary, charming, educated, and modestly attractive guy; besides, as luck would have it, to a mild degree so unaware, or innocent or from another world, that he apparently didn't have the least idea about what big game he had in front of himself. Totally harmless we thought too. But, hello, how we were fooled! Suddenly he was transformed into a slavering wild animal, without warning armed with an ancient 16mm Arri, zooms in on us and re-veals his real ego behind the polished facade: the documentary film-maker's ugly snout rooting around in all sorts of mythological shit. So nice to meet a star there! And then we all kept a good face in a wicked performance during several strange days with earthquake, rape, incest, theft; all in the best Olym-pic style. Can you ask for more from a happy vacation, on Greek islands? As you certainly can understand it never happened!

Pen has kept me closely informed about your latest doings. As usual she did a splendid job; that is a valuable girl. Now it is finally my turn to reenter the game, before she gets too fond of you again. New pictures are to be obtained this evening. Don't forget the cassette, otherwise you will be stopped right at the door. And don't forget the password to the very inner-most: Tone sent you!

The address?

You'll certainly find it. You with your nose for books!

Center and periphery are absorbed into each other. At a long distance, in a wide perspective, from up high or deep beneath, everything falls together. As if someone consciously amuses himself by framing the whole in over-explicit structures and thereafter leaves it to its fate. If you get closer, then it turns out every now and then that this so-called reality isn't fully so simple and surveyable as it first seemed. It suffices for a short while to open up near-sighted eyes from pedagogically disposed atlases or colorfully arranged historical accounts to realize that life thrives better in bloody throbbing chaos than in cosmically transparent ether. For millennia, philosophers and all kinds of so-called scientists have lived well by chewing on these obvious relationships. Still, after all of these thousands of years there isn't much consensus, or the common vision that someone called it, in these existential questions. In any case, if you really take the pains to stare more closely into people's consciousnesses and look at what actually stirs there.

For example, and first of all: is it one and the same reality that is in question, is it yours or mine that counts or is there a third?

Secondly: you or I who independently enters us into history, or someone else who enters us; who quite superbly edits, puts things right, cuts the strips of life as he wants, rearranges, makes double copies, dissolves, pushes in necessary extra effects and strange background music in the final mix? Puts the finished copy in an appropriate folder to await shipment, allows the digitally punched file card to remain in the computer catalogue?

Thirdly: ancient silver thins out on shrinking black and white rolls. The colors die out implacably in cool casemates. The videotape demagnetized by overzealous archive workers. The paper in voluminous novels decomposed into its chemical parts because of economic demands. Will anyone remember, will there be anything to remember? Pictures dissolve, the figures vanish into thin air. But, if every detail is just as important for the unfinished narrative as all the links in the DNA chain for your life, then who has the responsibility for the accelerating devastation? The last man? The first?

The irritation in the clam, in the membrane's fine secretion between muscle and shell, gives birth in due course to the pearl. This also occurs far to the north, strangely enough; outside of exotic Baltic islands, in the sea under the seals. From Salvo Reef it carried stirred-up currents after a hard northwester onto Norsta Aura's beach. Glimmering cool mother of pearl. On fire, it burns an invisible hole between meandering lifelines in the palm of the boy's hand, to fill with longing. He carries it with himself through landscape and cities, the form, the invisible formula for all the beautiful in life. Mystery. Hiding place and memory.

At the same time, light years away, space belches, spews gravel and specks of dust out of its throat; everything is still intervals, moments. That they later on played with a magnifying glass and telescope has in no way facilitated intelligibility. Still everything overlaps, a paradoxical grimace in the star of timelessness. Then it is just a matter of being there. But, even if no one will recognize himself, you can be certain that there will always be some presumptuous type who possesses the absolutely most natural explanation.

Once and for all inscribed in copper, engraved on dusty plates well-hidden among the sealed briefcases in sleepy cabinets, the hand raised in an archaically sensitive gesture, with inflated shiny cheeks enthroned on the oils in the museums' proud halls: the old whore Notoriety, the harlot Honor, the hooker Celebrity never give up. Envy and Gossip quarrel as never before at her feet; everyone feels invited to the party. The stench around Fame is the same, the sounds as well, but the instruments different; bassoons and the clinging bell-pieces of the trumpets replaced by well-programmed synths. Everything is recognized. The forms easily recognizable under the shifting market conditions of fashion, History's faithful lackeys and weapon bearers: statues, paintings, engravings, photographs, films, videotapes; the same old perfidious messengers. the unique has become shabby celebrity, the voyeurs have a look at each other, the cunts ruffle up, the cocks fit in. The star light is darkened by the brightness of searchlights. The heavens turn aside while the laser draws new star pictures, new names in the sky, creates phantoms out of nothing.

History's metamorphoses tell a lot about the desire to be different and an absolutely ordinary John Doe at the same time, famous but still the same sweet girl in the neighboring house. In the most reliable fairy tales it turns out bad for the one who tries to be someone other than the shepherd boy he is in spite of everything. The frogs don't at all grow in the trees. Besides, what happens with the myth's heroes is often so disgusting that it is not even possible to put it on television without common sense beginning to howl for censorship. The self-confident one aspires to embrace both himself and the audience, great or small, the family's bosom and the electronic screen's rays. The everyday is chock full of entertainers with a thousand shifting roles, all at the same time hams and spectators, parquet and stage flow together into a single protracted soap opera between nine and five, through tiring night shifts in overhead cranes under the foundry's roof, in the sighing halls of the nursing home. This has absolutely nothing to do with personal satisfaction. Only outer attention counts. The correct hour's correct behavior, even our own temperament's brakes screech.

What is Honor, happy Falstaff questions and answers himself: a word. Today he would presumably have added, a picture.

The idols evaporate. The playing fields, mirror fields become empty.

So blink little star there, while you can; before the copper gate closes!

The car ran leisurely northward along Sepulveda Boulevard. The signs pointed down to Redondo Beach or up to San Diego Freeway. Gradually the window displays grew denser around the airport. The way home. Long before he reached Imperial Highway he had decided. Now it was going to come off, now he was going home. He turned into the terminal and booked a seat on the flight the following morning, checked out of the motel and went on down to the general consulate at Wilshire; sent a telex with flight number and arrival time so that the transport department could pick him up at Arlanda, thanked them for all the help and bother with his equipment; asked them to say hello to his brother in Washington. They promised to do it.

Not without certain difficulty he packed all of the equipment into the trunk so that it didn't have to lie in the back seat and entice a break-in. It was already afternoon and the stream of vehicles was getting thicker on the way down toward Santa Monica; the parking prices scandalous on the vacant demolition sites where newly built condo skyscrapers with guaranteed ocean view were soon going to shoot up or futuristic shopping cathedrals of glass and concrete would become ever wider, garnished with plastic and neon.

What a change since the first time he was here to depict the young California generation of the white freedoms and the black revolts, the flowers in the rifle muzzles, the pot dreams floating over pillows and mattresses in the small rooms, the clenched fists and flaming fires in Watts; the awakening out of the previous generation's lethargy, the earnest games, the flirting and sniffing between the sexes that at the same time changed over into their antitheses, militant feminism and armed gays. At that time all of the older environments were still around to be depicted. The camera wandered around between the run-down restaurants of the forties and the bars where refugees from the old world, the Europe of fascism, gathered in groups around Schoenberg and Brecht and Mann; there were even all the thousands of unknown or forgotten emigrants; the low bungalows of the twenties along the palm avenues, the pleasure piers, the innocent massage parlors and illicit brothels where you went down in your Bugatti or ordinary old Ford to have a good time after hard days of work in the studios.

Now everything was as if completely vanished. Even the new pedestrian street was already in the process of decaying in the shadow of the most recent growing castle, the shimmering glass monstrosity of a shopping mall. Gone all the wonderful houses that had been decaying at a humane rate, antique stores and billiard parlors, 24-hour cafes, bike shops, pawn shops and barber shops, seventh class hotels, friendly drunks and old whores who usually offered something to drink both before and after. Instead, trendy high fashion boutiques, architectural offices, computer repair, bank branches, armed guards, police patrol cars, surveillance TV's.

But the wind was the same, rustled in the hanging flakes of bark on the eucalyptus trees, in the overgrown coconut palms' green herringbone curtains along Ocean Avenue where unpleasantly pushy squirrels were still fed bread crumbs by the very last silver-haired old people. The new era's joggers strutted past smelling of perfume in glossy togs with their eyes far away and their ears filled by a thump thump suitable for running from handy fashionably colored cassette players, dangling on thin threads from their waists.

He walked from telephone booth to telephone booth. Finally he found one with a fairly complete copy of the Yellow Pages left and checked under the rubric Beauty Care. He called up. Beep. An ordinary answering machine voice reported that unfortunately all of the day's times were already filled but suggested nevertheless a personal visit, in the event of possible cancellations. Or leave your own telephone number and address for later contact. Beep.

The address given, 106 East Third Street, shouldn't be too far away, about where the shore drive from Malibu turns up the steep hill and merges with the I-10 freeway in toward the center of Los Angeles. The problem was just that the parlor in question had clearly been swallowed up by all the stylish halls of Materialism. After an hour's desperate zigging through over-glassed galleries into the yawning abysses of department stores he discovered here and there that old signs had been preserved, hopefully in the vicinity of the original placement. Besides, there were ingeniously incomprehensible information signs set up for strangers unacquainted with the surroundings, and many seemed to be just that, where all levels of the building were de-scribed, super-imposed in three dimensions and slightly displaced in rela-tion to each other, so that you could understand all the more clearly on what floor and, for example, where the various Beauty Salons were located. The architect of the sales castle had obviously been carried away by the dream of succeeding to inscribe a star in a sphere, in spite of the fact that the orders naturally were first and foremost to produce a profitable combined depart-ment store and parking pavilion. From this collision between economic reality and artistic vision, this muddle of cars, merchandise, people and talkative cash registers had been born. The central square was the obvious center of the crowd, the pulsating heart of the dragon, where sooner or later all checks and bills ended up in strategically well-placed bank branch offices.

Right there, pressed in between the armor-plated steel and glass win-dows of First Califorina Bank and City Bank, is an amazing anomaly; a sim-ple paneled gable juts out a few yards on the hard plastic marble floor. Either the original color is flaking quite a bit or, otherwise, some versatile master of the art of trompe l'oeil has produced a late monumental work. Two steps lead up to a deep green gate with accompanying door clapper of worn yellow metal; above, a well-centered miniature window with black-painted eyebrow marks. Windows with small panes on each side, hung with thin pleated curtains that effectively prevent every unwarranted observation. On the right doorpost the numbers 106 are screwed on, possibly original, weather-beaten verdigrised copper plate, otherwise even more evidence of masterly fakery.

Hans Jörgen Kineman hesitated below the high glass roof dome, close to the fountain with the odd caramel-colored water. Complementary colors continually merge with their opposites, suddenly everything becomes gray for a few seconds before the whole coloratura is played back in constantly new variations of richly-toned color arrangements. Muzak out of invisible loudspeakers provides contrapuntal accompaniment with gentle modulations and increasingly tranquil rhythms. Round about, people of all ages and skin colors were sitting and just staring at this magnificent work of art, stuffing themselves with huge ice creams, slurping ice slush with a weak coca-cola filling, throwing quarters into the fountain and wishing for even more money to buy things with and carry out to the station wagons.

Finally, he summoned up his courage, wriggled out of the grip of the soporific sound gruel and trudged up to the door with firm steps, turned the handle and stepped in.

Everything, of course, looked just like you might expect in such a place; rooms filled with small booths and screens where good-looking young men and women made other – if possible – even more beautiful and at least on the surface just as young women and men comfortable. The mirrors reflected ardent lips and pink cheeks, the air vibrated from the scent of choice soaps, perfumed eau de toilette, mixed with the sweep of mysterious chemicals, burnt hair ends, lilies, orchids, narcissuses. It was like stepping into a latter-day Dardelian inferno, infected by neo-dandyism and snobbery's most exaggerated bacteria.

In a pretty, gold-ornamented mirror he caught sight of himself; a rather odd figure in worn blue jeans, baggy in the back, orange shirt with TEXAS in white letters right across the chest, the beloved worn mocha jacket hanging over one shoulder, backpack in hand.

"Is it a question of a reservation?"

The girl at the low counter got a blank screen on the computer terminal.

"That probably wouldn't hurt."

Perhaps a hint of a smile passed over her face, a costly wasted second, but immediately she looked at him again just as immutably serious and businesslike.

"Of course, we can't guarantee anything. All treatment is at your own risk. In this business no insurance is valid."

"Like in the cruel world of art," he added, already on the way to forgetting his real mission:

"There is supposed to be a place here, Old Danish Beauty Parlor; have you heard about it?"

Mainly followed by a quick:

"So, no treatment."

She had already hit the return key and turned away. Nothing is more clearly cruel than body language. He promptly left the room.

The Skipper's still hangs on, half dangerously hovering over the pier's north side. Far below, around high posts and powerful dolphins the breaking swells wash against the broad beach; farther out, while waiting for the right wave, twilight's late surfers ride fiberglass boards in richly colored wet suits. The sun plunges quickly, tosses an ever more savage, muffled red violet shimmer over the steep, crumbled cliffs below the boulevard. There is something almost enchanting about this pier in Santa Monica; no hurricanes seem to be able to finish it off, it constantly rises anew, no violent waves finally succeed in smashing this remarkable thousand footer that has dipped its legs in the water for decades, with its back full of bars, restaurants, game parlors, the carriage-house with the merry-go-round. To the north, in the dark below Santa Monica mountain the lights are lit in Malibu; the clouds swarm to the south above the luxury houses that are beginning to replace the slums in Venice. The picture windows glow. The sky is still absolutely clear, but the blue slowly whitens to gray. Soon the shimmering contrails of the planes going to Tahiti and Honolulu will be swallowed up by the night.

One more time the same feeling seizes him, or is it a madness or a knowledge, like so many times before during all the trips, throughout his own life as well: everything is still there as it always has been, where he has been, change has nothing to do with time, rather with growth and presence, life constantly in progress. Time is an evil invention of autocratic swindlers who to make doubly sure also invented death, war, nightmares, nuclear weapons to satisfy the most morbid of desires: to establish borders, raise taboo poles, determine the course of the story; even confine language itself into precisely regulated syntaxes, freeze images, let music do itself in.

The abalone is small and extremely expensive. The dollar has undoubtedly shrunk. No splendid silvery sea otters turn around in the water any more, reflecting the very last light in their wet and shiny up-turned bellies. He pays and asks at the cash register. Sorry, no one seems to know anything about the place in question. There aren't many cars left down in the parking lot. The evening breeze stiffens. Sand drifts in from the beach, hits against the cars' sheet metal; a thin fine rustle is mixed with the roar from the breakers and the monotonously rhythmic non-stop pop from the turned-up loudspeakers of the surfers' strange vehicles. With the side window rolled down he lets his arm hang down outside the door. Sharp grains of quartz really bite hard in the wind gusts. At longer and longer intervals the headlights from the traffic stream along the coast road sweep down over the concrete paving stones. Round about some cars rev up their motors before they completely blow away with howling tires. In others, people are getting ready to spend the night. Hell, why not. If the race is after all over he can just as well stay in the car instead of spending the last night in yet another anonymous motel. The night is warm, the Icelandic wool sweater easy to get to in the luggage. He pushes the driver's seat as far forward as it goes, lowers the backrest , tries it. Sure, he can still crumple up and turn in in a car. He closes his eyes, the canvas gets light. At once the images begin to roll, hypna-gogic ones, the title-texts pass, the chat becomes more dense, he is no longer chasing after vanished images of female phantoms, all are there, together, the smoke gets thick, scanning voices, the human bricklayers move in constant-ly changing choreographies, in slow motion, toward each other, with each other, from each other; he too is there with the camera on one shoulder ready for action, in the first rank, with the heavy tape recorder chafing on his other shoulder, the tear gas drifts between the universities and he is there and it is also Lönnroth up at Berkeley talking with Njál and Delblanc doesn't dare to go across campus to the lecture hall, sits at home instead and makes a fragile bridge of asses to the calm Uppsala; far away in Västerås Mr. Gustafsson himself sinks farther down into Sephardic writings and women, dreams about Texas.

You should be in the jungles of Vietnam if you really want to under-stand, not here, all of your comrades are there, no one will comprehend his both/and, that you never can understand the one without the other, some third is not necessary; the carpet-bombs grow, the sparkling cold winter eve-nings of the torchlight processions; the crammed documentaries, balance, objectivity, impartiality, cowardice; everything at the same time or not at all. Many also went mad, changed beyond recognition, moved out into the country; others dressed up in wide milky lilac mahjong pants and discov-ered that there are tender children to love. When the war was finally won, they were the first of all to stand outside the American embassy and line up for visas, in trim suits, with ties, with their pockets full of unimpeachable travel funds from the CIA or author stipends; all of the old comrades, the writers, the journalists, the TV producers, the chameleon-like Lagercrantz-es, the glib Lidmen, the Isakssons devoid of poetry. Now valid were broad, critically humane perspectives of the achievements of Western civilization. Asia was allowed to drown quickly under reeducation camps and new hem-orrhages. South Africa could always be resorted to. Latin America seemed explosive and interesting, certainly worth staking a career on. Soon

Marcuse and McLuhan were gathering dust at the antiquarian bookstores. But the old techno-anarchist Buckminster Fuller could just as well stay on the bookshelf with his instructions for the space ship Earth. And Myrdal's Asiatic drama was actually not a bad structural, radical analysis at all. The mytho-poet Norman O. Brown too smiled alongside leafed-through Watts and Snyder. The air completely filled by the vibrations from a new powerful synthetic socio-aesthetic-political criticism, and from a young middle-aged Myrdal, of course; it was suddenly downright teeming with newly promoted professors.

Ever trendier and approved by Rolling Stone the music poured out of the loudspeakers, the tribe increased powerfully with new families after Woodstock and Electric Kool Aid-Acid Kid; the intervals shrunk or expanded, difficult to determine which; reality's blueprint was fingered from all directions. He too suddenly stands in a kitchen window and tries to understand, but a screaming newly born son doesn't want to burp as he is supposed to do according to Spock, while she is away at her eternal seminars, and it had still never been anyone's idea, actually, that life should look this way, for anyone.

With a jerk he sits up; must have dozed off, just a few seconds, checks his watch. His head is full of gravel. Stretches out, his muscles whimper. The night thunders on, noise from the sea and highways close by. The Tivoli of pleasures grinds on on the pier, now more like a magnificent glow-worm. He digs out the light backpack, stuffs down the sweater, wallet with dough and passport, the cassette, of course. Give up? He? Never!

He makes sure the trunk is properly locked, laces up his jogging shoes and tries a few light, almost dancing steps over the parking lot. Perhaps not fully so timeless as he prefers to imagine himself he trots over to the spiral staircase and the unsteady bridge that leads over the freeway to the boulevard. If the conceivable time shrinks to zero, space's hovering point is still there!

The Grotto of the Muses lay where it should, an out-of-date remnant in the shadow of the steel and plastic and glass mountain of late modernism. Just as friendly and open at night like the first time he found it, the door invitingly ajar to an outer sea of nicely shining newly published books in shelves and on meandering counters, upstage the inner nooks' millions of unsorted morsels. Late evening strollers were browsing. He left his backpack at the cash register. The girl nodded without looking up from the guitar, quietly trying a sliding blues arrangement; long straw-yellow hair hung down over the neck of the instrument, sometimes getting caught between finger tips and strings; perhaps she wanted it that way on purpose; blonde, muffled sounds.

He rooted around in the antiquarian mishmash, mostly at random, a hunting dog still uncertain which track to follow; after a while more concentrated, as if he had gotten the scent. The inner part of the Grotto of the Muses is strange in such a way that it isn't at all a book shop or even an antiquarian book shop in the usual sense; it is rather a question of a single huge unsorted archive where all kinds of printed matter, all the way from scandalous gossip magazines to esoteric doctoral dissertations, are shoveled into an ever more confusing chaos. The only guiding principle seems to be that all the material should have some connection to the muses. But since the boundaries between the respective ladies' areas of responsibility are undeniably vague and the relationships between them so obvious and strong, besides new artistic techniques and areas of activity constantly arise, so a customary library order and classification is completely impossible and has been replaced by the strictly neutral labels of chronology; century, decade, lustrum, single year.

"Young man, consider time as constantly shifting furniture, glowing remains from the great star. Clues, there is plenty of guiding light in the intervals, sufficient in any case so that in the end you can find what you seek; if it isn't stuck in the moment, of course, or been blown away on the irritating dust specks of chance. Here we buy everything, accept everything, but sell nothing. The youth outside ought to take that up."

He was certain that it had been completely empty in the room when he came in, just his own breathing and heart beat were heard. But there without a doubt stood an ancient woman in front of him. For a short moment she turned her eyes toward the moiré glass door that separated her inner space from the well-lit trade on the other side. She was thin and transparent, her wrinkles fine but at the same time so deep that they reached through her skin all the way down to her skull. Clear traces of rouge could be seen on her cheeks, remains of eye black, violet blue mascara, extremely fine streaks of lipstick around her mouth. But when she again turned her face toward him there was no trace whatsoever of age in her eyes; the pupils were large and firm, the iris sparkled in all conceivable shades of green and gold.

He immediately looked away with his eyes. The room seemed to be the same one as a moment ago, but yet not. Over-cluttered book shelves, rickety ladders, chairs with piles of newspaper volumes, sky globes on the shiny round mahogany table; masks where there was still room on the walls, grinning, smiling with their empty eye sockets; the lyre, scrolls in one corner, slate-pencil and blue gray board nearby; a double flute. Some bobbins, a roll of film, a funny old Paillard with external mechanism; inside the showcase an elegant antique watch without hands, a splendid golden dusty Oscar statue; bunches of other insignificant old trash, difficult to make out in the dark.

"Perhaps I can help you with something?"

"Just a moment, please!"

With throbbing temples he rushed after his backpack, picked up his wallet and looked in one of the compartments for the well-thumbed photograph 3 x 4, developed already in Athens: shadows and green tendrils, a rock wall, two female figures, or possibly a double exposure. A face looking straight ahead with a smile frozen just before it exploded into guffaws, the other one a profile half turned away, closer but still strangely indistinct. As if the focus wasn't really adequate for it or an ill-disposed ray of backlight had irritated the film at the delicate moment of exposure; of course, it could even have to do with the photographer's shaking or a normal banal error in development. Whatever; the picture seemed somehow diluted there, on the way into or out of itself.

Without a word she took it and shuffled into the vault. Inside the showcase shimmered a strange animal figure. At that distance it resembled a strangely shaped Dalecarlian horse with an unusually long neck. The saddle blanket was painted a pretty red, with a white cross under the thin cracked lacquer. On the neck could be seen markings that perhaps represented a ladder, or small boxes. The key was in the showcase door. He turned it and opened it. The little horse felt solid and heavy, cut and carved out of heavy wood; distinct traces of a chisel, knife and mortise chisel could both be seen and felt in the hand. He turned it over.

On the belly the artist had cut a heart. He leaned over under the ceiling lamp to get better light. An inscription. A few finely cut letters. At first he couldn't believe his own eyes. But the words were still there even after a second and third reading: my dear Tone, from HJK!

"Have you found something interesting too? There is so much here after the previous owner. Junk that actually has no business at all here."

He gave a start like an ancient school boy, caught red-handed at some delightful prank. Ashamed and confused he put back the childishly carved animal in its place alongside the ugly, gilded statue hotly desired by so many. He glanced carefully at the witch. Clearly she was not thinking of petrifying the disobedient child. On the contrary, she smiled at him. Besides didn't she look strangely much younger? Was it something with her hair? The color? The length?

"She's probably the one you're looking for? Or possibly her? Although she is, of course, much more beautiful on this picture."

She spread out two newspapers in front of him, on the one hand the Parade of the Stars from the early thirties, on the other hand a very fresh copy of the National Enquirer.

"All right, just stay there. Now I know where I can look for more."

She stood there, with her arm stretched out.

"The key," she smiled, "I need my key to lock up. Those mementos are not mine, you see. I am only keeping them for a dear old friend."

But then she changed her mind, put the little horse back on the table, alongside the newspaper file.

"Look, just hurry and put it down in your backpack. No one will notice that it is gone; I'm the only one who knows and I am sure that the owner won't mind ..."

This time she didn't shuffle away. A very young back and the sound of high piercing spiked heels returned in between the shelves.

Hans Jörgen Kineman began at once to go diagonally through the articles. He took notes in a notebook. The Cinderella story that became a true story. Memorized, hammered into his skull; there was so extremely much to plow through. Stared incredulously at the scandal sheets' flaming headlines: Milou, knocked up again? Greek orgies! Deed of man or work of God? The cover's faces.

"Hello! Mother! Are you there?"

He turned around. The girl with the straw-yellow hair looked as if she was scared stiff.

"God, I got so frightened. I didn't know that there was anyone inside. We actually closed, a long time ago."

"You were playing, perhaps didn't see when I got my backpack."

He hung it on one shoulder.

"That explains things."

She was wearing a coarsely knitted shawl loosely hanging around her neck; she straightened out one of the edges. Her hands were thin, nervously gathering the files.

"I must ask you to go now. This way, please! I closed a long time ago and locked outside. But you are welcome back tomorrow. We are always open."

"I know."

She pulled the door shut, checked carefully that it was really locked.

Before she jumped into her open Rabbit, he came out with his question.

"I have no idea about that place. I only know that mama worked there once!"

She took off in a hurry. He looked at his watch, squeezed the hard lump in his backpack. He could sleep another time. Now he had to be close.

Within the whole pile of hotels along Ocean Boulevard the place was completely alive with more or less dubious massage parlors, dance halls with low profiles outward, intimate restaurants, clubs for the most curious of activities. These brothels mostly never lasted very long. But, if one was closed, it wasn't long before another arose nearby, in some humble, wood-paneled bungalow, with a deep shadowy porch where you discreetly hid yourself while waiting for someone from inside to answer the signal with a searching look through a crack in the door. Some of them were almost to be considered as simpler imitations of Beverly Davies' real luxury spots in Belmore or down in the very center of this metropolis, which was hysterically growing in all directions. There you could order intercourse with Garbo or Pickford and fuck more or less disguised copies with the accessory willing arms, breasts, lips, legs and genitals.

It was here that little sweet miss Tone gave birth to her only child, a daughter. After a short time in hell, as a cocktail waitress and occasional dance partner at one of the more unknown of these establishments, Sweet Lorraine, right at the curve where Sunset turns off up toward the mountain, she changed her life abruptly, without understanding why such a talented girl would throw away her spectacular career for the rather unglamorous one as manicurist, hair nurse or on extremely rare occasions, as a versatile Scandinavian finger tip masseuse; a career that, by the way, was well-deservedly crowned when she received the film academy's great distinction as best make-up artist.

Her old star dreams she left to her child, baptized as Tilde Louise, partly after her own grandmother, partly after the enviable wife who according to God and all worldly laws had the man she once loved so greatly; the thin worn-out woman who in a way gave her this new life through a smarting blow right in the face by the fine lace glove-covered hand with the hard envelope full of money. And who thereafter crying fell around her neck, kissed her passionately and wished her all the luck in the new world!

Her beauty and innocence she preserved very consciously over the years, in spite of the fact that the attacks on them in no way decreased. And around the city signs popped up with the Old Danish Beauty Parlor on them; especially near great arterials, where she with an unerring sense for the right, cheap and apparently completely useless pieces of property bought in to block after block. With the motto Drink, Look, But Don't Touch, the movement gradually spread out to comprise even bars with stand-up comedians and stripteases. Especially at the end of the second world war and the Korean crisis' so tragic years for her, with her daughter's death in childbirth and a renewed role as mother for her own granddaughter, the business turned in such a way, that the good name and reputation for quality of the operation day in and day out was questioned. Not the least by infamous gossip reptiles and corrupt city planners with a pronounced nose for others' hard-earned money. With good help from old, now attractively graying customers and gentlemen from the right circles, with the right connections, one more time sweet little Tone's business changed; now to Tone Incorporated. This time she no longer needed to stake her remarkably well-preserved body as capital, dancing on the tables before the vulgar crowd's salivating corners of the mouth, desirous looks and half-open money-bags. But, the flesh was still amove on the board of directors, and many had trouble checking their old lust when madame chairwoman swept into the reverently restored original location at Third Street, East 106.

However, no one escapes his fate; it is registered from the beginning, however open the end might seem. With the spectacular move from the original address to West 106, thereby to make room for her newest investment, moreover Santa Monica's most spectacular newly built shopping center, its existence was further embellished. The mayor, with special greetings from the governor in Sacramento, after a proper bill in the state senate, for an eternal period of time registered the Old Danish Beauty Parlor as an Official California Cultural Monument; with a commemorative plaque attached to the wall and its very own mark on the Map of the Stars!

History seldom becomes better if you tell what really happened. Possibly truer. The fantastic, the unbelievable, the distasteful, the sleazy; the stench, the sweat, the belches, the groans. In large sweeping summaries all of this sort of thing has a tendency to disappear. No one any more believes in stories where the wild flourishes freely. Informants who want to retain their credibility are careful to see that their lies are verified by like-minded people. Ambiguous truth suffices all the more rarely as proof. Everywhere there abound naturalists and realizers, pompous interjectors and book canvassers, the so-called dead certain, self-appointed inspectors of common sense and good taste. They all have one thing in common. They stink, in spite of the fact that they never dared to get close to a dung hill, even less wallowed in one to find out about normal human understanding or the mechanisms of the divine lack of wisdom. It is easier to forget, omit, cut out, censor and thereby meet today's fawning assessment; perhaps even allow themselves to be invited and enticed into participating in the dreary rituals of the predestined.

The story never gets really dangerous before it is clear that it has no other authorization but itself; the art of foreseeing what has already happened. Of course, there always appears some splendid wiseacre to disarm, point out obvious flaws in logic, the absence of civilized chronology; the dangers for a society that allows reality to imitate the stories' campaigns and even worse, let unverified reports from the muck ooze out. Preferably you should ask for absolution from everything that is real and genuine. Waiting for chance to coincide with purpose can take a long time. But only in these rare moments does everything become possible, there is room for impossible beauty; the triumph of the vulgar, the sweaty civilization of earth; all honor and all light that obstinately emerge through the intervals where the heroes are pushed away by cocky sheriffs and sensitive hangmen. Who dares today in full earnest to speak out loud about the vital days of being when strength and beauty, but even weakness and ugliness, agree about life without any supervisors whatsoever?

There isn't much to add to the actual story; most of it is well known, also to you, even if the variations are legion. In the end it has to do just as much with you as with him, the man with a thousand names.

I knew my way back to the parking lot: a one-floor bungalow with facade of weather-beaten horizontal wood paneling. Two steps led up to the porch that seemed to wander around the whole house. The door was ajar, a deep green gate with a worn clapper of yellow metal. A streak of light fell out and floated more and more dimly away among the shadows. The wind was fussing with the palm leaves high up in the night darkness. The roar from the sea could no longer be heard, just a muted growl from the traffic on the other side of the shopping cathedral. The wind also took hold of the sign. It was squeaking around the chains it was dangling from. The gleam from the nearest streetlight illuminated the text: ORIGINAL OLD DANISH BEAUTY PARLOR. The number 106 could be dimly seen on the wall close to the door-case, as well as the large plaque with the bear, the state of California's heraldic animal in half relief. Between powerful paws the beast was holding up streamers with the text Cultural Landmark. There was a glow from the gaps between the curtains, which were not completely drawn. In one of the windows hung a lopsided, red violet neon tube: OPEN.

Dark and calm. An ordinary spring night in Santa Monica, even a little cool; an anonymous side street a few blocks behind Ocean Boulevard. An out-of-the-way place where development generously allowed a few shabby and rather worn-out blocks to remain. Some cars whisked by, one turned into a garage ramp just opposite with a creaking body. A noisy couple were rolling over each other in their house. Again calm and dark. I was still looking carefully around, as if I didn't have anything to do there.

I was sweating copiously.

Nothing was forcing me, other than an innate curiosity and desire, of course, for the pictures.

Without any great hesitation I pushed the door open.

When the unfamiliar begins to feel well known, there is reason to be on your guard. I wasn't prepared for anything. There was no cause for anxiety or fear. In spite of this my heart was thumping; like a widespread extra vibration right under the skin. The pores were struck by an acute inundation. I wiped away some drops of water from my upper lip. In the dark reflective glass of the ticket window I was met by an expectant, almost a little triumphant smile. But it was pushed aside.

"Stop there, young man!"

The window was pulled open a few inches. A thin, diaphanous hand crawled out onto the narrow marble counter. Deep white wrinkles between high black veins. At first the fingers lay still, then they began to move, impatiently drumming an inaudible rhythm.

"The museum is open during the day. The evenings are only for subscribed, private performances."

Calmly and without visible haste I untied my backpack and pulled out the videocassette, pushed it into the window which fell down with a thud. At the same time the light was turned up imperceptibly. I found myself in a reception room of some sort, with sofa, table, a few easy chairs. Behind the lounge suite a velvet drape that partly covered a sliding door with magnificently painted door mirrors; a Baroque throng of pig-pink cupids, light blue wings, flower-adorned vessels and grain wreaths.

Life is most often simpler if you let reality remain as metaphors, don't give a shit about importunate symbols and stupid paraphrases. Everything still has to do with everything else. Plato destroyed a lot with his philosophy, and what was left was taken care of, as is well-known, by Rousseau with the result known to us all: a society that isn't suitable for anything but gods. It is certainly difficult enough to find yourself an ordinary, banal and proper hero's role. Language doesn't do much either to improve the situation, neither as mirror nor as window. When you stand there, in the middle of life, you just stand there and try to understand what is actually going on beyond all well-known knowledge, catch a glimpse of something else, perhaps new, beyond all partitions and walls. And the soul plods on in tiresome circles, presumably already lost from the beginning, continuing along ever nastier paths in toward a darkness that is neither blackness, blistering light nor pure intellect, leads nowhere: just panic and sweat and trembling, confusion and surprise. It is a matter of keeping on, keeping a straight face all the way to the glades where the pure, wonderful light returns, where the mysterious regions of the green fields and groves meet with music and dance. A very pure now, a new space; free and loose of all bonds.

The door is pushed aside, the drapery pulled to the side.

The quiet murmur, the thin music that filled the outer room like a weak organ stop was still there at the same remote, turned-down level even inside the salon; somehow filtered through sensitive membranes that only let through the very most essential: the sounds from bright cymbals, a screechy flute, glass tambourines.

At the same time as I stepped over the threshold there was a flash by my head. I ducked as fast as lightning, diagonally to the side, completely instinctively.

"That really could have turned out bad!"

A half-dressed waitress was standing in front of me. Around her neck she was wearing a fluffy thin veil that also was barely draped around her breasts. In one hand she was holding a substantial pair of scissors, in the other a lock of my reddish gray hair!

"Please, this way."

My eyes slowly got used to the subdued dark. More of the room grew forth, sometimes hastily illuminated a bit more by showers of dissipated rainbow light from the slowly turning faceted globe up in the ceiling dome. Here and there you could see obscene embossed plates of stucco or ordinary plaster inset in the walls. Shabby Silenuses with splendid phalluses, rooting pigs, cheeky leopards, a boy with a piece of cloth over his head; roughly the way it is in the Villa Farnese. In between, obvious and poorly done copies of Pompeian murals: ritual hand-washings, raised bowls and ships, genitals, exposed breasts and buttocks under whirling garments. Everything was marked by the extraordinarily poor taste that is the distinguishing characteristic of American art when it is at its very best, but here of course completely adequate considering the room's original function, the reception place, the field of battle where the victims are selected for continued joyous intercourse.

She went in front between the small tables toward the long halfcircle-shaped bar, which in part consisted of an inset grill with slowly turning pieces of meat. When we passed, the girl tossed the lock of hair on the glowing blue coals. A quickly disappearing blaze flamed up, the air singed; that was it. She climbed up onto one of the high stools and threw out her hand toward a round silver tray, filled with dark, coarsely baked cookies. There were also porcelain bowls with liquid honey and olive oil, wrinkled black olives, pink and white onion slices as well as a dish with something that mostly reminded you of finely ground flour, mixed with the sharp little ears that adorn the kernels of unground seed grain. The dish looked quite prickly.

"Taste it. Just dip in and sprinkle!"

She showed how, but noticed at once my considerable reluctance.

"Guaranteed healthy, pure organic products. Is it this mess you are wondering about?"

With her little finger she made a hollow in the little white pyramid, held it out. I licked it off with the very tip of my tongue. It tasted about like damp oatmeal flakes.

"Flour, ordinary flour?"

Her face was split by a smile, her eyebrows flickered up high on her white, made-up forehead.

"I am Cynthia," she said and handed me a well-filled glass with finely etched garlands around the edge, raised her own. I was obviously not completely successful in restraining the somber sigh that was caused by the thought of the painful bill that is always the consequence if you offer unfamiliar ladies drinks in locales like this.

"Why this sudden gloom?"

"The thought of coming economic catastrophe."

She giggled so that she almost choked.

"Relax, guy, it's on the house."

I took another gulp, moderately calmed; those girls know their stuff, know both the written and unwritten rules. The wine tasted far too sweet, almost like lemonade.

It was pretty peaceful in the place; diverse gentlemen of various ages at the tables, the half-naked girl at my side, an apathetic colleague of hers was strolling absent-mindedly back and forth on top of the bar between beer glasses, drinks, ash trays, bowls of salted nuts and chips. Occasionally, she crouched down in front of one of the men, parted her clean-shaven legs and did funny little tricks in front of them until they satisfied her appetite with a folded-up dollar bill in one cavity or other between her shiny thighs. There were videocameras inset in the bar. A large screen on the black glass wall above the shelves with liquor bottles reproduced in absurd enlargement, the intimate details of the private parts and all the dark movements that were a part of it.

A sharp shoe tip playfully nudged my shin.

"My name is Cynthia," she pointed out again and held out the little dish with the flour hotchpotch.

"Cocaine?" I wondered.

"Even worse," she answered with a laugh.

"What do you mean?"

"If I don't say any more, then I haven't said anything."

I dampened the tip of my index finger, ready to taste the white powder. But I stopped myself.

"Dear Cynthia, do you know whether any of the chicks in this establishment is called Circe?"

She stiffened, but didn't answer.

From behind I was surrounded by a sharp smell, like from smoke or burnt spices: galanthus, turmeric, cumin, white cinnamon!

"Thanks, sweet little Cynthia, that's enough now, I'll take over the party now. Besides, it will probably soon be time for you to go up again?"

A propeller whirl of well-manicured fingernails winked her away. Pen's better half, the spiritual theater critic from yesterday evening, sank down alongside me, after he first with a grimace pushed away the tray with cookies and other delicacies.

"If I were you I'd be careful of that. Skoal instead!"

Emery raised his foamy beer glass and downed it with deep loud gulps at the same time as he turned around and, squinting, looked at the place over narrow slipped-down reading glasses.

"Nice that the general public is really beginning to come back. But it always has, of course, as soon as society begins to smell decadence and bodies. The vicarious forms of art for some reason have their best periods when things get critical. Grotesque really. Pay dearly. Lethal to touch the artists. Mere watching instead of total engagement. Life exchanged for texts and peep shows. Total theater, muck days at a stretch. No place any more for pauses, intermissions, room for silence and reflection. Really comfortable conditions for culture. Shit! Queer place to meet for the likes of you and I. What do you have there? I'll be damned, isn't it an old pancro glass. Let me see!"

I pulled off the thin platinum chain over my head and handed over the light smoke-colored glass with its circular edge of ivory. How many times hasn't it saved me over the years from difficult-to-assess situations, seen to it that reality was correctly exposed, revealed the sensitivity of colors, given the clouds a place in the sky, made contrasts clear, lifted up men's faces from the great common darkness, revealed intervals, given light language, a voice to my pictures. Without it I feel absolutely naked.

"I don't know whether you've ever thought of that," he said and changed his glass into a monocle, "but surely the old philosopher is right when he claims that the eye is the first circle and that its field of vision forms the second. And then it is replicated everywhere in nature, endlessly, this first picture. We spend our entire lives trying to understand and interpret this the most original of forms. Life is actually nothing other than a single long apprenticeship so that you are supposed to understand the simple truth that around every circle you can draw a new circle. Consoling thought! No end in nature, everything moves in circles; flowing, variable, without fixed limits."

"A circle damn well has to be round."

"Who says so?"

"This sounds just as dippy as if I were to claim that time doesn't exist."

"Not at all. Nothing says that you aren't right. Try to remember: duration is at the most a relative concept, isn't it, approximately just as firm as the snow flakes in April or the waves that come up on the shore. As a matter of fact, we are all victims of a very unfortunate understanding: that time exists. During really dark hours I can also imagine that it is completely normal, absolutely correct and unusually convenient always to adjust to current conditions and regulations, subordinate yourself to the controllers, suppress your own little ego. If you claim that time doesn't exist, then it doesn't exist. Stick to your guns. Who can contradict you, prove the opposite?"

"In effect, everyone I have met."

"You obviously have to begin by getting people to distinguish between time and time. There is chronological time. It is stiff and hard. The time of bigwigs and thralls, the one that leads to the era of the slave camps. But, then there is also soft time, psychological time if you will. Completely lawless, it lives on your own conditions, where you are; also here, in this room. It is transparent and clear. It is the one that allows you to see, be seen. Un-

273

fortunately, there was some fundamental error in the programming already at the beginning; clock time knocked out space time. Just like so much else gone wrong and turned into a mess for us: first came the god, then the laws and finally man. The devil only knows how it would have looked here in the world if it had been the reverse. For it is not time that ultimately is the master of life, my friend, neither now or then; it is exclusively duration that prevails! This whole fantastic story about Pen and Mary Lou, about your lost roll of film, is a rather fine confirmation of it, don't you think?"

He held out the pancro glass, examined me carefully before he handed it over.

"The little Pen told at first actually got me to guess that you were a very ordinary rogue."

"An old-fashioned filmmaker, with extraordinary high work ethics, that's what I am" I filled in for the sake of completeness and tried to sound convincing.

"Isn't that roughly the same thing!"

I courteously joined in with his laughter. Yet, there was something in that man's presence that made me ill at ease. It had nothing to do with his fashionable image or the elegant didactic conversation with a tone of mild indulgence. No, it was just his presence that bewildered me and made me distrustful. The whole situation was way too well directed for my documentary temperament. Finally, I couldn't help but ask:

"How does it happen that you are here just tonight?"

"Presumably the same reason as yours."

"Namely ...?"

"This movable art, of course. These unusually well-shaped works of art, lovely coeds from the College of Communications at UCLA, moonlighting housewives from Westwood. Do you have some other errand, perhaps?"

He nodded ambiguously to the side. Cynthia drew near, ominously lowered her perfumed bottom ever closer to our places at the bar. He

274

stuffed a five-dollar bill into her ass and got up, looked around the place; as if he were searching for someone. He nodded to acquaintances, blew kisses, raised his hand in greeting; but I couldn't avoid noticing how carefully, even a bit uneasily, he at the same time was searching with his eye for some person, some sign. Nor did I miss the short, hardly perceptible nod and corresponding happy smile when he found what he was looking for.

"Fellow, it's soon show time. Circe's own hour. Presumably you have to take a pee first too?"

More people had come in, the place was swarming and murmuring, voices were heard and laughter and clinking glasses over in the half darkness; the globe up on the ceiling was turning slowly and casting an indistinct blue-violet and greenish gleam. I gulped the last slurp of wine and picked up my backpack from the floor. Something told me that I shouldn't return. Moreover, it would certainly be wisest to make my way to the car right away and curl up in the back seat, try to get a few hours of sleep before the following morning's tiresome trip home. But nothing induced me to change my course and direct my steps toward the exit. We crowded ahead along the bar's half-circle toward the door with the his and her symbols. Before we got there he stopped and dug down into one of his pants pockets, took my hand and stuffed something into it. In the dark it was difficult to see what it was. Possibly some dried cactus buds or mushrooms, perhaps pieces of bark, or even little hard twisted pieces of a root it never hurts to carry in one of your pockets. I stuffed a piece in my mouth; it tasted bitter and familiar. I was ready.

Now I knew who he was.

"You go ahead," he said.

A fat girl clad in a bloody blue and white checked apron was guarding the door, she held out a restraining hand to me. I had noticed her earlier; she was helping the grill cook pick intestines and other viscera out of the animal bodies that were slit down the front before the actual meat was cut up into suitable pieces.

"No one comes in here, in here, in here," she hummed and nudged me playfully in the midriff.

I said my password.

Without any further hesitation I opened the door. They gave me a couple of substantial terry cloth beach towels and gave instructions about the closest way from my little undressing booth to the shower and steaming whirlpool. Thereafter I was taken, fresh as a baby and stinking of balsam, into a significantly larger room with unpleasantly reflective black glass walls. They stretched me out on the bed. The actual slaughter was carried out under adequate hygienic forms and ceremonies. The whole thing went very painlessly, handled almost clinically, according to well-practiced and reliable rituals. For recently arrived viewers it is easy to find fault with, perhaps also regret, that so many obscurities still remain; in spite of all serious attempts at completeness. It is always easy to poke fun at the expense of the participants, especially if you yourself think you are sitting securely with the answers in your hands, righteous and washed clean, with a curly tail and your self-confident mug in the air. To be sure, from many points of view it would be desirable to have an unequivocal and clear-as-glass continuity, especially now that the whole procedure is well known in most of the details. You can hardly any longer speak about any secrets. There are exclusively local circumstances that determine the outcome, the commitment of the performer, the efficiency of the implements, the possible resistance of the body; the bonding agent, the membranes; what it is that holds everything together for the longest time without being seen.

The fascination in the presence of the mysterious which only exists for those already initiated, the promises of the titillating exposure of marvelous orgies, the fear before the meeting with this unknown other are obvious consequences of the long shots and risks that individual freedom offers in rich measure, if you dare to accept; profitable material for comparative phenomenologies. As a matter of fact, it deals with something quite different, everywhere present, ominously simple: glimpses, conjectures, the trace of hastily flaring-up fragments; darkness and light, rapture and agony.

The skin of the gutted he-goat was hanging from the ceiling; the skull too with the powerful crooked horns. It was dripping, the body still warm, from gutted and rearranged bowels. Just before the drapes were pulled, when the lighting was increased in the whole place and I clearly saw the girls dancing on the bar outside the glass wall and in the darkness beyond divined the uninterested general public, I caught sight of the operator's black gown, the camera's eye. The cassette was waiting at the back door of the establishment, with greetings from the management. Everything conducted admirably discreetly.

"Damn mess," said the young black guy who finally stopped his taxi and took care of me.

It was easy to go along with that. Everything had happened very suddenly, on the way to the airport. At the intersection with Jefferson, right after Marina del Rey, where there was a red light I drove into a car that had already climbed up onto another one, and it was bang-bang behind me, and soon there were quite a few of us who were stuck in the morning fog from the Pacific Ocean. I wriggled out, took my backpack and hobbled up to the nearest telephone booth. Police and ambulances were soon at the scene. Others needed them more than I.

When we have something to report from our constant wanderings around the world and greetings from Mr. Eco then the operator immediately takes care of the conversation and puts us through to the right editorial office. If something serious or very important has happened there is, furthermore, a code word to resort to. I have never before used it. Now I did.

"Who's calling?" wondered the guy at the exchange.

"Odysseus."

It wasn't many seconds before I had Sickan's uneasy voice in the receiver. I reassured her quickly, reported briefly that there had been trouble with the rental car, that I would presumably miss the plane and that it would be just as well to cancel the pickup at Arlanda. No, it was nothing serious. Home in Sweden it was a radiant May afternoon. She promised to call Astrid and report the delay.

"Downtown," I said, "to the Greyhound terminal."

"Damn mess," he said and drove off. The first wreckers were already there and they began to lift away the wrecks with their cranes. A police car with a blue light on parked alongside my smashed Camaro. They lifted up the equipment box from the trunk. It looked whole. The address label was fluttering in the dawn breeze. Everything would certainly get home. I squeezed my backpack on and checked what was in it. The leather handbag with passport, dough and tickets. The funny wooden horse. The cassette with my social security number.

It was beginning to really hurt. Half my knee seemed to be missing and besides there seemed to be too many ribs on the right side of my chest. I looked at the reflection: a pale resolute face in the side window.

You never really get done. There is always something missing in the travel expense account; never do so many hand-written receipts, vouchers and receipts seem to satisfy the Cyclops' unjustified demands for a tenable account in all regards.

0000

The man who is coded with the designation 0 pulls up his hand from the sea when he is so near the shore that it is not possible to stop. Not even the ferryman succeeded in giving him a new face. Through tin-plated layers of skin earlier features grunt. The scars for example show up as stains. Everyone knows what price the heroes must pay for their return home. Yet it is never difficult to find new sponsors.

Between rough barns and cold-bricked pigsties he feels his way on. The path leads from the sea. The temporary space in his backpack contracts to an increasing lump of irreplaceable baggage. He had learned to balance far too early. The islands succeeded each other. It became more and more sparse between the straits. He had expected a more powerful sea instead of the scent of sour salt licks. The navigation mark was overgrown by pine forest. He dug the oar down into the ground.

About crucial parts of the country they still know strangely little. Speculations are in the majority. Moreover, delightful spots for example have never interested wholly competent geographers. It is even claimed that you have to let yourself be satisfied by the poets' assertions, excuse individual expressions of opinion.

Development goes on, he thinks.

Sail-makers come aflocking to begin the unmasking. From the remaining shreds and torn remnants new foresails and jibs are sewn. The stench from the cities blows in over the point. Lacunae are continually formed anew and roll ever farther in over the island.

The pictures are piled in the darkness. The limestone kilns smoke. Time heals all wounds, all space.

Possibly we can, still provisionally, use the designation 0.

She went ahead and got all the ice cream at Konsum, crammed the ice chests full of vanilla and pistachio and chocolate almond, strawberry, raspberry, nougat and lemon ripple. Steam came from the plastic bags with crushed ice. The coldness burned her hands when she carried it out and filled the trunk. On the way to the beach she stopped at Blue Thorp and looked in to tell The Old One that he obviously was welcome. Strangely enough he wasn't at home. She yelled one more time through the open kitchen door. No answer. She looked in. Empty everywhere. Strange! At this time of day he was usually always sitting on the porch, after yet another day with his tools, enveloped by thick, stinking pipe smoke; a warm cup of tea on the table, a substantial biography of some unknown British thirties politician on his knees. There were a couple of half-empty beer glasses on the sink. Alongside, a funny little wooden horse. She had never seen it before. Undoubtedly it reminded her of the Danish horse on the mantelpiece in the dining room up at Austers; Pegasus, the unknown ... But this one was coarsely carved, awkwardly painted under flaking varnish. She took it in her hand, lifted it. It felt massive, almost unnaturally heavy for its size; at least in comparison with the other one's ingenious lightness, with all the secret drawers in the grotesquely long neck. The kitchen clock showed four thirty. Certainly an hour left before the buses arrived.

That weather can change appallingly quickly! Yesterday the heat out on Auren, the on-shore wind drove in the sun-warmed sea. Good luck, though, that the front passed without catastrophic rain showers on all the people over at Lauters. She hopped out of her clothing and took a quick dip. Some frozen August tourists watched her, crouched in the protection of the fishing booths at Fitegarda. They could gape as much as they wanted. Still wet, with her skin goose pimply in the mean offshore wind she pulled on her sweater, took her panties and the rest of the garments in her arms and rushed half-naked up to the car she had parked alongside the wide-eyed staring strangers. She glanced toward the rushing sky. Clear blue reefs could be seen in all the gray, brooms of sun were already sweeping the water outside of Kamben. There was still a lot left to squeeze out of the summer.

In front of the house everything was almost ready. The tables placed in a neat square around the thick trunk of the elm, under its tight dark-green hissing crown. Ulla and her girls came out from the kitchen and helped carry in; thank heaven the ice cream fit in the big freezer in the laundry room, among recently caught flounder and last year's salmon, chanterelles and raspberries from the summer harvest.

The jeep with Bamse and Ler and Långhalm and a few more thundered into the field near the barn; way too early!

"You were perhaps thinking of welcoming them that way," nodded Ulla.

The girls giggled.

She hooked up the window in the bedroom before she stretched out flat on top of the bed. Only one minute she intended to rest. The wind tore into the curtains. Time after time they were sucked out by the swirling gusts. She brushed her still wet hair from her forehead. Her fingers continued down over her body in a slow caressing tickle. Her breasts still felt flat. But her nipples stiffened. She turned on her side, with her hands squeezed between her thighs. Actually, of course, she should have gone up and closed the window. Otherwise these curtains would be ripped apart too, like so many others this windy summer. Just one second of rest she intended to allow herself. It had been a successful day, so far; but tiring too. Too much respectful rubbish about lagoon harbors and long distance trade; of course, who would have expected anything else. Well-polished, totally dull associate professor scholarship. You could actually make so terribly much more out of all that valuable knowledge. Seriously relate it to the pictures that accompanied the keels and oars and sails to the north, the stories from Troy that were carved in the stones; the signs were indeed still full of song. That no one had heard before! Archaic, remote fresh Homeric winds. The impression so clear, everywhere. That no one had seen! Didn't they want to see; or hear? Tomorrow it was her turn. With delight she was going to let the heads roll, methodically impeccable; the guys' so-called scholarship once and for all send off to the national curiosity park of footnotes.

She smiled content, yawned, rolled over on her stomach and burrowed her face down in the pillow. It was damp and smelled of good newly washed linen, splashed with a few drops of sea. She closed her eyes. Rest. For a second, only. She deserved it.

Before the bus got half way to Broa he regretted it. What in the hell did he have to do at Lidingö? No boats. No friends home. There were still a bunch of jobs left on his father's old Finn hull. The cracks in the plastic around the foot of the mast had to be fixed, for example. And actually, he was quite curious about that huge party mother had arranged for all the daft archeologist fools. On the ferry over the sound he made up his mind. Erik laughed and he exchanged his Visby ticket for a return to Ajkes. Money back in an instant. No uncalled-for Swedish Railroad bureaucracy there, no.

On the sound, large shiny spots of calm were mixed with light ripples that were trying to ruffle up the water surface, but with lousy results. It remained a mirror of the sky, viscous, almost oily. A rather large sailboat was drifting forward without steerageway. Apparently it lacked a motor. The helmsman was gesticulating wildly, flinging his arms toward the slack main and shaking his head. The ferry gave way, heeled over. The vessels passed dangerously close to each other. The backwash shook the rig. There was a metallic rattle when the boom went out toward the port shroud. The sail snapped. Something about that boat gave him a start. He rushed aft over the deck toward the back bascule, pressed between the tightly packed cars; yes indeed! For certain it was an Elvström cruiser, the same unusual sort he had admired in Viken's harbor last week; perhaps even the same one!

He sat down way out on the sail club's guest pier, below Stux, beyond the real old ferry berth. The clear blue above Norra Gatt fades over into blue gray. The front that mother had been so afraid of, that it was going to drown the whole party at Gamle Hamn, was passing. With bunches of good squally wind for the one who likes that sort of thing.

The Other One looked like he usually did at this time of the year; his face full of white sun wrinkles, his hair in half-long wisps, roughly like on pictures of old hippies. The man smiled and tossed the youth the end of the rope from the foredeck. The interval shrunk. The seal pup tied it fast, smiled back.

The Old One was moderately amused by this party up at Austers. The last days had been completely crazy. The shed cleared out and emptied; emergency spot in case of rain. All the tools tossed up in the loft in a single mess. No respect at all for others' property. No respect for anything now, neither for experience nor for age. No one possessed the noble ability to be able to listen or carry on a clever conversation any more. Couldn't tell stories either, for that matter. At least he had tried. Had he?

He straightened up and continued what he had promised in a weak moment, nailed together simple but durable cross-legs for the planks that were going to function as long benches around the tables. The dull pain in his back stuck with him, he couldn't get rid of it any more. And the strength in his muscles was disappearing, however much he swore and cursed. Strangely enough the pain drew discreetly away when he was sawing and hammering, like now. He enjoyed his skill, the precision, how everything fit exactly; the lengths, joints, the neatly countersunk screws. Once he had built a boat for his son. Now it was lying tossed away and unused somewhere inside of Folke's barn. A great shame. Now only fiberglass and alloy and plastic, hardening epoxy glues, were suitable; chemicals that ate into the nose. Once he had also made a horse, a real wonder. If anyone had the desire to listen, he would gladly tell. Sometime it had to be done, before forgetfulness finally spread too widely.

But if no one wanted to listen?

He searched for the tobacco in the huge pocket of his overalls.

Besides, there was another horse, his very first one; the one he gave away.

He smiled far inside his memory, stretched his arms. Forgot the damn aching, the more and more hunched body of old age. Drove out the last planks with the wheelbarrow, lit his pipe, tried out the benches before he walked over the meadows, home to Blue Thorp.

He had done his part. Under no circumstances did he intend to honor the evening's filthy habits with his presence.

A strange sailboat was cruising in the head wind outside of Håpuhällen, dangerously close to the reef. Either a vacationing madman or someone who knew the water. Likely the latter. Now he pounded again and stretched a last cross-leg against the pier in the shade of the pine grove at Fifang.

He fixed a pot of tea and sank down in the easy chair on the porch, with an old wooly gray military blanket over his shoulders. A few half-grown lambs were trying to get through the wire fence. Sometime he should take the time and replace it with a really old-fashioned wooden fence, of split young pine trunks and lithe juniper withes; restore the landscape to the way it looked once on the shore meadows.

There was a draft around his thin neck. The kitchen door had probably blown open. It too needed repair. Life became more and more full of shoulds, of the sort of things that constantly had to be repaired because no one else did it. He turned around. In the backlight it was difficult to make out the guests.

"Hi father. You don't possibly have a couple of beers at home, possibly?"

You are dimly seen behind the pillar in the shed, sweaty, very wet from all the dancing and wine. The rest of the story is well known, it doesn't need to be rehashed, everyone still knows how it goes. Work is waiting, the show must go on. Everything remains to be discovered. The home pocket's heat. The joints. The keys of the alphabet, the rainbow, the stars. The faces and the animals. Nothing of this is reserved to returning seafarers. Everything is equally open to all; the bitter and the smooth, the sugar, the salt, all the spices. It can be fetched in the intervals, to be sure. But still more between the people. Language, scents, twilights; the inexplicable closeness.

It has been said before. It can be repeated.

There is just the first man.

And the second.

Two small children.

And the bed in the tree.